DEAD ON ARRIVAL

A MAGGIE AND JOE MYSTERY

DEAD ON ARRIVAL

JACKIE GRIFFEY

FIVE STAR

A part of Gale, Cengage Learning

GALE
CENGAGE Learning·

Detroit • New York • San Francisco • New Haven, Conn • Waterville, Maine • London

LIBRARY OF CONGRESS CATALOGING-IN-PUBLICATION DATA

Griffey, Jackie.
    Dead on arrival : a Maggie and Joe mystery / Jackie Griffey.
  — 1st ed.
    p. cm.
    ISBN-13: 978-1-59414-846-0 (alk. paper)
    ISBN-10: 1-59414-846-5 (alk. paper)
    1. Widows—Fiction. 2. Police—Fiction. 3. Wrongful death—
Fiction. 4. Murder—Investigation—Fiction. I. Title.
  PS3607.R544D43 2010
  813'.6—dc22   2009037806

First Edition. First Printing: January 2010.
Published in 2010 in conjunction with Tekno Books and Ed Gorman.

Printed in the United States of America
1 2 3 4 5 6 7 14 13 12 11 10

To all the members of The Penpoint Writers Group in Little Rock, my local fellow writers, for their support, critiques, and fellowship; and to Alice Duncan for her usual professional expertise editing *Dead on Arrival* and making it the best it can be. Thanks and cyber hugs to all of you.

CHAPTER ONE

Maggie laid aside her magazine, glancing up at the clock. She'd be sleepy if she wasn't so mad.

One A.M.

She pricked up her ears at a sound. Footsteps came slowly across the porch.

Maggie got up and went to the door. Not caring how much noise she made, even hoping she woke up a few people on Jupiter if any of them were like her mental case of a husband, she ran the last couple of steps and flung open the door.

The door slapped against the wall and Maggie stopped, frozen speechless, with her mouth open.

A young uniformed policeman stood there clutching his hat in his hands. He was young, nice looking, and terribly uncomfortable. He glanced nervously back at his partner in the Memphis, Tennessee City Police car at the curb.

Neither he nor Maggie spoke. The young patrolman was obviously wishing he were somewhere else. Anywhere else.

His partner, an older policeman, gave him an encouraging nod from the car, but made no move to join him. He swallowed and got on with it.

"Mrs. Murphy? Mrs. Horace A. Murphy?"

Dread seeped into Maggie like something contagious, the heat of anger replaced by a chill and the feeling she'd been kicked in the stomach. She managed a very small nod. She took a breath.

"I'm Maggie, Margaret Murphy. My husband is Horace Aloysius Murphy."

"Ma'am, I'm sorry to tell you, there's been an accident—"

A figure appeared beside him but neither Maggie nor the policeman saw it.

The unseen spirit beside the policeman was a young man in a leather jacket. He materialized out of thin air, looking uncomfortable. Unseen and silent, he gazed with worry and compassion on Maggie's upturned face.

Horace's spirit had come home. He was there to let Maggie and the police know, somehow, that his death was wrong, dead wrong!

Maggie's misery showed plainly as she listened to the officer. Pictures of Horse, which is what his irresponsible, motorcycle-riding friends called Horace, flashed like a kaleidoscope across Maggie's memory. Horace's smile. His arms reaching out to hold her close. His sweet generosity. Horace on his motorcycle, grinning back at her.

Tears Maggie wasn't even aware of rolled down as she tried to concentrate on what the policeman was saying.

There had been an accident? Had to identify? Oh, God! Identify! Oh, God!

Maggie's cold hands clenched till the nails bit into her icy palms.

Motorcycle left the road and hit a tree.

Snatches of what the policeman said insisted on getting through the turmoil in Maggie's mind. Her beloved juvenile delinquent would never grow up, never have children of his own, would never know how much she cared for him and worried about him. Slowly, Maggie's sudden bruising, breathtaking hurt settled to a less breathless, more continuous ache in her heart. Tears blurred her vision.

When the recitation was finally over the officer looked relieved but sad. As he reached out to touch her hand, the young police-man looked as miserable as Maggie felt.

After that, Maggie didn't remember whether she had thanked him for coming or not. She didn't remember closing the door after the policeman left. She didn't know if Horace was there or had faded away when the officer left.

In a state of shock and disbelief, she drifted into the house and over to the couch to pick up the phone on the end table. It was cold in her hand; she leaned back against the couch, feeling weak.

She didn't remember pushing the right numbers either, but her Aunt Myrtle's groggy voice answered.

"Mffft—hello?"

"Aunt Myrtle. Aunt Myrtle . . ." The words were barely audible.

"Maggie? Is that you?" Aunt Myrtle was suddenly awake, glancing at the clock. "Are you all right?"

"No. No, I'm not." Something like a sob made it hard to get any more words out. "Horse, Horace—there's been an ac-cident."

The words trailed off and Maggie realized her fingers hurt from gripping the phone so hard.

"Accident. Horace? Maggie, are you all right?"

Maggie couldn't speak.

"Are you at home?"

"Yes." Maggie's tears rolled down onto the phone. She felt like laughing at that, an eyelash away from hysteria.

"Just stay right there. I'm coming." The dial tone came on.

Aunt Myrtle got there in minutes. She pried the phone out of her favorite niece's hand and took over.

The following ten days went by for Maggie Murphy as though they were happening to someone else.

The zombie that looked like Maggie Murphy ran on automatic. It brushed its teeth and managed to get decently covered when it had to go outside. The rest of her life was directed by Aunt Myrtle.

Horace's last paycheck was sent to Maggie, along with a small amount of money he'd had in some sort of retirement plan she didn't understand, plus some other information about benefits. She understood that she would have hospitalization for only the next sixty days and there was a little bit of extra added to his last paycheck.

She sat stunned, holding the correspondence, as if hoping all the information would somehow soak in through her fingertips.

The small amount of extra money talked the loudest. She would deposit it tomorrow. Some shred of logic was still working well enough to register that much.

The golden truths Aunt Myrtle extracted from the company's correspondence and what felt like brain bruises in Maggie's head were: Maggie had Horace's last check; there would be only one more. Those plus the little dab he had in the retirement fund, which was what the extra money was, amounted to just under two thousand dollars.

"He had just paid the rent and monthly bills," Aunt Myrtle commented. "That's one good thing."

Good for thirty days, anyway. Maggie nodded, thinking. *I've got to get busy and find a job.*

The now familiar painful ache twisted her heart again. *Oh, Horace, I need you!*

Aunt Myrtle was still going through the papers Maggie had laid on the coffee table.

"Did Horace have any insurance? Any kind at all?" Aunt Myrtle asked hopefully, her eyes busy with the papers.

Horace's transparent spirit appeared and paced as Maggie and Myrtle talked. He got a guilty expression when insurance was mentioned.

"No." Maggie sighed with a sad half smile. "Horace thought he was immortal. Him and that motorcycle."

Aunt Myrtle eyed another stack of papers on the coffee table and saw the top one was another bill.

"There's something else sure as death and taxes, and it's monthly bills."

She raised her eyebrows at Maggie, sounding hopeful. "Maybe you can get on full time at the day care center now? You've been there a while, what do you think?"

Maggie shook her head. "No, that's out. They're closing one of their places, and I got notice last week they won't need me anymore. I'm going to have to find something else, and fast."

"You will, you will. Don't panic yet."

"Thanks. For all you've done." Maggie's eyes went to the urn that held Horace's ashes. "I didn't know how to go about any of this. I know Horace would probably want to be scattered over a raceway or a cloverleaf somewhere. He told me so once."

Horace stopped to examine the urn and grinned like an eight-year-old at the reference to a racetrack resting place.

"He mentioned it at some race we went to . . ." Maggie bowed her head. "But I just can't. I can't do it. Not now, anyway. I don't know what I'd have done without you, Aunt Myrtle."

"Oh, you'd have done all right and you'll make it all right from now on, too. You're young and healthy." She grinned, trying to cheer Maggie up. "And you don't have warts on your nose or a wooden leg. You'll get a job and everything's going to be all right."

Horace grinned at Maggie and gave Aunt Myrtle a thumbs-up.

Maggie laughed a little through her tears, making both of them feel better.

"Come on home with me. We'll have supper and there's a good movie on. Bring Horace with you." Aunt Myrtle waved an arm in the direction of Horace's urn. "He always liked a good movie."

She kept talking, not giving Maggie a chance to settle back into dull-eyed depression. "Hollywood's got more trouble than we have. And heck—those poor devils have to sell it!"

They stopped by the store for salad things and a frozen pizza.

At Aunt Myrtle's, Maggie started putting things up in the kitchen shelves and Aunt Myrtle suggested, "Go out and look at my rose bed. I just put in a pretty new pink one. Down on the far end."

Getting a sudden idea, she turned to look at Maggie, her expression thoughtful. "Maybe Horace would like to rest in peace with the roses. What do you think?"

Maggie stopped, her elbow holding the refrigerator door open. "Can we do that?"

"I don't see why not. Some people put their ashes on the mantel. Some people scatter them where they were told to scatter them before—before—what's wrong with a rose garden?"

As she closed the refrigerator door, Maggie leaned against it, picturing Aunt Myrtle's roses. "I like the idea better than scattering, and I know you aren't going to move after forty years here."

"Right. This was my mama's house and now it's mine. There's a shovel out back in the shed if you want to do it now."

Aunt Myrtle got on with her work stocking the shelves from the grocery sacks. "But there's no hurry. Whatever you think."

"I don't know. I think my decision maker's still on break or something." Maggie sighed. "I'll go out and look, though. Think about it."

Maggie went out to look at the roses, moving as if she needed a tow. Horace started after her but faded and disappeared as if he hadn't got the hang of appearing and disappearing yet.

As soon as the door closed behind Maggie, Aunt Myrtle went into action. She grabbed the phone like it was a hot bargain on sale and dialed quickly, keeping an eye out the window. Her ring was answered promptly.

"The *Herald,* Hank Hanover."

"Hank! I've got to talk fast!"

A slightly nasal twang intoned, "The number you have reached is not in service at this time—"

"Nice try, Hank. Listen, Maggie needs a job and she needs it now. How about it?"

"I don't have one, Cuz. The best I could do is a couple of days a week. Three if she can stand in for the senior citizen who calls himself my only columnist."

"Stand in?"

"Yeah, he hasn't showed up for work for a couple of days."

"How old is he?" Myrtle blurted quickly.

"Forget it, Cuz. His DOB is nineteen-oh-hell and he will probably outlive all the other nervous-frantic cases here. But I do need someone to write the column till he gets back. And do general office work, of course."

"She can do that."

"How do you know?"

"Because she's smart and she can type, and she can do it. Start her off with the two or three days and try her out on the column. What have you got to lose? You said you need help, didn't you?"

"Well, send her over tomorrow. But I'm not promising a thing."

"I am. Blood kin is blood kin!" Myrtle's voice had dropped an octave and sounded grim.

"Are you threatening me, Cuz?"

"You finally caught on!"

13

"You've been reading too many of those whodunnits and 'cozy' mysteries." He made a prissy little gesture as if she could see it over the phone.

"We'll be there tomorrow."

"We?" He didn't get a chance to argue. He was holding a dead phone.

The lettuce and salad things were nearly all reduced to bite-sized chunks when Maggie called to her aunt from the door. She looked happier and so did Horace, who accompanied her.

Horace came and went a couple of times, as if practicing his entrances, until Maggie spoke and he stopped to listen.

"Hey, I'm taking you up on the rose bed plot. The new rose is beautiful and the climbing one is Peace." Maggie gushed about the roses, looking pleased. "The pretty new pink is a hybrid. Did you know that? Silly question!"

"Yeah, I know. I'm picky about my roses. Besides which, it said so on the tag it had on it. Do you need any help?"

"No. I'll be back in a few minutes."

The door closed again as Aunt Myrtle checked to see if she'd got everything they needed out of the refrigerator.

Looking around the pleasant, homey kitchen, Maggie's aunt remembered some of the sweet things Horace had done for her favorite niece and blessed him as a good guy. The rose bed was a beautiful, appropriate place, and she knew Maggie would feel better after Horace lay in it.

Right now that was the most important need, making Maggie feel better. That and finding a job.

Myrtle looked around, checking things on the table again. *I'll handle Hank*, she promised herself. Hank had admitted he needed help, and that was half the battle.

Aunt Myrtle straightened, smiling to herself, as she watched Maggie from the kitchen window. She was nearly finished planting Horace, and the roses were beautiful.

When Maggie came in to wash her hands, the tossed green salad looked good and Myrtle was taking the pizza out of the oven.

"I buried the urn at the end where the new rose is, since the ground was a little looser there. I put your mulch back, too."

"That's good. Timed it just right. Want a Coke or root beer?"

"Either one. Everything looks good, including the salad. I'm glad you thought of having pizza." Maggie raised her eyebrows, teasing her aunt. "You checked the label to make sure they didn't put any calories in this stuff, didn't you?"

"They know better! But I think my personal fat factory can operate without them. Don't worry. Just enjoy."

Maggie shook some dressing onto her salad without looking up. "I buried the urn up to the rim around the top. It looks all right, and I know where it is in case either one of us wants to move it for some reason. One of Horace's friends had his ashes scattered over his favorite fishing hole, isn't that a hoot?"

Maggie caught her lower lip between her teeth and fought back tears.

"I've heard of stranger places." Myrtle patted Maggie's hand. "Maybe it's not about places anyway. A friend of mine said she wanted to be cremated and her ashes scattered because she wanted to be free, not in a grave or a mausoleum somewhere."

"Maybe so. Anyway, he's been cremated like he wanted to be, and he had his organ donor card in his billfold so he can feel good about that, too."

"Did they tell you anything about the organs?"

"Yes, I think they have to. They took a kidney and an eye cornea. I didn't want to know any details."

"Maggie, I'm so sorry. He was a good-hearted person, and everybody liked him. And he enjoyed life." She reached over to squeeze Maggie's hand again. "You've got a lot of good thi to remember."

"I know. I've got a lot of good memories to hold on to. And they told me he didn't suffer. He never regained consciousness. They kept him on life support to take the organs and check with next of kin. I didn't even know enough to ask about what happened. I guess there's some kind of report. I'm just sort of numb right now."

Aunt Myrtle shrugged. "I'm sure there is some kind of accident report. But right now, you've got to take care of Number One. And you'll be all right. We'll go see Hank tomorrow."

"Oh. Cousin Hank at the paper?" Maggie's expression was dubious.

"Yes. I'm pretty sure he's got something for you to do." Aunt Myrtle kept her eyes on her plate.

"Aunt Myrtle—" Maggie's tone demanded the truth. "Did you threaten his family jewels if he didn't?"

"I didn't have to. He knows me," was the grim answer. "And this is a family matter."

Maggie swallowed the last bite of her pizza and didn't comment, not wanting to think about it. "Do you have any of Mama's funeral salad left?"

"It's in the 'frig, help yourself. And just leave it out here. I'll have some too."

Tasting the Jell-O salad, Maggie remembered some of the times her mother had made it before she and Maggie's dad were killed by a semi on the freeway several years before. Aunt Myrtle noticed the fleeting sadness.

"You want to stay over tonight? There's an old movie on, as I said."

"No. If you don't mind taking me, I want to go home. You an get back in time to watch the movie and I've got to get used all that emptiness sometime. Thought if you don't mind ping, I'd get a paper on the way home and start looking for a job. A full-time job, I mean."

"That reminds me, when I talked to Hank at the *Herald* about using you two or maybe three days, he mentioned a column someone was doing. But whoever is doing it hasn't showed up for a couple of days. Who knows, it may work into something." Aunt Myrtle sounded optimistic but Maggie raised worried eyes to hers.

"You're sure? Hank said so? Two or three days for sure? Now?"

The answer was a positive nod. "I said we'd be there tomorrow." The words sounded chiseled in stone.

"And you didn't—lean on him?"

"You have to lean forward to get ahead. Haven't you noticed? I just asked, is all. He's always needing help at least part time, the way they move on. You can't ever tell, and it's a start."

"It sure can't hurt." Maggie's expression brightened. "He won't throw us out, I guess. We're kinfolks, after all, like you said."

"And I'm practicing my judo." Aunt Myrtle pointed that out with pride, looking superior if not downright invincible.

"You still taking that martial arts course?"

"No, but he doesn't know that. I switched to aerobics till my muscles started objecting and reminding me I'm facing the big six-oh on my next birthday. That's when I forgot about all that muscle building. Now I just move around enough not to take root anywhere."

Maggie insisted on washing the dishes before she left and floated out into the night on hearty assurances from Aunt Myrtle and a few glimmers of hope about Cousin Hank's temporary job offer.

Despite her guilt about Aunt Myrtle having to drive at night she felt better on the way home than she had since Horace's accident. They stopped for her to get a paper and a diet drink before Aunt Myrtle pulled up into her driveway.

Maggie waved goodbye and marched bravely up the steps of the dark house, not looking back.

I'll leave the porch light on next time. Then she frowned. No, Horace said that just lets all the burglars know there's no one home. I'll leave a lamp or something on inside.

She closed her eyes. Her hand gripped the cold knob. Standing in the door as her Aunt Myrtle's car picked up speed, there was an empty feeling inside where her heart was supposed to be.

I miss you, Horace.

The dark closed around her as she entered the quiet house. She didn't see or feel Horace as he joined her with an encouraging pat on the back. He put his arms around her briefly, but they just went through like a gentle breeze. He put his hands back in his pockets and faded away.

Maggie hit the light switch. She tossed the paper on the end table by the phone and went to brush her teeth before looking at the want ads, not expecting much, since she'd checked them recently.

There was nothing new or that sounded promising. The paper didn't have much to offer but lots of professional placement services. She made a face at the pie-in-the-sky ads. *I doubt these places have any jobs anyway. It's always worded so generally, nothing specific. And all these technical requirements! If I had those skills and degrees and 'ain't I wonderfuls,' would I be reading this?*

Maggie snorted in disbelief at an ad that appeared so frequently she had noticed it before. *Got to be something wrong to have that much turnover.*

Maggie tossed the paper aside and put on the shapeless gown Horace had laughed at, her mind still on job possibilities. She mentally went over the exact amount in her purse and her checking account. A lot of the money was already spoken for with no more in sight.

After our stop at the *Herald* I'll start knocking on doors just in case Cousin Hank isn't as afraid of Aunt Myrtle as she thinks he is. A wave of affection warmed her heart as she remembered her aunt's determination about the job.

Horace appeared and bent to kiss her on the forehead just before she closed her eyes.

CHAPTER TWO

The next day Aunt Myrtle's car pulled into Maggie's driveway behind the old car, which looked like it had found its final resting place. Maggie and Horace referred to it as the heap. She tooted the horn twice.

The door opened and Maggie's head appeared. Myrtle noticed a mended tear at the bottom of the screen.

"Be right with you. Brushing my hair!" Maggie called. She wore a skirt and a t-shirt advertising pizza.

It seemed the harsh morning light was showing up in unsympathetic, glaring daylight all the flaws, perils, and patches that surrounded her favorite niece.

Aunt Myrtle got out of her car and was looking down at the heap in the driveway when Maggie joined her.

"What ails this beast?"

"You've got me." Maggie shook her head. "But I think it's got a lot to do with old age."

"Don't say that!" Aunt Myrtle clapped her hands over her ears in horror.

Maggie wrinkled her nose. "Don't be so touchy, you're not old." She smiled at her favorite relative affectionately. "You wouldn't be so much in demand for chauffeuring and such if you were in anywhere near the shape that heap is in."

"Thank you, I think." Aunt Myrtle got in behind the wheel and settled her tall and well-upholstered but not fat frame, reaching for her seatbelt.

"This is no Cadillac," she admitted. "But what it lacks in prestige it makes up for in efficiency. It runs on bubbles and fumes!"

Maggie smiled. "Looks like a BMW to me after trying to coax the heap to just run, then stop somewhere near where Horace applies the brakes." She fastened her seatbelt, recalling the heap didn't have those either.

Aunt Myrtle drove defensively, facing whatever traffic hazard might come their way.

Seen from the corner of Maggie's eye, her Aunt Myrtle's profile bore so much resemblance to her mother's, Maggie's heart warmed with affection and not a little humor. The pretty, nearly sixty-year-old face looked straight ahead like an Irish setter on point and held every bit as much determination.

On point for a job for me! I love you, Aunt Myrtle . . .

"Getting there early like we are, in case Hank does tell you to take a seat and start typing, you'll have a full day's work. After all, he did say he that he could use you a couple or three days."

Maggie gave a small nod without answering. She reminded herself to get the recommendation they had promised her from the day care center as soon as she could. She mentally crossed her fingers.

At the paper there was a strip of parking slots in front of the *Herald,* which also served as the real estate office. Aunt Myrtle evidently didn't feel a bit guilty about taking up room in the small area, and Maggie was afraid they wouldn't be there very long anyway. So there was no use worrying about it.

It's not as if I'm looking for input for my worry list. Here I am, a new widow and facing my twenty-fifth birthday when all the cosmetics companies tell you your skin starts drying out. She tried laughing at herself instead of crying, and looked briefly at her reflection as she closed her car door. Her aunt was already out and on the move.

There goes Aunt Myrtle. Marching in there like she's ready to take over!

She followed Aunt Myrtle in. What else could she do?

Not seeing Hank anywhere in sight as they entered the outer office of the newspaper, Aunt Myrtle looked around. She approached a chic, young black woman who was gazing critically at her flame-colored fingernails.

Before speaking, Aunt Myrtle looked down at the nameplate on the cluttered reception desk.

"Ah, excuse me, Fatima?"

"Yes," came out bored to the bone.

"We have an appointment to see Hank Hanover this morning."

Fatima glanced at her a second with beautiful but uninterested eyes then yelled, "Hank!"

From somewhere off to their left came a shuffle and Hank appeared with an armload of papers.

"Oh, hi, Myrtle. Maggie." He greeted them pleasantly, or maybe just wasn't much interested one way or another, Maggie thought.

"Come on back to my office." Hank led the way, Maggie picking up the loose pieces of paper that fell from his collection of whatever it was as they followed.

In the office Hank laid the papers on the desk and took the ones Maggie handed him to lay on top of them.

"Have a seat."

Maggie perched on a step stool near the door, and Aunt Myrtle eyed something that might have been some back issues in the only other chair.

"Will that ink rub off?" Aunt Myrtle peered suspiciously down at the papers.

Hank eyed her flowered dress with the white background.

"'ll soon know."

Myrtle knew Princess Grace wouldn't sit there, Princess Grace being Hank's wife. But a little ink was not going to stop Aunt Myrtle. She promptly sat and waited for Hank and Maggie to take it from there.

"I really don't have a job to offer," Hank began. "But I can use you a couple of days for maybe a couple of weeks till some of my help comes back, settles down, gets out of jail, or all of the above. They sort of wander in and out as hunger demands." He explained mostly to Aunt Myrtle.

Maggie smiled at his candor. "Right now a couple of days sounds good to me, since what I've got to compare it with is nothing. You won't feel insulted if I put in applications elsewhere, will you?"

"No, feel free."

"Aunt Myrtle said something about a columnist that's gone missing, that maybe I can try writing a couple of things to see if you like them or they can be improved enough to do?"

"Probably be a waste of your time. He'll straggle back in, always does. Sure could use some help right now, though. Of course it would be typing and general office work, not just the column."

"Well, my typing is pretty good. Last time I checked, anyway. And my typing fingers fit around a broom handle . . ." Maggie eyed a pile of papers that appeared to have fallen from the chair Aunt Myrtle was sitting in.

"That's the spirit." Hank began looking happier.

"I know a regular job is just daydreaming right now." Maggie's voice was hopeful. "But, just in case, how much do you pay the columnist?"

Hank's happy cloud deflated as he evaded a direct answer.

Maggie said with a sinking feeling, "Oh. You do pay him, don't you?"

"Yes!" Hank hurried to clear that up. "Yes, I pay him for

circulation. He just does the column because he likes to, and it impresses his cronies down at the synagogue to see his picture every week."

"Down at the synagogue?"

"Yes, he's Jewish. One of his friends gives him a hand sometimes. And he goes to the local senior citizen meetings, too. He does very well in circulation. Says he likes to have something to do."

"Circulation?" Maggie had no idea what that was, outside the human body.

"He and his friend who helps him sometimes pick up the papers when they're ready. They take them and put them in the boxes." He quickly added, "But you won't have to do that. Just help in the office and if you can manage, get a column together, until our resident genius comes back."

"All right, I'll sure give it a try." She asked curiously, "What kind of column is it? I'd be a total loss at sports or mechanics or anything like that."

"It's 'Help from Helena.' It has some household hints, some advice. Just general things. It's a women's column, but Fritz likes to have his picture on it anyway." Hank smiled and Maggie could tell he must like the old fellow. "He likes to impress the ladies, too."

Maggie tried to remember some of the columns in the daily paper. She wasn't much of a fan of any of them. She'd have got cold feet if she could afford them.

"Right now we need some warm bodies to help in the office. And the column, of course." There was an expectant pause.

"I'll do my best. Two days for a couple of weeks then?"

"Make it three," Aunt Myrtle broke in. "I'll bring her over here."

Hank turned to Maggie, "Car trouble?"

Maggie nodded.

"Okay, three days a week for two weeks." He got up and beckoned.

They followed him back out to a big desk, which had a place for a typewriter but no typewriter, and had three untidy piles of papers on it.

In one of the stacks there was a back issue containing the "Help from Helena" column with a small picture of an elderly man at the top.

Hank beckoned to a man across the room. "I'll get you a typewriter over here," he told Maggie.

The man Hank beckoned to stuck his cigar in his mouth to free his hands, and brought the typewriter.

"This is Floyd Graves. His job is copy, sometimes sales, black hole."

"Black hole?"

"Through that door—presses, resident devils and gnomes."

"Oh."

"You've met Fatima?"

Maggie nodded, "Sort of." She exchanged a smile with Fatima.

"That's Tim Thompson's desk over there. He's out selling ads right now—I hope to God! Office boy's Carl Peabody. You'll know him when he comes in. He's the only one young enough to be the gofer except Fatima. And I think it's against her religion to touch anything that looks like free help."

This was completely ignored by Fatima, who was working on her nails.

Maggie put her purse in the desk drawer and Hank waved a combination dismissal and goodbye at Aunt Myrtle, turning to go back to his office.

"Let me see what you come up with by quitting time," he threw back over his shoulder at Maggie.

Aunt Myrtle's voice stopped him in his tracks. "When's that?

Quitting time?" She pinned him down.

"Must be around five o'clock, because there's never anyone left in here then." Another relevant thought hit him. "Lunch is any time you have the money and the urge at the same time and there's at least one warm body left in here to answer the phones." Hank went back to his office.

"Lunch—" Aunt Myrtle began.

"No problem, Aunt Myrtle. I can see a convenience store from here."

"Okay." The love in Aunt Myrtle's eyes wished her luck. "I'll be here at five."

CHAPTER THREE

Fatima watched the door close behind Aunt Myrtle and turned a lovely smile on Maggie.

"Welcome to the asylum."

"Thanks. I'd be embarrassed for you to know how glad I am to be here," Maggie smiled back. She sat down and glanced over the three rats' nests on the desk before starting on the first one.

The phone wasn't too busy, and Maggie learned to tune it out and concentrate on her work, not even noticing when Floyd came in and out. By two o'clock, with an eye to what was in the back issues and some almost legible handwritten notes from Hank, which included brief but harsh critiques along with things he'd lined through, Maggie had an outline of what she was going to write. She pushed the pile in front of her back a little to make room to write better and tackled the job.

Finally, having done the best she could, she laid the pad with the rough draft on it aside. A hand appeared in front of her face. It had a can of soda in it.

"You didn't have lunch," Fatima accused. "You thinking of giving me some competition down at the agency?" She narrowed her eyes, but her lips turned up at the corners.

Maggie gratefully took the Coke. "Agency? You model! I should have known."

"I get a job once in a while. I guess you're working here part time now?"

"Yes and no. I'm looking for a job, and Hank said he'd let me work here three days a week for two weeks." There was a pause and Maggie added, "Any typing or anything else I can do, plus hopefully, get a couple of 'Help from Helena' columns done. Just while the man who usually does the column is gone."

Fatima nodded. "He's been gone. This is the third day now." A slight tinge of worry crept into her voice. "Ain't like him."

Maggie glanced at one of the columns with the picture in it and tried to imagine the elderly man in person as Fatima lightened up. "Usually he just parties too hearty and sobers up the next day. Must have had a high-heeled good time this time. Or maybe he got sick."

"Guess so. Hank said he'd be back." Maggie glanced at the pad before her. "I've got an outline done for the 'Help from Helena' column. His byline says Frederich Wartz. How come a man is doing a column named 'Help from Helena'?"

"Helena means the town. Helena, Arkansas, not a woman. Whoever started it was from there. I think it was Helena, Arkansas—it was before my time." Fatima dismissed it and sipped her Coke.

"Oh, I see. The town. Well, I'll take out the rest of this stuff I'm through with and get it written up, and see if Hank thinks it will do."

"It'll do."

Fatima got up off the corner of the desk, making even that limited bit of movement look glamorous.

Maggie asked nervously, "Do you think Hank will mind if I make a personal phone call?"

"You planning on telling him?"

"No."

"Then he ain't gonna mind."

"That's true. Thanks for the logic input." Maggie grinned and reached for the dog-eared phone book.

She chose what she hoped was the right extension at the police department and punched in the numbers.

Horace appeared, looking hopeful as she asked questions, then faded when she gave up and hung up the phone.

"Well! I learned a lot, none of it having anything to do with what I wanted."

"What you want? What kind of report you looking for?"

"I wanted a copy of the police report on my husband Horace's accident if there was one made." She gave the phone a contemptuous sneer. "And the phone company says, 'let your fingers do the walking.' Big joke! I'll just wait till I can call from home."

"Did I hear you say his name was Horace Aloysius?"

Maggie nodded. "The name's after some long-dead family member." She wrinkled her nose. "Some of his friends called him Horse. I'll bet the relative he was named after had to fight every time he had to answer to it in school or maybe." She gave a little laugh. "He just died of embarrassment with a name like that."

"It's not funny! You don't know how bad a name like that can be!"

"Oh, come on, Fatima isn't so bad," Maggie pointed to the nameplate on the reception desk. "Sounds exotic and mysterious. Glamorous even." Maggie tilted her head, studying it. "Fatima. It's an Egyptian name, isn't it?"

"I don't know. I just know it's mine and it's paid for."

"Paid for?" Maggie's eyes widened, wondering if there was some new government department where you had to go and pay a tax or a fee on your name. If there was, Horace hadn't mentioned it. Fatima's voice broke into the worrying Maggie was getting so good at now that the bills were hers to take care of.

"Yeah. Paid for. Lots of models have a professional name, so

29

I picked me out one. It only costs a few bucks to make it legal, so why not?"

"No reason, I guess. Sounds like a great professional name to me. Exotic, as I said." She looked sideways at Fatima. "Don't suppose you'd like to share the original?"

Fatima's dark eyes checked the area before answering. "Momma liked the Old Testament names. She named me Queen Esther Johnson!"

Maggie bit back a giggle. "I don't blame you, then! And you're as pretty as Queen Esther must have been." Maggie felt generous since she'd landed her part-time job, and grinned. "I'll throw in the Queen of Sheba too."

"We are friends!" Fatima beamed briefly. "Unless you tell anybody about the original. I'd swear you lied, of course."

"Of course. Deal!"

Maggie went back to work. After another forty or more minutes of writing, rewriting, muttering and proofing, she had what she hoped was a passable finished column that might have a chance with Hank. She leaned backward then forward and stretched her arms like a cat after a nap to ease tense back muscles as Fatima watched sympathetically.

Maggie got up and placed the wannabe column carefully in the center of her desk with a chipped-up ashtray for a paperweight and started cleaning off the rest of the desk and its immediate vicinity. At least that was something she knew how to do. The job turned out to be like washing a wall with no stopping place. She crammed everything she could into the dented trash can and saw Fatima shake her head when she looked up as if she had read Maggie's mind.

"This can looks like it might have accompanied the last columnist on some of his adventures." Maggie eyed it critically. Fatima stifled a comment and reached for the ringing phone.

Both arms around the plastic sack full of trash, Maggie

headed for the back door. If Hank saw her pass his office, he didn't comment, nag about the column, or offer any help. It was only a short walk to the wooden enclosure that held the commercial dumpster out back. The wooden gate was latched, making it necessary to set her burden down.

Why couldn't they be this organized inside?

Picking up her burden again, she stepped inside and was met by the granddaddy of all bad smells. She coughed, feeling like gagging, it was so strong. The awful odor that greeted her got worse as she lifted the sack to throw it in. Part of a back issue blew against her leg as she let go the bag and she bent to pick it up. There didn't seem to be any stopping place there either. She picked up some other debris and drink cans that hadn't made it into the dumpster.

Trying to hurry, the thought occurred if this was a high school project she would probably get points for neatness on her column, since there wasn't much neatness anywhere else around there.

Grabbing at everything that didn't look too repulsive to touch, her hand hit an old athletic shoe. It didn't move.

She drew back her hand and straightened up, feeling strange inside. She tried not to breathe in any more of the bad smell than she could help as she stepped around the side of the bin. She stopped there, looking down on the body of a man.

Her first instinct was to turn around and run, but her weak knees didn't seem to get the message to move.

She put her arm up over her mouth and held her breath. The stench was at its worst there. Or maybe it just seemed worse because now she knew what it was. The man's shirt was bloody and there was some blood in his white hair, too. She recognized the face. The face beneath the bloody white hair was the one she had seen at the top of the "Help from Helena" column.

She got moving and didn't stop to latch the wooden gate.

31

She didn't stop till she was standing in front of Hank's desk.

Hank was busy writing something.

"Hank? Ah, Mr.—"

"Hank's sufficient." He kept writing.

Maggie took a deep breath and waited as he jabbed his pen at the paper to make a period and looked up in annoyance. "What the hell are we talking about?"

"I-I think I just got on regular."

Hank struggled between a frown and a puzzled look. "Regular? Got on regular? That's my decision, isn't it? When did that change?"

Maggie consulted the watch Horace had given her for Christmas. She suspected he'd liked it for the second hand, which was good for measuring acceleration speed. She pushed the thought aside. "About two minutes and twenty seconds ago."

She turned and went out and heard him get up to follow her. Horace appeared and fell in behind Hank. His worried look was back again as he watched Maggie's back. He tried to give Hank an encouraging pat on the shoulder, but his hand went through as it always did. He shrugged, just walked with them and watched.

Maggie hadn't fastened the wooden gate, and it was swinging open in the slight breeze. Standing aside to let Hank pass, Maggie gestured at the shoe on the other side of the dumpster. Horace looked from Maggie to Hank as if satisfied she would be all right and disappeared.

Maggie walked slowly over to look down on Hank. He was kneeling beside the body.

He glanced up at her. "Yeah, it's him, all right. It's Fritz Wartz."

He reached over and gingerly lifted some of the white hair

with two fingers. Jagged points were carved into the flesh of the forehead.

"A star!" A chill ran down Maggie's back and she shuddered.

"Yeah. We'd better not touch anything. I'll call the police."

Back inside, he went into his office and Maggie went back to her desk, looking as strange as she felt. Fatima came around her reception desk, asking what was wrong with her.

As Maggie filled Fatima in, Floyd Graves came from the back with ink stains on his hands. Tim Thompson had come in and looked up from his desk. They listened quietly to what Maggie told Fatima until she finished.

"I knew it wasn't like him to stay out this long," Floyd said.

"Hank call the police?" Tim asked and looked at the boy coming in. "Here comes Carl."

Tim went to the boy and told him Fritz Wartz had been found dead.

"Old Wartsy?" Carl exclaimed. "He's—he's dead?" He looked around at all of them as if it couldn't be true. "I just talked to him when I was in last week, and he was fine. What happened?"

"He's been killed. Maggie just found him out back by the dumpster. By the way, this is Maggie Murphy. She works here now."

"Hello, Carl."

"And this is Tim." Floyd nodded at Maggie. Tim nodded.

"Old Wartzy." Carl sat down by Tim's desk. "But what happened to him?"

"We don't know yet. We'll know more when the police get here."

The questions were halted by the arrival of a plainclothes detective who looked like he could and probably had handled about everything, and a younger uniformed policeman. The detective and the policeman were escorted out to the scene of the crime, then the detective and Hank went into his office to

talk. The policeman came to wait in the outer office.

Maggie tried to get on with her typing, but was making more errors than progress. Horace had come back and wandered around, studying the faces in the office and peering at Maggie until he stuck his hands in his pockets and faded again, looking as nervous as she was.

Exasperated at two wrong letters in one word, Maggie pulled the sheet out of her typewriter and gave up trying to work. She spoke to the policeman.

"Could I ask you a question?" she asked timidly.

"Sure." His smile was nice. "If it's an easy one."

"I guess it would be for you." Maggie smiled too, noticing how good looking he was when he smiled.

"My husband was killed in a motorcycle accident recently. It happened on his way home, so it must have been in this precinct or whatever they call them. Would there be a report on it? A one-person accident like that? I'd just like to know what happened, whatever they can tell me."

Immediately, Horace was back and interested. He peered intently at the policeman as he answered.

"Motorcycle accident. What was his name and where was it?" The nice-looking policeman took out a little notepad.

Maggie told him the little she knew, feeling lost with so little information.

"The car that found him would have reported it. I'm sure it will be easy to find. Would you like me to look into it for you?"

"Yes, please." She hesitated, wanting to ask for a copy. She decided to do that later.

The policeman closed the little notepad and returned it to his pocket.

He's not wearing a wedding ring. Maggie's heart fluttered and she blushed at noticing about a ring. Fortunately, the policeman was putting away his notepad and didn't notice the look, but

Horace did.

There was the sound of the outer office door opening, which filled a silence that was getting a little awkward. The policeman got up, his eyes swiveling to the people from the coroner's office who were coming in the front door, single file and all business.

Maggie was fascinated as the good-looking policeman with the nice smile reverted to an official, efficient stranger in uniform. Horace gave him a speculative look.

Straightening the things on her desk, Maggie left it and went to the back door where Hank stood watching all the activity he could see from there. He looked around at Maggie.

"Here comes the detective. He said he wanted to talk to you," Hank told her quickly then stepped forward and held the door open for him.

The detective glanced at Maggie.

"This is Maggie Murphy," Hank said. "Detective Alan Hill."

"I'm going to borrow your office if you don't mind. I won't be long."

"Sure." Hank turned and went toward the outer office.

Maggie just stood there until the detective motioned her into Hank's office. He didn't shut the door and sat down at Hank's desk. She started toward the chair Aunt Myrtle had sat in when Hank hired her. She noticed it still had the same back issues in it. Horace turned from studying the uniformed policeman and hurried back to go into the office with her.

"I need to ask you a few questions, Miss Murphy."

"Mrs." Maggie quickly made the correction. Horace smiled approval at her pointing that out to him.

"Mrs. Murphy." He nodded, added it to the paper he had picked up to write on. "You found the body?"

"Yes, sir."

"How did you happen to find him?"

"I had been working on a column and had some trash to take

out. When I went out to the enclosure, I noticed a bad smell. Then I saw this foot sticking out. He, the body, was lying beside the dumpster."

"How long had you known him?"

Startled, Maggie answered, "I didn't know him at all."

"How did you know who he was?"

The detective's eyes were on her. Maggie thought he'd be an impossible person to lie to, not that she would or had any reason to. Neither of them moved; he waited.

"His picture was on a back issue of the paper. It was on a column he wrote for the paper and I saw it, is how I knew. I just came to work here today and I happened to see it. Then Hank— Mr. Hanover—I got him to come and look. And he said yes, it was Mr. Wartz."

Horace stood listening, peering at Maggie. She sat quietly, her hands clasped in her lap.

"So you didn't know him or anything about him. Hadn't seen him until you found him out there by the dumpster?"

"That's right, sir."

Detective Hill wrote something briefly and looked up. "That's all I need to ask. I would like your address and phone number in case I want to ask anything further, but I will get it from Mr. Hanover."

"All right. I'll be glad to help any way I can." She reached for a piece of paper on Hank's desk. "In fact, I'll just jot it down here for you."

It didn't take long, and she handed it to him.

"Thank you, Mrs. Murphy."

Out in the office, Fatima buttonholed Hank. "Was it really Wartzy? You saw him? It's really him?"

"Yeah, it's him. Maggie recognized him first, from his picture on the column."

"The police are here," Fatima observed. "Maggie didn't say, but being dead and having a bloody shirt, must be he didn't fall into the dumpster by himself?"

"No. He was beside the dumpster, not in it. And somebody killed him."

"Heck, his column wasn't that bad," Floyd volunteered. Tim smiled.

The comment broke the tension. "No, if bad writing was a motive for murder, none of us would be safe. There's a chest wound and some scratches, I guess you'd call them, on his forehead. We'll know more when the police tell us. But it is Friedrich Wartz. Our Wartzy, and he is dead. Don't even know when it happened yet. That's all I can tell you."

All of them turned as Maggie and Detective Hill came out, followed by the patrolman who had gone to wait in the hall. Horace trailed along with them.

Hank walked out with the detective, and the policeman beckoned to Maggie. She went to him and he handed her a card, closely watched by Horace.

"My name is Joe Driver. You can reach me at this number. I'll look up the information you asked about and call you here, if it's all right."

"Yes, it's all right, but let me give you my home number too, in case you need it." She wrote her number on a blank memo and handed it to him.

"Thank you."

Horace glanced from Maggie to the policeman and back, and stuck his hands in his jeans pocket. He left when the policeman did, giving him a thoughtful look as he disappeared.

Fatima raised her eyebrows at Maggie. "Home number? You gave him your home number?"

"He might not get to call till after regular hours and I do want that report."

"Maggie?" Hank called from the hallway.

"Yes, sir, I'll be right there." She quickly got the column and took it into the office.

Hank took it, gesturing impatiently for her to sit.

CHAPTER FOUR

Joe Driver started the car and Detective Hill fastened his seatbelt. As they pulled out into traffic, Alan looked at the name, address, and phone number Maggie had given him.

"Maggie Murphy. Must be short for Margaret. Pretty young lady. Must have been quite a shock, finding that body."

"I'm sure it was." Joe was noncommittal.

"She wasn't wearing a wedding ring."

"No, she's a widow."

Alan raised his eyebrows. "Oh, you're a faster worker than I am."

Joe grinned. "Not guilty. I didn't ask. She asked me to look into a report on her husband's fatal accident. He got killed on his motorcycle."

"Think there was something other than accidental about it?"

"No, she just wants to know more about how it happened, I think. And she is pretty. I did notice."

"Well, good. I was beginning to worry about you." Alan chuckled.

Maggie sat waiting to hear Hank's verdict on her first effort at writing a column. His expressionless face didn't give her much hope.

Hank laid it down in front of him when he finished. "It's better than Fritz ever did, not that he was in line for a Pulitzer." Hank chopped down any rising hopes.

"Here's a couple of changes I think we should have. For future reference, we don't want to get involved in anything controversial or ask for any input. We're not a sounding board, and Lord knows, I hope, we have limited space because we'll be making room for paying advertisement."

"Yes, sir."

He proceeded to help Maggie polish her column and Horace left, looking bored.

It took Maggie another hour to make the changes Hank wanted, but she felt better on the second trip to his office.

"Yes. This is good. Add a little humor every chance you get." He smiled. "I guess we're going to have to talk salary, since you are going to be regular. If you still want to be regular?"

"Yes, I do need a job." She added cautiously, "But the reason I need a job is to pay my bills." Maggie glanced up, her eyes meeting his. "I've got to make enough to do that. Horace made enough to cover the necessities and was up for a raise, and I worked part time, but it was hard making ends meet, even then."

Hank asked how much Horace made and other questions she wouldn't have answered except for a member of the family. Finally, Hank had enough information to satisfy him. "I'm thinking double Horace's salary and insurance at our group rate. What do you think?"

"I—why, I think it's wonderful!" Maggie was pleased. "My insurance Horace had on both of us will run out sixty days from—" she found it hard to finish.

"The rates aren't much." Hank rescued her, quickly changing the subject. He rummaged in a bottom desk drawer. "And they're very good for one employee, and still good for an employee and spouse."

"Fine. I was worried about that. The insurance, I mean. The salary and insurance both sound good to me. Thank you."

"Shouldn't take long to get the paperwork done, since we've

come to an agreement."

Maggie took a deep breath, making room for the joy and relief expanding in her chest. "I'd have taken less," she said with an embarrassed little laugh.

"I figured you would. But you'd have been putting in applications all over town too, wouldn't you?"

"Yes. If not this month then next month, when it got to be obvious the bills are for more than I've got and nothing left for emergencies."

Hank smiled. "Emergencies. I know what those are. Everybody's got 'em. They just go by different names. Okay, you're now a full-time employee. You'll have to take a physical for the insurance, but the exam won't cost you anything and the health insurance is at the employee's rate, with the paper picking up most of the premium. That's legalese for we pay most of it so everybody will take it and be protected. We get a better rate that way and the coverage is good. Eighty percent plus the big calamity coverage. You know, cancer and all that. I know it's good, because my wife checked it out and told me so." Hank rolled his eyes. "Nobody gets ahead of Grace." He grinned. "If I was still sending out resumés, I'd put 'suits Grace' on them for sure."

Maggie laughed, stomach full of butterflies, feeling good. "Thanks for the job, Hank. I'll work hard and make you glad you hired me. I guess hours are eight to five and lunch is like you said?"

Hank nodded. After a couple of seconds he asked, "Aren't you going to ask when's payday?"

"No, I wasn't going to ask, but I sure would like to know." Maggie admitted it seriously, thinking about her limited funds.

"Next Friday. Ordinarily you wouldn't get one for another two weeks, but I'm going to pay you a week's salary for saving me trying to find someone and covering the office work and

41

column too."

"Thanks. I can sure use it. And as I said, I'll work hard."

"And show up for work? Nobody gives a hoot how smart you are if you aren't here."

"Yeah, that too." Maggie's smile was wall to wall as she left.

At five o'clock, Aunt Myrtle waved from the door and Maggie covered her typewriter to leave.

As soon as she got seated in the car Aunt Myrtle demanded, "Okay, why the big smile? Hank die and will you the place?"

"No . . ." A sudden frown eclipsed the happiness on Maggie's face. "But speaking of dying, I'd forgot the downside of my good news."

"Good news? Downside? Speaking of dying?"

"The man who did the column—he—we found him dead. Out by the dumpster in back."

"Dead? Out in back? Did he have a heart attack or something?"

"No, Aunt Myrtle. Somebody killed him. The police have been here. No one knows who did it. Hank heard some of the coroner's people say it looked like he'd been stabbed at least once. And I saw a lot of blood."

"Stabbed? You saw a lot of blood?" Aunt Myrtle's knuckles turned white on the steering wheel.

"I found him."

"You? Oh, good Lord! How—how?"

"I was cleaning up the desk after getting an outline of the column done. And when I took out the trash, there he was. Lying in back of the dumpster."

"Oh, you poor thing!"

"It's all right. It was just a shock. Then after the police and the coroner and everyone left, Hank read the column I did. He made some changes and it was okay, I guess. Anyway, he said it would do. Then we talked about a regular job, and—" Maggie wound up breathlessly, "to make a long story short, I'm hired!" She couldn't hold the smile back any longer. "Full time!"

"He paying you enough for gas to get to work?" Suspicion oozed from the words.

"He is, Aunt Myrtle. Better than I could have got anywhere I was planning on trying to get on. And I've got group health insurance, too." Maggie gave a short bark of laughter, remembering her conversation with Hank. "And the insurance is good, Hank said, because Grace looked it over and she said so!" She giggled.

"He's right about that. If Grace approved it, it's good. And it's great about the job. Congratulations!" Having checked out the important things, Aunt Myrtle grinned too.

As they pulled out of the parking lot, Maggie added, "I do feel sort of guilty though. About getting the job I need and the poor man who had it being dead."

"You didn't dash out on break and kill him, did you?"

"No," Maggie laughed.

"Then whoopee! I'll stop on the way home. I've got our dinner fixed, and I'll get some praline ice cream for dessert!"

The next day was a happy one for Maggie. She looked at back issues of the *Herald* and some of the notes and cleaned out the desk, in addition to getting some correspondence typed for Hank. She even peeked into the black hole where the presses were, at the big machines looming like the silhouettes of hibernating monsters. But she didn't go in. They were so big and it was so dark in there, she stepped back from the door quickly, afraid an evil, inky little gnome of some kind would leap out from behind some of that mysterious monster machinery and get her.

She swept the office and earned a thumbs-up sign from Floyd behind her back. Not all communication in the office was verbal.

That night she picked up the ringing phone and recognized

the policeman's voice.

"Joe Driver," he said. "I tried to call you last night—"

"I had dinner with my aunt," Maggie explained. "Were you able to find the report?"

"Yes." He sounded like he was smiling. "Do you like pizza?"

"Doesn't everybody?" Maggie's smile matched his.

"Probably so. I just haven't asked everybody. I've just got off work and there's a pizza parlor near your address. Would you meet me there so we can talk about the report?" Hank appeared and listened, interested.

"You mean Garlic Pepper Heaven?"

"That's it."

"When?"

"In about fifteen minutes?"

"I'll be there. It's in walking distance."

"Walking distance? No car?"

"Not right now—"

"I'll swing by and get you. Exercise is for after you eat."

"You don't have to convince me. Thanks."

At Garlic Pepper Heaven, Joe ordered their pizza with everything and a pitcher of root beer when she nodded her approval of the drink.

Horace wandered around looking at everything and everyone, but never getting very far from their table. He came to stand close when Joe Driver started talking about the report.

"I read the report and talked to the man who found your husband. I guess I can get you a copy during office hours tomorrow?"

"No, that's all right. I thought I wanted one, but I only wanted to know what it said, other than . . ." Maggie held her breath a second and didn't cry. "Other than just the motorcycle hit a tree."

Horace put his arm around her briefly then concentrated on

what the policeman was saying. Horace got a hopeful-expectant expression on his face, reached over and touched the candle on the table, but the wick didn't light. With a frustrated expression he watched while Joe squinted, reading the notes he had taken.

"They saw him. Or rather, saw the light shining upward where the motorcycle was wrecked, about ten-thirty—"

"Ten-thirty?" Horace put his hand over Maggie's, but she didn't feel it. She was feeling guilty, remembering how mad at him she had been because he was so late.

"That's right. The motorcycle left the road and ran into the tree. Didn't look as if he'd tried to stop, the report said. There were no skid marks and none approaching, so no phantom vehicle caused the accident."

Joe watched Maggie's face. "The one who found him pointed out to me in the report that there was a dead dog a little distance away. A bloody spot on the highway showed the dog was hit and then must have wandered, wounded, and then died. Your husband may have swerved to miss the dog. Anyway, he ran off the road and hit the tree."

Horace looked at him as if he couldn't believe his ears and shook his head. He turned and glanced at Maggie.

She sat silent, picturing what must have happened. "It would have been like him," she said at last. "To try and miss the dog. But you're sure it was ten-thirty they found him?"

Horace narrowed his eyes again, listening intently.

"Yes, the report confirmed that. He was alive, and they called an ambulance and got him to the hospital, but he never regained consciousness. They put him on life support because of the donor card and notified you. I'm sorry, Mrs. Murphy."

"Maggie," her smile was weak as she fought tears.

"There's one other thing. I called about the motorcycle. It's still at the impound lot where they took it, if you want to see it. Or I can have it taken to where they might be able to fix it. But it evidently looks pretty bad. I told them to hold it so you can decide about it." Horace nodded at that, looking glum.

"Thanks. I appreciate your checking on it for me. I won't need a copy of the report, but thanks for the offer. I just wanted to know a little more about the accident. And now I know he was trying to get home." Horace looked at her, his love showing in his eyes. "Ten-thirty you said they found him."

Joe nodded, "Could have been earlier, but not by much. He would have been gone, so ten-thirty must be pretty close to when he hit that tree."

Maggie nodded. "I'll have the motorcycle sent over to the shop where Horace usually had it worked on."

"I'll tell them at the lot. You can have them look at it and decide what you want to do with it."

Maggie nodded, bringing her mind back to the present.

Joe didn't see Horace bend and kiss Maggie on the forehead before he faded, and she didn't feel it. "Here's our pizza."

At the office the next day, Maggie arranged for the shop near their house to pick up the motorcycle, though she didn't know what to do with it. As she hung up the phone, she heard Hank's voice.

"What's that about a shop?"

"I'm having Horace's motorcycle taken there." She tried to ignore the ache in her heart. "Not that I know what to do with it."

"Is it a shop near your house?"

Maggie nodded. "Horace always had his work done there."

"Get them back and tell them to tow your car over there, too. I'm paying," he hastily added. "We'll see what can be done to get it running. It's best to know if you're going to have it or shoot it." He turned and went back to his office as she dialed.

He's right. I can't impose on Aunt Myrtle forever. Maybe Hank ill take it out of my salary now that I'm on the payroll. If not, I'll see what kind of arrangements I can make. Oh, Horace, you married a naive nincompoop! I'd still be trying to get a report if Joe hadn't helped me.

That weekend Maggie went to the shop to check on the bike and the car, expecting the worst.

"Yes, ma'am?" The man with the shop cloth wiped his hands.

"I'm Maggie Murphy. I came to see if I'm going to have to shoot my car." She smiled up at him. "How bad is it?"

"I think it's got a few more miles in it. It's just had the brakes done." Maggie was grateful for that news as he continued. "Right now it needs a battery and a heater hose and an alternator, which ain't exactly cheap. But beats buying another car."

"Can you give me an estimate so I can tell how many of the family jewels I'll have to hock?"

"Yeah, and if you want to fix it, I'll cut the tow bill in half. Be right with you."

"Mrs. Murphy?"

Maggie turned to see a boy about seventeen or eighteen years old. He wore faded jeans and a ratty-looking denim jacket.

"I'm Happy Harris. "I—I knew Horse. He—he was a really neat guy. I liked him."

Horace appeared, eyeing Happy expectantly.

"Thank you, Happy."

"I called the impound lot and they said the bike had been sent here. I was with him, the night, that night."

"You were?"

"Yes, ma'am. He and three friends were having barbecues outside at the Hog Pen. I work two jobs and I dozed off, but I heard him say you were expecting him at home and he had to leave early. He sure thought a lot of you, ma'am."

A tear spilled over as Maggie listened. Horace bowed his head.

"Thanks for telling me, Happy. I got someone to look up the report and they say they found him about ten-thirty, a lot earlier than I thought. I wasn't notified till about one in the morning. I'm glad to know he started home early. When it got to be one o'clock, I was really worried about him."

"One o'clock?" Happy looked surprised. "He left, must have been about nine or nine-thirty, I don't know exactly. Had some kind of hassle with the others. I didn't know but one of them, Jack Gardner, and I don't know him too well either. Anyway they were pissed, excuse me." Happy blushed. "I mean, they were mad at him because they wanted him to do something or go somewhere with them and he wouldn't. Said it was a bad idea and he'd rather be home with you."

"Thanks, Happy. That means a lot to me and I appreciate your telling me. I can see the bike is pretty well torn up."

They stood there looking back at it. She said, "Do you want it? Think you could fix it? Is that why you came to look at it?"

"I thought maybe about fixing it. I've been wanting one and I've got some parts." Happy again looked back toward where the remains of the motorcycle rested near the back wall. "But I wanted to see it, too. They, the others, they put something in Horse's Coke. They thought I was still asleep when he went to the john, but I saw them. I didn't know what to do. Horse took a few sips of it when he got back and set it down. Then I acted like I was just waking up and stretched out my arm and knocked it off the table."

"Knocked it off the table?"

"Yes, ma'am. I didn't know what else to do. It couldn't have been vitamins for them to do it behind his back like that."

Horace's eyes never left Happy's face, but he tried to grip his arm to thank him. His hand went right through, and Horace didn't try again as he listened.

"Are you sure? Do you know what it was?"

"No, ma'am. And he didn't get enough to hurt him. But it was a weird thing to do. Maybe they wanted him to pass out and go to sleep there and get you mad at him so he would go on and do whatever they wanted them to. They wanted him to look at something and talked to him about the plans they had about something they were excited about. I didn't get much of it so I don't know what. But I do know about the drink, and it was a weird thing to do. But he left around nine or nine-thirty, going home. I left at the same time he did."

"Who were they? These friends? You said you knew one of them?"

Maggie pressed Happy for information. Horace's eyes bored into Happy's, willing him to talk.

"The only one I knew was Jack Gardner. Lives over on Sycamore Street. He left earlier than that, before the drink thing. Had something he had to do."

"Well, as you said, whatever it was didn't hurt him, thanks to you. And I do thank you for telling me about his leaving early to come home. You can have the bike if you will pay them for bringing it here from the impound lot." She smiled at him. "Have we got a deal?"

Horace nodded, his eyes approving the gift.

"Yes, ma'am. Thank you!"

Maggie went to the shop manager's office door and looked in. The mechanic came out and handed her a form with the estimate on it. "This should do it for now, get it going so you can get to work in it."

Horace looked over her shoulder and nodded approval before he disappeared.

"Thanks. I'll look it over and see if I can raise the money. It's okay to leave it here a few days, isn't it?"

"Yeah, we won't get nervous about it for about thirty days."

"Good," Maggie said gratefully. "Oh, and see that boy out

49

there? His name's Happy Harris."

"I know. He hangs around a lot. What about him?"

"I told him he could have the motorcycle if he'd pay you for the tow from the impound lot. Is that all right with you? And would you let him have it for half the tow bill, like on the car?"

"Yeah, I can do that. Probably make my money back in parts." He grinned. "He'll be glad to get it. You let me know about the car."

"Yes, sir, I will." Maggie's mind was in a sad turmoil with questions she couldn't answer. *Horace, wherever you are, I know you were trying to get home. I miss you, Horace. Right now, I've got to see about the heap so I'll have a way to work . . .*

CHAPTER FIVE

When Maggie showed the estimate to Hank, he took it and put on his glasses. He looked at all the parts listed and the other writing, some of which was pretty bad.

Seeing Hank struggle with the estimate, it crossed Maggie's mind that maybe they should have Grace read it. She stifled a grin as he looked up.

"This sounds reasonable." This was accompanied by a brief nod. "When will it be ready?"

"I haven't told him to do it yet. Anything over a hundred dollars always called for a summit meeting between Horace and me and a hard look at our checkbook balance. If there was a balance, I mean." She looked down at the paper he'd handed back. "You think it's all right, then?"

"It's two hundred and twenty-five dollars including parts, labor, and tax. I think it's fair. If you want to, I'll go on and pay for it and take it out of your salary ten dollars a week." Hank gave her his foxy smile. "That won't hurt so bad." He pointed out. "And it will leave you gas money to get to work, which I'm sure Myrtle will see as my main motive and gross selfishness on my part."

"I see it as help, and I'll take you up on it. Thanks. I'll go call him and tell him to get started on it now. Then I need it to get to work."

Inspired by a regular and sufficient salary, Maggie happily threw herself into the job and made friends by helping with

51

anything that needed an assist. She got her promised first paycheck Friday and turned in her form for the group insurance. The car was to be ready Monday or Tuesday. By the end of the day, she was so high on security she had to reach down for her phone on the desk when it rang.

"The *Herald,* Maggie Murphy," she practically sang.

"Joe Driver." Joe smiled into the phone when he heard her voice. "You sound glad it's Friday."

"Yeah, good day. I don't remember thanking you for finding out about Horace's accident. I really do appreciate it. And besides it being Friday, it's payday and I'm getting my car fixed. I should get it back Monday or Tuesday."

"Sounds like you're on a roll of good luck. What would you think of a picnic with no ants and you don't have to fix a food basket?"

"Sounds like 'a rose without a thorn,' as the saying goes. Is there a catch?"

"Yeah, there is. Me."

"You?"

"Yeah, I go with the invitation. Do you like barbecue? Ever go to the Hog Pen?"

"Yes. Both. Are you—is this a date?"

"We don't have to call it that," Joe hastily assured her. "I want to go and I don't like to eat alone and we can call it whatever you want to."

"I call it friendly. Timely. Are you already off? I mean . . ." She hesitated.

"I know what you're thinking. I've been on foot before. I can come by and get you there at work if you want me to."

"Yes, that will save my aunt a trip. Hopefully, I won't have to hitchhike more than a couple more days."

"Fine, I'll see you in a few minutes."

They were a little early at the Hog Pen. People were just

starting to come in. Joe ordered for them and they had their choice of the tables outside in the shady patio. Maggie set their baskets and plastic utensils out, and Joe went back in for extra napkins and drinks.

"Hey, Jack," someone called. "Jack Gardner!"

A young man of about twenty-five or so stopped and looked around at another young face framed in the Hog Pen's service window.

Maggie quickly covered the few feet between them. "Are you Jack Gardner?"

He stopped and looked at her suspiciously. "Yes?"

"I'm Maggie Murphy, Horace's wife." Horace appeared beside her, looking daggers at Jack.

"Oh?" He seemed lost for any other comment.

"Happy Harris told me you were with him and Horace the night—the night he . . ."

"Happy has a big mouth." Jack Gardner frowned and turned away.

"Please. Wait a minute," Maggie implored as he took a step.

Horace tried to put a hand on his arm, but it went right through. He glared at Jack as Maggie spoke again.

"I wanted to ask you something," Maggie started again.

Jack turned to give her a brief look, but shrugged and turned away.

"The lady said she wants to ask you something," a voice from somewhere above said with quiet authority. Maggie's imagination pictured God or at least a guardian angel behind her as Jack Gardner stopped immediately.

Jack and Horace's eyes took in the man now standing beside Maggie. Joe still had on his uniform and didn't look like it would matter much to him if he didn't.

Jack said sullenly, "What? What did you want to ask me?" Horace's eyes approved of Joe's support and returned to Jack.

"About that night. Who were the others there with you? You and Happy and who else was there and—I don't know, really. Just—things like, what did you talk about? When did he leave? I—I just want to know about that night. Happy said Horace left about nine or nine-thirty?"

"Yes. That's about right, I guess. We didn't talk about nothin' in particular, just hangin' out."

"Who were the others?" Maggie repeated the question. Joe lowered the napkins in his hand looking like he might grab Jack if he decided to do something foolish, like run. "You and Happy and Horace, and the other two. Who were the other two?"

Jack looked right, left, anywhere but at Joe. "Raid Wilson and Mick Lewis."

"Raid and Mick?"

"Raymond Wilson and Michael Lewis."

"Do you know where they live or how to get in touch with them?"

"Why would you want to do that?"

"The same reason I wanted to talk to you," Maggie said quietly. "You were the last ones Horace was with before his accident, and I just wanted to know about it. Wouldn't you, if you lost someone close to you?" Maggie appealed to him.

"These two, Raid and Mick, do they work anywhere?" Joe asked. "Or do you know their addresses or phone numbers?"

"Raid worked at McCorkles's Parts Shop a while and Mick dropped out his junior year in college and was lookin' around. He's a computer freak. He'll do all right," Jack added with a touch of pride. "But they're not here now. Haven't seen either one of them around. Not since that night, come to think of it."

"All right, thank you. I didn't mean to bother you," Maggie apologized.

"S'all right . . ." Jack eyed Joe's uniform as he left, appearing as unfriendly as he dared as he hurried away. Horace followed him.

"I didn't mean to cause so much trouble," Maggie apologized again as they got settled at the table.

"I wouldn't classify that as trouble. He should have had more consideration. You had a right to ask a few questions about your husband's last hours."

Maggie looked uncomfortable, not meeting Joe's eyes. "I was curious about something else too, but now I don't know any more than I did before. Or even how to ask about it if I should get another chance."

"What do you mean? What is it you're curious about?"

Maggie took a deep breath. "It's probably nothing. But, as I said, Horace was here with those friends the night he had the accident. They were inside here, at the Hog Pen. And Happy Harris not only told me when Horace left, that he left early, but he said someone put something in Horace's drink. Happy saw it."

She recounted what Happy had told her about seeing the hand putting something in the drink when the others thought he was asleep. Joe listened closely when she told him all the details and about Happy knocking the drink off the table after Horace had only had a sip or two of it.

"So, well, I guess it doesn't matter anyway since he didn't drink it all. But Joe . . ." Maggie's frown was worried. "Why would they do that? What was it they tried to put in his drink? And why? Happy didn't see which one did it. I guess I'll never know," Maggie answered herself. "Anyway, I appreciate your finding out about the report for me, and I do know now he left early to come home like he'd promised he would."

"I'll just write those names he told us down in case we run across these other two." Joe put the names in his memo book, then added, "But Jack Gardner says he hasn't seen them since that night, so it's unlikely we will." He put away the memo and smiled at Maggie. "Let's not let Jack Gardner's attitude spoil our meal."

"Spoil our picnic without ants? Certainly not," Maggie happily agreed.

She turned her attention to the food before them. "This looks good."

The Hog Pen lived up to its reputation, and the barbecue was so good the meeting with Jack Gardner was soon forgotten. Maggie and Joe sat in the candlelight and sunset, enjoying nachos and root beer and getting acquainted until dusk claimed the patio.

They swapped brief bios. Maggie was a widow, but she had a good job and loving relatives around her. Joe was divorced but not soured on the world or matrimony.

"Remind me to tell you a few funny things about that experience. The divorce, I mean," Joe remarked. He looked more relieved than despondent about his matrimonial flop. "Part of it was good for a laugh, anyway."

"I've told you enough of my troubles to qualify you for about all the equal time you think it will take," Maggie admitted ruefully.

She looked down at the debris on the table. "If you're ready, it's time I was getting home and reporting to Aunt Myrtle. Some might think it's bothersome to have nosy kinfolks, but it would be a lot worse if nobody cared enough to ask any questions."

"You're right about that." Joe nodded with feeling and got up. He started helping clear the table.

At home, still feeling good about having barbecue with Joe, Maggie dialed her aunt's number.

"Well, you're home!" Aunt Myrtle exclaimed when she heard her voice. "Everything else close up on you?"

"No, I was having a good time." Maggie giggled, unrepentant.

"Okay then, all is forgiven. Wasn't this supposed to be pay-day?"

"It was. And Hank paid me a week's salary just like he said he would, and I got my insurance papers filled out." Maggie detailed all the week's good things. "So now I'm working, on the payroll, have insurance, and get this!" She paused dramatically. "And Monday or Tuesday I'll have my car back so you won't have to chauffeur me to work anymore. How's that for great news?"

"The chauffeuring wasn't supposed to be on your worry list, but all that other stuff sounds good too. It's nice of Hank to pay you the week's salary, but he's getting a good employee, too, remember. And what about the car? Was it really bad? Don't go into details, because I wouldn't know what you're talking about. Just what was the financial damage, and will it go?"

Maggie laughed, "Of course it'll go. I wouldn't be able to drive it away if it wouldn't. And Hank looked at the parts and labor and thought it was fair, and the mechanic says this will fix it for now. 'Fix it for now,' loosely translated, probably means till something else falls off or rusts out. It's old, you know."

"Just don't make any more references to old, thank you. How much?"

"It's a little over two hundred dollars, and Hank is going to pay it and take it out of my check ten dollars a week."

"He wants you to get to work," Aunt Myrtle said grimly.

"He said you'd say that," Maggie laughed.

"He thinks I'm a cynical old woman. But I'm not old, just cynical!" Aunt Myrtle giggled too. "I'm glad it's worked out so well. You're going to be all right, just like I said. Wait a minute. You only told me you had a ride home. So where is this you were having such a good time tonight?"

"At the Hog Pen, it's—"

"I know where it is. I like their barbecue. Anything else you want to tell me?"

"Like who I was with?"

"Yeah, like that?"

"Remember the nice-looking policeman I told you about who came out with the detective when Hank called about Mr. Wartz? His name's Joe Driver, and that's who I was with. He called me about quitting time and asked if I wanted to go have barbecue."

"He wore his uniform?"

"Yes, he'd just got off from work. Why?"

"I don't know. I guess I just somehow thought he'd behave himself if he had on his policeman's uniform." She laughed at herself again with Maggie.

"He was a perfect gentleman. You don't have to add him to your worry list. He's really nice, more like a good friend than a potential boyfriend."

Aunt Myrtle pointed out suspiciously, "It's those awfully nice, sneaky ones you have to watch."

"Oh, Aunt Myrtle . . ."

"Hank invite you to their wing-ding Saturday night?"

"No. But Fatima and I have been talking about it, and he probably will."

"He will. I'm going too. I'll come by and get you. The food's always good and you don't have to listen to the addlebrained conversations. You just have to concentrate on Princess Grace to keep her from making you part of the domestic help."

"Oh, she couldn't be that bad. And I won't mind helping her out if I need to."

"Don't say that too loud. She takes advantage every chance she gets."

"I haven't been invited yet."

"You will be. I'll come get you tomorrow night."

As predicted, Saturday morning Hank called and invited

Maggie to the party.

"You don't have to come if you don't want to," he added.

"I want to. Aunt Myrtle said she was coming and would come and get me if I got invited."

"Good old Myrt." Hank grinned. "Sorry I didn't think to mention it before. See you tonight."

The phone immediately rang again. "Forget something?" Maggie asked before she heard a voice.

"No? What something?" It was Fatima.

"Oh, Fatima, I'm sorry. I was just talking to Hank."

"Oh, the party?"

"Yes. I never have been inside his new house, but I've heard a lot about it. Aunt Myrtle is going to pick me up. Are you going?"

"No, I don't spend any more time with Grace than I have to."

"Princess Grace?" Maggie was curious. "I wondered about the name."

"You'll find out. What I called for, I'm going to my momma's salon to get my hair trimmed, and I remembered you said you wanted to get yours trimmed and shaped too. You want to go?"

"I'd like to. Is it very expensive? I haven't been to get anything done in dog years!"

"No, it's not expensive. She has a lot of regulars. She'll trim and shape it for ten dollars if she doesn't have to do anything else. That's relative's rates, and my welcome to the *Herald* present."

"No, no. Getting a job was present enough! But I appreciate the relative's rate. I won't get my car till Monday or Tuesday. Where is the salon so I can tell Aunt Myrtle how to get there?"

"No need, I'll come get you about ten o'clock."

"Okay, it's—"

"I know, it's on your personnel sheet. Who do you think di

the typing before he suckered you in?"

"Yeah, what was I thinking?" Maggie laughed, "I'll be ready."

They parked in front of the Sunday Best Salon and Maggie looked it over, as well as the shop beside it. The other shop called itself the Triple H Gift Shoppe, with Herbs, Health, and Happiness circling the big H in the middle. There were bottles, herbs growing in pots, and all sorts of interesting things in the windows flanking the door.

"Say, that place looks interesting."

"We can go look around if you want to when we get through. My momma and dad own the building and some cousins of mine run the shop."

A friendly, heavyset black woman met them at the door of the salon and hugged Fatima. She appraised Maggie quickly, and to Maggie's delight, opened her arms to embrace her too.

"Momma, this is Maggie. The friend I told you about. This is my momma, Sharon Rose Johnson."

Maggie said, "Happy to meet you," as she hugged back. "I really appreciate your giving me the relative's rate today." She turned her head. "As you can see, about anything you do will be an improvement. I haven't been to a salon in a long time and need some shaping."

"Anything in particular you got in mind?"

"No, just some shaping done by a professional like yourself."

"I told you she was smart." Fatima smiled at her mother as she went to work.

"I haven't had any professional attention since a friend of mine took a cosmetology course five years ago. She used to call me and say, 'Come over and bring your head,' to give you an idea," Maggie smiled.

When momma was finished, the trim and shape was a huge success, and a few streaks had been added for glamour as well.

Maggie was pleased and it showed. Momma was pleased too

and wouldn't take any extra for the streaks. Horace appeared and looked the new hairdo over. He grinned at Maggie. He stepped over and gave her a big hug, even though his arms went right through her.

"Come on," Fatima said. "We'll go look in the herb shop a little before I take you home." She led the way through an inside door to the Triple H Shoppe.

"Fat Rosie that runs this place is my cousin, so distant I don't know what the actual connection is. We call her Rosie. Fat Rosie if she can't hear us. And that other one that's about half here is our old auntie, Evil Elvira. She was a slave and claims to be about a hundred and thirty, except there isn't any proof, her not having any birth certificate. She does have one of the old papers where she was sold to someone so long ago it just might be true. She wasn't above working a spell or two to get her way or make some money back then, before she got too old to remember the spells." Fatima giggled. "At least that's what they tell on her. She's not really evil."

Rosie looked up from her magazine and waved to them. Elvira had her head back, napping in her padded rocking chair. They looked around a while and Maggie bought some chamomile tea and scented soap. Fatima bought some aromatic bath crystals, and they went to Rosie to check out.

"This is my friend, Maggie Murphy, from where I work," Fatima introduced her. "Maggie, this is my cousin Rosie and our Auntie Elvira."

Elvira opened her eyes at hearing her name. She recognized Fatima with a sleepy little smile.

Then she saw Maggie, and her eyes grew frightened. "She got company!" Elvira mumbled, staring wide eyed at Maggie.

Horace's eyes met the old ones, and he quickly retreated to look back through the front window at them.

Maggie nodded at the elderly lady and smiled, not sure what

she had said or if she could hear very well either as they left.

"What did she mean? She called me company? Or did she say I've got company?" she asked Fatima as the door closed behind them.

"You don't want to know." Fatima changed the subject, talking about the bath crystals and other nice scents Rosie had in her shop.

The new hairstyle won rave reviews from Aunt Myrtle when she picked Maggie up for the party.

Maggie felt presentable in a long black skirt and a sequined top she had bought several years ago and worn only once. She touched her new hairdo self-consciously.

"You look really nice," Aunt Myrtle assured her. "I hope Grace is jealous as all get out and it shows!"

"Shame on you, Aunt Myrtle. I was just hoping I don't look tacky."

"Tacky? Why, with that new hairdo, you'll be as popular as a bone in a dog yard. Just you keep an eye on that policeman if you keep seeing him. That uniform of his isn't tattooed on!"

"So far, I haven't seen any indication I need to worry." Maggie was surprised she felt so disappointed about that.

Aunt Myrtle slowed, looking for a parking place and Maggie turned to look at the house.

"Goodness! You mean that's Hank's new house? That's some mansion!"

"Yeah, it's really something. Grace is right to be proud of it," Aunt Myrtle admitted grudgingly.

When they got inside, there were some members of the family, a few people she had seen come by the office, but mostly strangers to Maggie. One she recognized because he had come in recently to ask for Hank.

Myrtle went to greet someone, and Grace came to Maggie

with a large tray of canapés. Maggie took one; all of them looked delicious.

Grace was beautiful and well dressed and the soul of gracious politeness, even when she was cutting someone down. Someone who needed cutting down, Maggie thought loyally.

Maggie was admiring her, thinking the Princess Grace name fit, when she handed her the tray.

"Would you mind?" Grace smiled her beautiful, gracious smile and gestured across the room.

Maggie took the tray. It was heavier than it looked. Grace disappeared as if by magic, leaving her standing there feeling awkward. Maggie self-consciously approached the group near the door and offered the tray, then several more people helped themselves as she turned away.

Then someone abruptly took the tray out of her hands. It was Aunt Myrtle.

"What did I tell you? She's slick, isn't she?" Myrtle set the tray down on a nearby coffee table.

A flash of light distracted them, and Maggie saw Hank standing with a portly, gray-haired man near the punch bowl.

"Who is that?"

"Don't know. Some politician with his hand in the till," Aunt Myrtle guessed. "When I get enough of these finger food fancy sandwiches that I won't have to raid the refrigerator when I go home, I'll be ready to leave. How about you?"

"I guess so. They do have a nice house. I'd like to see more of it," Maggie said wistfully.

"Come on," Aunt Myrtle grinned and took her hand. "We'll dodge Grace and play nosy kinfolks!"

Feeling like a conspirator, Maggie went with her and looked at the rest of the house. It was lovely, but too big for her comfort.

"Must cost an arm and a leg to keep heated and cooled," Maggie said when they got back to the finger sandwiches.

"Yeah, houses are like old women." Aunt Myrtle grinned, "Paint and upkeep get higher every year."

Chapter Six

Maggie got lucky. Her car was ready Monday, and the shop mechanic's helper drove it to the *Herald* to deliver it to her. Hank wrote them a check and went out with her to look at it again after they left. The shop had washed it and the old car looked better than it had in months.

"Looks like it's set for a while, anyway," Hank observed. He opened the hood and peered at the new battery. "It's a Die Hard. I wanted to make sure."

"Thanks. Thanks for the advance to pay for the repairs. Thanks for the job. Thanks for the week's pay. Thanks for everything, Hank."

"You're welcome. You've never tried to get dependable help, or you'd think I'm as selfish as Myrtle does." He smiled. "You dating that policeman who came out on Wartz's case?" Hank added, evidently embarrassed for asking. "Or do you have plenty of nosy relatives already checking on that?"

"You and Aunt Myrtle aren't nosy, and I guess not. I thought the policeman was nice, but he hasn't called for a few days now." Maggie shrugged, trying not to look disappointed. "Maybe he just felt sort of sorry for me."

"I doubt that." Hank eyed the new hairstyle. "Well, whatever nosy warnings and advice Myrtle's already given you—listen to them."

Maggie laughed at his passing the buck on fatherly advice and went back to work. She was putting a sheet of paper i her typewriter when she heard Hank's voice behind her.

"You know anything about computers?"

"Yeah." She nodded. "They cost a lot of money." Maggie said it as she made a half turn away from her typewriter. She wondered what Hank was getting at with a question like that.

"Other than that—you think you could use one if I got one? The word processing part is way ahead of typewriters—at least, according to the salesmen. What do you think?"

"I used one briefly at the day care center. They had their program already installed on it, so all you had to do was log into their records. Didn't even have to turn it on, since it was always on when I got there. So I didn't have to do much. Or know much," she added apprehensively.

"What about the word processing?"

"I've seen a friend's, and I think I could make use of it. But we'd have to keep the typewriter for envelopes and times when—when—well, sometimes the one my friend has decides not to work or the power goes off or something. Not to mention my vast store of knowledge would be about a three-sentence paragraph in 'An Idiot's Guide in How to Use a Computer,' and I'm not sure I could even follow directions if I had any." Maggie paused for breath before asking, "You really thinking about getting one?"

"Yeah. I'll ask a few more questions first and we'll see."

Hank went back to his office and Fatima grinned, giving Maggie a thumbs-up sign. "Hey! We're moving into the new millennium at last!"

"Sounds like it. They have all kinds of manuals, and it will be the word processing part I would have to use the most." Maggie tried to think positively. "And we'll have e-mail, is that what you're thinking? I have no idea how to do that!"

"I don't either, but they've got them all over the place at ʼool."

"School?"

"Sure do. Where I'm going to school they've got them everywhere. When I graduated last year, we—the family—decided I'd wait a couple of years to go to college, and I'm taking a class at night while I'm waiting. My brothers will be out then and they can help on my expenses and tuition."

I don't know what Fatima means by out. Sounds like prison! thought Maggie. "That's a great idea. You think we can handle a computer then?"

"Sure! Look at the airheads who send messages. We're as smart as they are, aren't we?"

"Certainly! And I think Hank is really serious about getting one." Fatima's confidence was contagious. Maggie eyed her desk, trying to picture a computer sitting there.

The phone interrupted her fantasy. Fatima answered.

"It's for you." Fatima transferred the call.

"Maggie Murphy."

"Maggie, this is Joe."

Maggie's heart skipped a beat. "Oh, I thought you'd forgotten me or I'd used up my mandatory sympathy ration or something."

He laughed at the mandatory sympathy ration and got serious. "I've been busy looking into something I think might interest you. I could come by and take you out for pizza—if you don't have other plans?"

"No, I don't have other plans. But I've finally got my car back. And believe it or not, it runs like it doesn't know how old it is! If you want pizza, that sounds good to me. You can pick one up somewhere or I can, and we can have it at my house so I won't have to come back for my car."

"All right. You leave at five?"

"Yes. I'll get the pizza and see you then about five-thirty?"

"No, I'll get the pizza. See you at five-thirty."

Maggie wasn't aware how broad her smile was when she hung up the phone until she heard Fatima's voice.

"Aha," came from across the room on a suspicious note. "Pizza? At home? Next thing, you'll be cooking spaghetti or he will be grilling steaks." Fatima added one plus one and got five by inserting a little suspicious nosiness.

"Don't rain on my parade. I thought he'd forgot my number or was just being nice because he felt sorry for me. He said he was looking into something that might interest me. I wonder what he meant by that." *Not that I care,* her heart sang. *He's coming over!*

"You're really getting interested in this policeman, aren't you?"

"Interested? I think he's nice and I enjoy being with him. And it sure beats sitting in the empty house looking at the walls, if you call that interested. You don't have to be in love or have designs on someone to have a good time."

"Sure." Fatima rolled her eyes. "While he's there, ask him if they've found out anything about what happened to our good old Wartzy."

"I'll do that. I'd like to know too."

Pulling into her driveway, Maggie was pleased to see Joe's car parked in front of the house. They met, he with the pizza, and she carried the half gallon of ice cream she had bought for dessert.

"New hairdo," he observed. "Looks nice."

"Thanks. A friend got me a relative's price deal I couldn't turn down," she explained, pleased he liked it.

She unlocked the door and went to put the ice cream in the refrigerator as he set the pizza on the table.

"Anything I can do besides sit here and be useless? I'm pretty good at that, but I can be trained for simple things," Joe offered.

Maggie dug a carton of cole slaw out of the ice cream sack and got out Cokes as she talked. "There's a pizza cutter in that drawer by the sink. You could get that."

Joe sat down with the pizza cutter poised, a comic, gleeful expression on his face as she joined him.

"One, two, three, slice." She grinned. "Hope you don't mind bottles. I don't have an ice maker and I didn't think about ice."

"No, this is fine. The way I usually manage would probably be a chef's nightmare. Come to think of it, my mother didn't think much of my preparations and culinary arts either."

"Oh, a no-frills chef, are you?" Maggie helped herself to pizza.

They ate in silence a few minutes, Maggie wondering what it was Joe wanted to tell her. She didn't ask, a little nervous about it. He paused once, appeared uncomfortable or undecided, and crammed another bite of pizza in on top of whatever was trying to get out.

When they were down to the last two pieces of pizza, Maggie said, "I've got some chocolate topping to go with the ice cream whenever you're ready."

"Not just yet. Maggie, I've got something to tell you. It's probably not important, but I think I'd want to know if it were me."

"Is it about Horace's accident?" Part of her cringed, reluctant to talk about it.

"Yes." Joe was taking it slowly and cautiously, probably because he really didn't know her very well, she thought. She gave him time, dreading whatever it was.

She took a sip of her drink and looked away.

"Alan Hill—"

"The detective who came out when we found Mr. War-

She pictured him, recalling a nice older man, most of his hair white, stout but not fat. Probably a little past the mid-fifties. He looked like he could handle any case they gave him.

"Yes. He and I both work once in a while for a private detective. He's retired from the force and Alan is thinking about joining him when he retires."

Maggie nodded.

"As I said, we're both working there when he needs us and we've got time, sort of learning as we go along. We call it Nosy One-Oh-One." He put down the crust of his pizza and smiled self-consciously. "We look into things, ask questions just for the experience, and also we're trying to establish useful contacts while we do it."

Maggie nodded again. She'd got comfortable and was still smiling about the Nosy One-Oh-One when Joe got to the point.

"What I learned about Horace's accident was about the organ donations. While I was asking around among people Alan already knows and making contacts in general, I learned about the tests done. The paperwork and tests and things for the donor organs. The blood taken from Horace had a little trace of rohypnol. It was only a trace in one of the tests."

"Rohypnol . . ." Maggie frowned. "Isn't that what they call the date rape drug?"

"That's it. Also known on the street as Roofies, ruffies, roche, R-2, rib, and rope—and probably some other things, too. It's an extremely powerful tranquilizer." He studied Maggie's puzzled expression. "Like valium but a whole lot stronger," he tried to explain.

"Yes, I've heard of that. A woman I used to work with took a tranquilizer sometimes. She had a lot of problems. I think she wound up in some rehab place. I don't know much about tranquilizers or any of that stuff."

"Rohypnol is a whole lot stronger than valium, as I said.

There wasn't very much of it, just a trace, but it was there. I got that from one of the lab techs." He smiled a little self-consciously. "Along with his phone number and e-mail address."

"Guess that gets you an A in Nosy One-Oh-One."

"I don't know. But it did get me a good contact for information and someone to ask questions about things I don't know anything about." Joe's face sobered as he asked, "Do you have any ideas about it? Horace didn't do drugs, did he?" Maggie didn't answer and he added hastily, "There wasn't anything else."

"No." Maggie shook her head. "No, Horace had a horror of what drugs do to people. I don't think there was even any aspirin in the house when he had his accident."

Joe said thoughtfully, "It would have been less unusual if it had been found in a woman who didn't know she had been given it. But a man?" He paused, waiting for Maggie's comments. "Wasn't very much, just enough to identify it and make you wonder why."

"I don't know why," Maggie said slowly. "But maybe I know who gave it to him."

"You do?" Joe's eyebrows shot up in surprise.

"You remember what I told you about Happy saying one of the friends with him at the Hog Pen put something into his drink? Could that have been what it was?"

Horace slowly faded in and stood listening intently.

Maggie smiled, picturing Happy Harris. "Happy's a nice, polite boy, about seventeen or eighteen." She searched for words. "Sort of a motorcycle groupie, I guess. He didn't have a bike of his own. And I believe him—about what happened, I mean. And there was not any other kind of drug we had or that Horace was taking."

"I remember your telling me that. What's his name again?"

"Happy Harris. Don't know anything except the nickname."

Joe wrote the name in his pocket memo. Horace looked on approvingly.

Maggie spoke softly, remembering her conversation with Happy. "He told me he had dropped off to sleep that night while the others were talking. They must have been there quite a while. Anyway, he said one of them put something in Horace's Coke while he was gone to the restroom. Happy acted like he wanted to tell someone when he talked to me. It scared him. He thought since there was the disagreement—"

"Disagreement?"

"Yes. He said it sounded to him like they wanted Horace to do something he didn't want to do and he refused. He said he had to go home, or I would be mad at him." She flushed, "I was! I'm ashamed now about how mad at him I was, and him trying to get home."

"I remember you mentioning it now." Joe thought back.

Horace started to touch her shoulder but Joe's hand was faster, reaching out to comfort her. Horace stuck his hands back in his jeans pocket.

"You couldn't know. Having a temper only qualifies you for the human race, Maggie. Tell me everything you can remember that Happy told you."

Horace tilted his head, listening, as Maggie continued, his eyes on Joe.

"Happy said he was afraid they had put poison or some kind of dope in his drink, but I didn't pay much attention at the time."

Joe nodded. He hadn't either. He'd forgotten her mentioning it.

"From the way he talked, whatever they wanted to do or talk about doing must have been something against the law. Or maybe it involved dope of some kind." Maggie stopped talking, looking miserable. "I just don't know." She shook her head.

"Happy didn't hear anything definite. It was just the way they were trying to get Horace involved in whatever it was. That's why Happy said he knocked the drink off the table. Do you think one of them got this rohypnol from somewhere and that's what they put in his Coke? I can't think of anywhere else it could have come from. You said there was nothing else in his body, and there was only a trace of it? And Horace couldn't have got much of it, thanks to Happy."

Joe sat silently, picturing the group and what had happened. "That would explain why he didn't get much of it, all right. That was quick thinking on Happy's part." Horace grinned at Joe, giving him a thumbs-up for Happy.

"As I said, I don't know much about it either. But from the little I've heard, it probably wouldn't take much to have at least a mild effect."

"You mean, they wanted him to pass out and have that accident?" Maggie's eyes widened at the possibility. Horace looked back and forth between them.

"Sounds like it to me. But why? Happy didn't hear what the disagreement was about? Anything about what it was they wanted Horace to do?"

"No, he only knew there was some kind of strong disagreement. That it must have been pretty important to them. And Horace wouldn't do it or even talk any more about it because— because he was coming home to me." She blotted the tears she couldn't stop, then got control of her emotions. Horace put his transparent hand on hers, looking miserable and sorry for making Maggie cry.

"Either there was just enough of that stuff in those few sips to slow down his reflexes and make him lose control, or that dog got in his way. Or maybe it was a little of both." Joe's eyes met hers. "There's no way to know." Feeling helpless, Joe shook his head and his hand came down on Maggie's, going right

through Horace's. "I'm sorry, Maggie."
Horace disappeared.

CHAPTER SEVEN

Maggie was glad to get to work Monday morning. *I'm probably the only moron in the working world glad it's Monday!*

As she took the cover off her typewriter, Fatima called to her. "Hank said anything else about getting you a computer?" She dusted the top of the reception desk with a piece of Kleenex. "Reason I ask is I want that typewriter when he does."

"Hasn't said yet. Maybe he's still just considering it. But I somehow got the idea he would. Maybe he's just at the shopping-around stage." She gestured at the typewriter on the last desk before the door to the press room, "What's the matter with that one?"

"It's not smart enough."

"Smart enough?"

"Long as I'm wishing, I want one with the read-out and some memory and all the other goodies I can get."

"I don't blame you. Hadn't thought of that. I'm sure he'll give you this one, though. And I'm pretty sure he's going to get a computer. Wish I was as sure I can learn how to use it as I am that he's going to get one."

Hank appeared at the hallway. "Got a minute, Maggie?" He turned without waiting for an answer.

"Sure, maybe two or three," Maggie said to nobody in particular as she got up to follow.

Entering the office, Hank gestured her to a chair. She sat down, thinking the loose pile of papers must not be important since she and Aunt Myrtle had been sitting on them since she'd started to work there.

The thought brought a smile to her face.

Hank smiled too. "Have a good weekend?"

"Yes, really nice. You?"

"Yeah, great. Which means nothing came up I couldn't handle or put off, and Grace was in a good humor." He stopped, the smile slipping a little. "Of course, I don't know yet how much that good humor's going to cost me."

Maggie laughed, "How do you figure good humor is going to cost you?"

"What makes her the happiest is skinning my head about something, spending money, or some of those brain ruffle organizations she piddles around with."

"Oh." Maggie tried for a stern look, stifling a smirk. "You don't approve of clubs for women?"

Hank looked blandly innocent. "Only if all else fails."

Maggie laughed again, picturing Hank, a club, and Princess Grace. She couldn't see Hank winning that one, or with a club for that matter. "Oh. Well, cheer up. It could be number three."

Hank dropped it, hoping for the best. "Car still running well?"

Maggie nodded. "Aunt Myrtle says not to let it know how old it is." She gave Hank a shrewd glance, wondering what he was leading up to. "I can say at the moment that my little chunk of the world is running good—car too."

"I've got an ulterior motive for asking," Hank admitted.

"You mean about the car?"

"Yes. If I promise never to ask again, will you take some papers to Josef Kranz so he can put them in the boxes? It's not far and he will take it from there. Floyd will go with you." He added, looking hopeful, "He knows where to go and can unload them for you."

"Yes, I'll do that. It will give me a chance to meet him and say I'm sorry about his friend. I guess they'll go in my trunk and the back all right?"

Hank nodded. "They will. There's not that many. I've already taken most of them." He looked at his watch. "I've got a meeting to go to. Pull your car around to the other side of the building."

Hank and Floyd loaded the papers in no time. Maggie and Floyd left for a nearby mall to meet Mr. Kranz.

She spotted the bank of paper boxes and a van that was even older than her car as she entered the big parking area. An elderly man stood near the van. He turned at the sound of the approaching car. The man looked so stern and merciless, Maggie drew in a deep breath when the cold, nearly colorless eyes met hers. Horace appeared beside her, sitting in Floyd's lap, and returned the man's evil-looking, cold stare.

Floyd said, "Looks as if he's left over from World War II, doesn't he? He's lucky to be left over, since he's Jewish."

"Oh." There was no time for further comments or questions. Ashamed of her first reaction, Maggie got out and smiled, extending her hand.

"I'm Maggie Murphy. I'm working at the *Herald* now. I was sorry to hear about your friend. I hadn't had the chance to meet him, but everyone speaks highly of him. I wanted to express my sympathy, and I'm pleased to meet you, Mr. Kranz."

"Josef Kranz." He made the smallest of bows as he took her hand. The *Josef* was clipped off at the end by a slight accent. There was a brief flash in the cold eyes of something that might have, years ago, been appreciation of a pretty face.

CHAPTER EIGHT

In the hallway ready to leave work, Joe turned at the sound of someone calling his name.

"Got a minute?" Lieutenant Alan Hill called.

"Sure." Joe turned into the break room head of him. "Let's have some hot chocolate. I think coffee would take the paint off the outside of the machine if any got spilled on it."

"Okay. I think the coffee is really tree bark and berries. Besides, I like chocolate." Detective Hill followed and stretched out his long legs under the break room table. He got as comfortable as the hard chairs allowed while Joe got their chocolate.

Joe joined him with the chocolate and blew on his. "You got anything new on the nogoodnicks I told you about in the motorcycle accident?"

"No. Not by name, anyway. Next I'll try things that might involve motorcycles or anything of any importance around that date to see what those guys might have been up to. Maybe there was something they needed help with and went on to do without Horace Murphy's help. What I wanted to ask you is, did you by any chance see that Josef Kranz who's supposed to have worked some with Wartz, the stabbing victim? Or did you hear your friend Maggie Murphy say anything about him?"

"No, I'm not sure she's even met him. Why?"

"I can't seem to catch up with him to talk to him. No one ʼms to know how to reach him."

"ʼll ask Maggie if she's heard anything about how he and

78

Wartz got along, or if he's moved or anything next time I see her. Or I can call her," he said with a smile. "It would be a good excuse to make contact."

Alan studied the tabletop as if looking for answers written on it. "This is beginning to look like one of those no-motive, no-connection-with-anything cases. Keep an ear and eye out for anything you can find out about him or these other two on the motorcycle thing while you're at it."

Joe nodded. He worked on the unanswered questions about Horace's accident when he had a spare minute, but without any success so far. He had also looked in all the plausible places for a current address on Josef Kranz, but couldn't find one.

"Kranz was actually working for Wartz, but it's Hank Hanover's paper," Joe said. "He was supposedly working part time helping Wartz take papers to the outlet boxes. I'll look into it further and try and find him."

Joe had also tried every source and directory he could find, trying to get a current address for Raymond Wilson and Michael Lewis. What they might have been up to wouldn't let him rest. He decided to try every avenue available on the computer when he got a chance to use it at work to see if there had been anything that went down about the time of Horace Murphy's accident that might have involved them. There had to be some paper tracks of some kind, somewhere.

Thursday of the following week Hank came out to Maggie's desk as they began getting the paper ready and laid the column she had submitted on her desk.

"Gets my paw print. It's okay."

"All right, I'll get it proofed and typed up."

"Fine. And Merry Christmas and Happy Birthday."

"What? Have I lost some months out of my life here without even seeing any aliens?" Maggie's eyes roamed the office i search of little green men with big black eyes.

Hank grinned. "Damned if I know. Strange things happen around here. What I'm trying to tell you is I've just bought you a computer to use. I got a PC instead of some big, complicated system that we'd never figure out what to do with."

"A PC?"

"Yeah, that's means personal computer. That's what they're called."

"Oh. Well, that's one thing I know now, but that's about it." She raised an eyebrow at Hank. "I'm glad you're not installing some complicated system, but what makes you think I can figure out what to do with this PC?"

Hank gave her a pained expression for her lack of gratitude. "Because you're smart, it will help in your work, and you don't want to get fired."

"No, I don't want to get fired. I'll have to work on the other, though. A PC?"

"Yippee!" Fatima was not one to hide her feelings. "When will it be here?"

"I said PC. One PC," Hank explained patiently, then glared at her. "What part of *one* did you not understand?"

"I know, I know. It's about time we got out of the dark ages around here, Daddy Warbucks. Any writer or secretary needs a PC, and I want that typewriter with the read-out and memory. I can have it, can't I? Nobody else in here needs it. Nod your head," she commanded. "It's easy, you can do it. Just tilt your head forward a couple of times and make me happy!"

Hank finally chuckled and nodded his head. "Okay, okay. That way, Maggie will have to learn to use the PC." He grinned as if he was proud of himself for arranging that.

"Thanks, friend!" Maggie made a face at Fatima behind his back.

"So, when's it going to be here?" Fatima pinned him down.

"Tomorrow. The place where I buy office equipment and so forth will bring it out tomorrow, set it up, and give you a few pointers. There's a manual and instructions and things that go with it."

"A manual. Why don't I feel better?" Maggie muttered, looking scared.

Hank went back to his office before anyone could ask for something else.

"Tomorrow!" Maggie looked as if it was execution day.

"Oh, you'll get the hang of it."

"He said something about a manual."

"Uh-huh, they all have those. You won't know what it's talking about till you've learned some things on your own. It's like getting a cookbook with your microwave. You have to find out some things for yourself."

"I'm sunk!" Maggie lowered her head to her desk and laid her arms over it.

"Oh, cheer up. Celebrate even! It's Thursday and you'll get a computer tomorrow and then there's the weekend. If the metal monster bites you, you've got two days to recoup and fight it again on Monday."

"Fatima, shut up! I thought you were my friend. How can you be so dratted cheerful when my job and my sanity are at stake—and tomorrow!"

"Maybe it's because I've got a job Friday night that pays so good I could buy me a PC too, if I wanted one."

"You do?" Maggie perked up. "Tell me about it."

"It's a couple of shots for a magazine. They want the full moon over the river for a background, a high-fashion thing. They asked the agency for me. Saw a catalogue thing I did."

"That's wonderful. Congratulations!"

"Thanks. I'm hoping to get some more jobs from them if this goes well."

"It will." It was Maggie's turn to be optimistic. "But wait. Full moon? Is this a night job? Silly question. Do you want Joe and me to go with you? Do you have many jobs at night like that?"

"No, there aren't many at night and when there is one, I'm not afraid of the buggers in the dark." Fatima laughed. "I just lay the trip on them."

"The trip? What are you talking about?"

"My brothers in college I told you about. Shad, Shack and Bed. They're triplets. They play football and the coach calls them the trip."

"Triplets!" The word held wonder for Maggie. "Triplets," she repeated softly.

Fatima nodded. "When Momma and Daddy got married and wanted to start a family, they had trouble. After seven years, they talked it over and Momma took fertility drugs. Then they had Shad, Shack and Bed, then they had me, then—that was enough!" She preened, putting on a false smug look.

"What did you say your brothers' names are?"

"Shad, Shack and Bed. You know Momma and her Bible names." Fatima rolled her eyes. "Their names are Shadrach, Meshach and Abednego."

"Oh, my Lord!" Maggie clapped her hands over her ears in sympathy.

"That's enough of my soap opera—what are you going to do this weekend?" Fatima followed that with a muttered, "I already know who with."

"I heard that! And yes, Joe and I are going to a movie Friday night and we'll see what the weather is good for on Saturday. And you don't need to worry about Joe Driver. My Aunt Myrtle will do that if he needs to be worried about."

They laughed together, the computer forgotten.

Hank heard them in his office. His face took on an faraway

smile as he chewed on the end of his pen, thinking about the new computer and all the good service he could wring out of its metal hide as soon as he could nag Maggie into learning how to use it.

The dreaded monster arrived about ten o'clock Friday morning, appearing heavy but harmless without any blinking lights or other intimidating characteristics. The modem, monitor, keyboard, and enough wires to plug in Mars and the outer rings of Jupiter were taken from boxes. Everyone not shackled to something by conscience or a deadline gathered around to watch.

There followed a printer, a scanner, speakers, gushes of delight from Fatima, and a terrified silence from Maggie. Maggie cast fearful eyes at the thing and the assorted wires and scary stuff with it.

"So, there's your very own thirty pounds of smart metal," Fatima told her with wide-eyed wonder when they had it set up.

Maggie put her hands together under her chin and prayed, "Thirty pounds of smart metal! Please, God, let me be smart too!"

Fatima giggled. "You will be." She peered into a box. "There's all sorts of brain cell fertilizer in here."

Hank came out of his office to see how things were going and ran everyone back to their work, where they stayed until he left the area.

The patient soul who had delivered the computer showed Maggie how to start it, shut it down properly and get to the word processor. Then, knowing darned well from tough experience that none of those little seeds of wisdom had taken root, he wrote down the instructions for turning it on, shutting it down and getting to the word processor. Then he put a bookmark advertising the store in the manual at the wo processor chapter, wrote his first name and the store's number under it, silently prayed for swift deliverance from this particular electronic illiterate in the usual thirty days and left Maggie to her fate. TGIF.

CHAPTER NINE

Maggie didn't have the distraction of Joe's company to get her mind off of having to go back to work Monday and face the computer. She wondered briefly what it was he had to work on this weekend.

Maybe it's something for Alan Hill and his friend? She smiled to herself as she thought about the Nosy One-Oh-One courses they were both taking and made a mental note to keep her curiosity under control. That didn't keep her from wondering.

And he did call and let me know he would be working. She still wasn't sure exactly what the status of their relationship was. She pictured his good-looking face with a smile on it, as if he were enjoying her company. *Well, I can dream, can't I? I know there are moments when being with him seems like more than friendship to me.* She shrugged and dozed off, looking forward to being able to sleep late.

Getting out of the tub the next morning, she put on her "po-folks bathrobe," a big, thirsty towel she had splurged on. She stood barefooted, contemplating her choice of what her closet offered to wear on a leisurely Saturday. Nothing seemed very exciting, but neither did the day ahead of her.

The phone rang, loud and demanding. The voice on it was too, but it was a cheerful and welcome one. She held the phone a little farther away from her ear.

"Thought I'd catch you before the police do," Aunt chortled. "If you're not too busy, come over for lunch chicken salad, potato salad, and ice cream. The no-guilt kind, if you want it."

Smiling at the rescue of her dull day, Maggie accepted. "The chicken and potato salad sound great, and I should definitely have the no-guilt if I have ice cream."

"Me too. That's why I got it."

"Can I come now?"

"Sure. But this is formal, so wear your thong sandals."

Maggie hung up, laughing, and scrounged in the closet for her thongs and whatever else this kind of *formal* called for. The thongs were the last pair left at the discount store where she found them. They were a strange, bright purple that went with nothing else in the closet, and she loved them. They were like going barefoot, except you had tough soles like the Hobbit in Tolkien's tales.

Aunt Myrtle met her at the door with a tall glass of ice and diet cola.

"Let's go sit in the swing and talk."

"Thanks." Maggie took the drink. "We can visit with Horace a while." She paused to look down at the urn as she passed.

"You don't have to rush off for an early date, do you?"

"No, worse luck. I'm not going to have one. Joe is working. He didn't say what he was working on and, of course, I didn't ask."

"Must be hard on policemen's wives not to ask questions," Aunt Myrtle mused thoughtfully, then brightened. "I've met a man who doesn't resent questions and likes to talk as much as I do."

"Well! I had no idea there might be one somewhere. Guess ' better find out about this. Where did you meet him? Who is 'ell me about him. And has he asked you out or does he ⁀w yet when he's going to?" Maggie giggled.

't know how much he's figured out yet, but he helped

me with my groceries and I think he's looking interested."

"You met him at the store?"

"Yes, I've seen him there before. He's been working there a couple of weeks and today he made a point to be there to help me with my groceries and told me he's not going to be there after this week."

"Oh . . ." Maggie frowned.

"No, no. That's not bad. He's a retired teacher, and he's only working there until he could find something for himself that's not full time, but something to do. He's going to work at the college in the administration building. In the registration and purser's offices. He'll just be working part time."

"Oh, so he'll still be living around here and he didn't want to miss getting acquainted."

"I guess. I hope. Anyway, he invited me for coffee, since it was time for him to get off work. I had so much frozen stuff I took my groceries home and went back to have coffee with him in the deli."

Maggie nodded, "I like their deli."

"We talked so much so fast, I don't know whose idea it was to get acquainted and learn more about each other. Sort of mutual, I think."

"Sounds like it." Maggie added primly, "I approve—so far."

Aunt Myrtle grinned happily. Her face lit up and she looked pretty and young again. "He does seem like a nice person. We're going to a movie Sunday night."

"Sounds good to me. I'm glad you've met an interesting friend to spend some time with. You know, of course," Maggie reminded her, "if this gets serious, I have to approve."

"You sound like me," Aunt Myrtle admitted with a laugh that made Maggie give her an impulsive hug.

"Naturally, you've got next-of-kin approval rights. But so far, it's in the friendship/something-to-do stage. Besides, I'm comfortable and not looking for any obligations or complications."

"You're right. I'll sure keep that in mind. Hey, you haven't told me his name yet."

"Oh, it's Doug. Douglas Hawthorne." Aunt Myrtle said, getting up, "Let's go have our salads."

Maggie fell into step beside her. "I should have been suspicious about all this 'no- or low-calorie' stuff." She smiled knowingly, then stopped briefly to pour her leftover ice on Horace's pink rosebush.

Monday morning at the office found Fatima happily using the typewriter with the read-out and the memory as Maggie cautiously and gingerly used the word processing part of the computer to do some of Hank's correspondence.

Everyone else had gone to lunch, and Maggie was having a diet drink with her homemade tuna sandwich when she heard Hank's angry voice.

"How in the name of Emily Post should I know? I didn't know anything about it! I don't know! Hell, I guess so, somewhere. I'll look for it. Yes, now. Bye." He slammed the phone down.

Hank stomped out, headed for the door. "Want anything from the convenience store?" he asked, looking annoyed to the max.

"No, thank you. I know I'm probably flattering myself, but is there anything I can do?"

"No. Thanks for the thought." He left abruptly, but later that afternoon he rang the phone on her desk. "Are you snowed under right now?"

"No, I'll be right there."

He looked up as she came in. "These three files are as close as we've got to personnel files." Hank waved an arm in their direction. They were expanding files that had expanded farther than originally intended, and some of the debris was sticking out through what had been creases but were now cracks.

"Will you go through these, one piece at a time, and see if you can find an address or phone number for Josef Kranz?"

"Yes. But maybe Floyd's got one?"

"No. I asked when I got finished going through my desk."

Maggie picked up two of the files after stuffing all she could back into them and balanced them in her arms in a huge, messy paper hug. "I'll be back to get the other one."

"Thanks. Grace is on her high horse because she invited Josef Kranz to speak at one of her patriotic drivel meetings and he didn't show up."

Maggie stopped to listen.

"She went with me to take the papers the last time and asked him. Maybe he didn't understand or something. I don't know. Anyway, he didn't show up. She can't find him. I don't want to find him, and all that evidently suits him right down to the ground. If he wants to keep it that way, he's doing a good job."

"I don't think I'd want to find him either," Maggie said slowly.

Hank paused, studying her face. "What does that mean?" He gestured her to the chair with the papers in it.

She sat, clutching the overburdened folders in front of her. "I don't know. I'd never seen him before I went with Floyd to take the papers to him, but he gives me the creeps. Maybe we shouldn't try to find him for her. I like Grace."

Hank lightened up a little. "She has her moments. Did Kranz say something out of the way to you?"

"No." Maggie shook her head. "In fact, he was very nice. He just looks like the German Gestapo guy who kills and betrays everybody in the old war movies."

Hank laughed. "I think he's Jewish like Wartzy, so I doubt he'd qualify for that role. But you don't need to contact hi

Just see if you can find any clues as to where he's got off to in all this stuff."

Detective Alan Hill hung up the phone on his desk looking beat and disgusted. It rang immediately.

"Homicide. Detective Alan Hill."

"Hi, this is Joe. I just had a few minutes and thought I'd check in with you. I'm looking around on the motorcycle accident I told you about."

"Making points with the pretty lady?" Hill inquired.

"I guess it's a little early in the game to be trying to make points—too obviously, anyway. I'm going to check on that address I got from the college on Michael Lewis this afternoon."

"Good idea. Get some experience, and who knows what might turn up? I tried my luck on something too, but didn't get anywhere."

"On what?"

"I thought maybe even if they've left the area like that contact told you—?"

"Jack Gardner. Yeah, he's one of the ones who were with Horace Murphy that night before he died."

"I was hoping there would be some kind of records from the phone company that might prove interesting. But there's nothing. Evidently, neither one of them had phones, or a phone wasn't in their names if they did. Zilch."

"I'm not surprised. I've only got the one address on this Michael, and nothing on Raymond Wilson. But maybe I'll get lucky."

"Yeah, good luck. Doesn't it sometimes gripe you how much more comfortably footloose and free the bad guys are with no ⁻ecords than us solid citizens with all the bills?"

"No," Joe laughed. "I like everything I'm paying on."

'Guess you've got a point. Didn't Jack Gardner tell you Michael was some kind of computer expert?"

"Yes, he did. Said he probably wouldn't have any trouble finding work."

"Maybe I can find an e-mail address or something. Anyway, good luck with your address. See you tomorrow."

Joe went home and changed out of his uniform before checking out the address he'd found for Michael Lewis. It was in an area of moderate-income homes not far from the college where there were quite a few duplexes and apartments sprinkled through the neighborhood.

The address was a small duplex with a separate, double garage at the back of the lot. There was no car in either side.

As Joe went up the steps, he noticed the *For Rent* sign on the left side and knocked on the other door. Getting no response and figuring the doorbell didn't work, he tried his hard-knuckled policeman's rap on the door before facing the fact there was no one home.

As he turned to leave, a feminine voice called to him. "He won't be back for a couple of days."

The woman standing beside the hedge separating the duplex from the house next door was small, white haired, and pleasantly attractive. Joe placed her about the mid-sixties. Words like *retired* and *comfortable* coming to mind, he walked over to talk to her.

"I'm looking for someone who used to live here. You say the man who owns the place is gone?"

"Yes, his name's Art Dunkin."

"And he's going to be back in a couple of days?"

"Maybe sooner." She smiled at something she knew and he didn't. Joe raised an eyebrow, amused.

"Every once in a while he and one of his cronies go down and play like high rollers at the casino, thinking they'll be playboys for a week or so. But he'll be back before the week is up. He's not that rich or that lucky," she confided.

Joe shared her smile. "Me either. That's why I don't go." He tore a page out of his little memo book and wrote his number on it as they talked. "Will you give him this and ask him to call me?"

She took the note. "You knock on doors like a policeman," she observed.

"I am, but this is not official. Why? Do you think he wouldn't cooperate with the police?"

"Oh, no. He probably will if he doesn't flush all his good humor down those slot machines." She added as she turned away, "It's just that he's got this little personality flaw."

"What's that?" Joe raised his voice a little to call after her.

"He's a jackass!"

CHAPTER TEN

For two days, between other things she had to do for Hank, Maggie had been combing the expanding files that were all the personnel information Hank seemed to have. She hadn't come up with any phone number or address on Josef Kranz, or even his name written on anything. When Hank brought out a letter to type, he eyed the folders.

"You through with this one?" He gestured to the one closest to him.

"Yes. No luck."

Hank pulled the trash can out a little and unceremoniously dumped the whole thing. "I guess there weren't any gold nuggets or anything that we might need to keep in there?"

"No. Didn't notice any little pearls of wisdom either."

"Watch it, Maggie, I'm the vice president in charge of sarcasm here. But I didn't think there would be. Wartz was his, Josef's, only contact here."

Maggie nodded, thinking, *And there's no way to contact Wartz short of a Ouija board, which I wouldn't doubt we've got around here in some of these junk stashes.*

Maggie asked aloud, "How did you know where to meet him last time? The time I went with Floyd?"

"He called to see how he was going to get paid."

Maggie's eyebrows drew together. "You said Wartzy paid him out of what you gave him. How did he know Wartzy wasn't going to pay him that time?"

It hit Hank right between the eyes. "Damn! You're right! I'll call and tell the detective that." A frown quickly followed. "No. I'll wait until we can get hold of Kranz. There may be some explanation we don't know about. Or he could have talked to Floyd or someone else here. On the off chance there is something to find, finish looking through the rest of that other file."

"I'm through. Just hadn't got around to asking if you want to keep them yet is all. If you'll bring me the other one, I'll get busy and finish it now, too." She looked up when another idea presented itself. "Or maybe he will call before I get through. To see what kind of job arrangement you and he can make."

"Could be. I'll bring the file out."

Maggie diligently examined every page, half page and all the scribbled-on unidentifiable shreds to no avail. There was no address or telephone number for Josef Kranz. When Hank came to check on progress a little later, she shook her head.

"Not a thing. Do you know where Mr. Wartz lived?"

"Yes, it's an old apartment house. Mostly elderly people live there; they use a pay phone nearby."

"Oh, I guess he didn't have any wife or family?"

"No." Sadness flitted across Hank's face. "Someone told me he had a wife once, but they were both young and hadn't been married very long. I think she was Polish. Anyway, they somehow wound up in a concentration camp, one of those awful ones where so many died. She died there, but he survived to be rescued when the allied forces came in."

"Oh, how awful. Then I guess he didn't have anyone but his friends you said he liked to impress with his column." She added, "And Mr. Kranz, of course. I'm sorry I said he looked like a Gestapo agent."

"Oh, nobody heard you but me," Hank assured her. "And I've got the finest forgetter in Shelby County, just ask Grace."

The third messy file had been disposed of and Maggie was killing time practicing looking up things on the computer until time to go home, when the demon machine turned on her like a lynch mob, hanging judge, and department store security guard all rolled into one.

This machine has performed an illegal act and will be shut down, the thirty pounds of smart metal scolded her.

Maggie gasped and stared at the screen in horror. Fatima looked up, and someone behind her snickered.

It was Hank who snickered. He glanced down at the last discarded file. "I was just wondering if you had found Kranz, but if you're on your way to jail then—"

"Don't pay any attention to him." Fatima came over, not looking worried at all. "These things do that all the time."

"What—what should I do?" Maggie quivered.

"Nothin'."

"Nothing?"

"No. Turn it off."

"But I can't! What about the proper shutdown?"

"We're already illegal, what have we got to lose? Trust me. Turn it off."

Hank nodded his approval. He didn't look worried either. Maybe he didn't know this thing might blow up the building or something else it might be connected to somewhere. Unclenching her fists, Maggie just nodded.

Half expecting to blow out power for the entire neighborhood, she reached down to the "absolutely essential power surge protector from mind-boggling catastrophes" the salesman told Hank they had to have. Braced to get electrocuted, or at least an electronic slam, she turned the hateful beast off. The monitor immediately went blacker than a pirate's heart.

"Oh, my God! It's dead! I killed it!" She watched as Fatima moved to where she could reach the metal monster. She reached down and turned it back on.

Floyd, Tim, Hank, Fatima and Maggie watched the gleaming demon in paranoid fascination. Carl Peabody was evidently as immune to worrying as the rest of his generation and stood there with them, grinning like the village idiot.

Then there was light! The metal monster lived! Maggie drew in a deep breath.

After a small paragraph to the inferior human operator about proper shutdown, the vastly superior machine began checking itself to make sure the moron at the keyboard hadn't done any damage. In a matter of minutes, the machine was good as new, but Maggie's face was red with rage.

"I didn't do anything!"

Fatima shook her head. "Can't argue with a machine. You can always start over. Don't know much about the rest of it and its program shenanigans, but I bow to nobody in Erase and Start Over." The rest of them applauded.

"It's too late to start anything else now anyway. Come on back." Hank beckoned to Maggie. "I want to show you something before you go."

The rest of them took this as dismissal and left so fast Maggie looked around for smoke. Fatima did stop to shut down the computer, for which Maggie shot her a grateful look over her shoulder.

The *something to show her* turned out to be a piece of real estate. Hank touched a couple of real estate ads lying on his desk as Maggie paused to glance down at them.

"You and Horace ever think about buying a house? Keep up with the ads and what's available?"

"What?" Maggie dragged her attention back to what he was saying as the outside door slammed behind the last employee leaving.

"No. We talked about it a couple of times but that's as far as it got." She gestured at the chair, "You mind if I throw these away?"

"No, toss them. Watch the spring."

When she picked up the papers, a little spring was visible in the middle of the seat. She folded about half the papers neatly and returned them to the chair before tossing the rest in Hank's trash can. "I didn't know this stuff was serving a purpose. But this looks better, doesn't it?"

"Grace would be proud of you." Hank dismissed the housekeeping. "So, are you tired of paying rent and throwing money down a rat hole?"

"At least nobody can repossess a rat hole," Maggie defended herself. "And if there's some kind of problem, I can pack up and move to another rat hole of my choice." There were other things she could point out, but those were the main ones that came to mind.

"Sometimes you sound just like Myrtle," he accused.

"Thanks, Hank. Are you trying to sell me a house? You, who should know I can't afford one?"

Hank leaned forward a little, his expression downright diabolical, temptation written all over his face. "Ah, but what if you could?"

"I don't know how I could. In fact, it sounds kind of scary to me."

"Scary?" Hank frowned. "How do you mean, scary?"

"I don't know any more about buying a house than I do about buying a car. I've never done it. What should I look for or beware of? What if everything looks all right and someone moves in next door and sets up a meth lab or something? Joe says there have been a lot of busts lately, and in unlikely places, too. And Aunt Myrtle watches the utility companies like they're training camps for crooked politicians—"

"Probably just the commissioners." Hank shrugged. "They're

the only ones with access to enough to make stealing tempting. But stop listening to all that negative drivel from the police and the Queen of Consumer Watch."

Maggie laughed at the title bestowed on her favorite aunt. "It doesn't hurt to be careful, and I can't afford to buy a house. Anyway, I don't think I'd even pay rent on the kind of a place I could afford to buy!" Maggie pictured herself sitting on a cracked concrete step, a ragged doorman beside her and a little embroidered sampler over the door that said *Hovel, Sweet Hovel* in faded letters.

"Aw, Maggie, don't be such a pessimist! I'm going to have to talk to Myrtle about being a bad influence on you—excuse me!" He got up abruptly and hurried up the hall, then came back. "Just thought I'd try to catch Floyd, but he's gone."

"If it was about Mr. Kranz, he probably would have already told you if he'd discovered where to find him."

"Yeah, you're probably right. Anyway, what I wanted to talk to you about is a place I've got. A new listing. And you can get it at a desperation price. Way below what it's worth, if you want it."

"I don't know, Hank. I've just barely convinced myself I can make it where I am."

"Well, I've just got it listed to put in my ads, so you've got time to give it some thought. But don't take too long." He picked up something and handed it to her. "Here's some stats on it. Take this and look them over."

"Okay." Maggie got up and took the papers he handed her, noticing one of the listings in his ad was circled in red. She pushed it aside mentally to think about the date she had with Joe.

"Goodnight, Hank."

Joe arrived at Maggie's door wearing a suit, tie, and an expectant smile. She stood there a moment taking in all his grandeur.

"Surprise! Or if it's more of a shock, I can lose the tie."

"No, you look too nice to classify this as shock. I guess I just associate ties with Sunday, funerals and collection plates." They laughed together.

"Me, too. But I still had a little money left at the end of my month. That's cause enough to celebrate. And I thought we might go to a place I know up by the river. Do you like Italian food?"

"Love it! Just give me a few minutes to change."

The restaurant was a nice one, with the candlelight she always associated with romantic dinners. Maggie's heart fluttered pleasantly when Joe took her arm to follow the waiter. The food and the service were excellent and gave Maggie and Joe enough time between courses to talk, admire the candlelight and scenery and enjoy being together.

Horace appeared briefly and looked the dining room over. He smiled affectionately at Maggie, gave Joe a thumbs-up he couldn't see and left.

Joe laughed about Maggie and Fatima's trouble with the computer and listened to her efforts to locate Mr. Kranz.

"I'm going to use every spare minute I have to get us a little more organized," Maggie vowed seriously. "I'll get some addresses and information on everyone first. When Hank asked me to try and find an address or phone number on the Mr. Kranz who used to help Mr. Wartz deliver the papers, I found nothing on Mr. Kranz at all. Floyd met him a couple of times at that sort of old folks' soup kitchen where they serve meals—"

"The one by St. Olaf's?"

"Yes, that's it. But there was no address, phone, or anything. I don't know how Kranz even knew Mr. Wartz had been killed."

"What do you mean he knew?" Joe pounced on it.

"He must have. Hank didn't pay him. Mr. Wartz was the

Herald's employee. Hank paid Mr. Wartz for circulation, and Mr. Wartz paid Josef Kranz out of his own money to help him sometimes. I don't know what kind of a deal they had. Hank probably doesn't either. But Kranz called and asked that Floyd bring his money with him for doing the papers that week, and to meet him at the mall where I drove Floyd the one time I took the papers. Neither Hank nor Floyd thought to ask him how they could get in touch with him. I hadn't thought about it either."

When Joe didn't comment immediately, Maggie made a face, "Fit right in, don't I?"

Joe relaxed and smiled, patting Maggie's hand. "Forget it. Kranz isn't on our worry list tonight. I'd like to talk to him, too. Maybe he'll call, wanting to keep the circulation job."

He glanced at a nearby table being served something that looked like Bananas Foster. "How about some dessert?"

"Yes, I'd like something sweet to go with some coffee." She promptly forgot Kranz and the computer, admiring Joe in the suit and tie he'd put on to take her out. "I think I've blown my calorie count for the rest of the month anyway." She grinned at him. "Is dating you going to be hazardous to my health?"

Joe's eyes appraised her with obvious admiration, "You've got a way to go before having to worry." He ruefully shook his head, "And I don't have enough money to be dangerous. That's one of the reasons Marlene decided to go seek her fortune elsewhere."

"Marlene?"

"My ex-wife. I think I told you I'm divorced."

Maggie nodded, fighting her curiosity with consideration, good taste and other stumbling blocks to satisfaction, as Joe continued.

"We were married less than a year. But that was long enough to see we were going to have to work on having anything in common. She liked to go out a lot, karaoke bars and places where they have live music. Country music was what she liked, and I put up with it."

He looked at Maggie with a pained expression. "It all sounded to me like some kind, any kind, of suffering accompanied by a bunch of long-tailed cats in a room full of rocking chairs. Whang, twang, dang! And somebody either dies, gets dumped or goes to jail."

Maggie laughed. "I know exactly what you mean. I had a date with a boy before Horace and I married who liked country music. We went to one of those so-called live music places. I stood for it as long as I could and finally asked him, 'Aren't there any happy hillbillies?' And he looked at me like I'd lost my mind and said, no, that happiness didn't sell beer." They managed to get their faces straight as the waiter came to take their order for coffee and dessert.

"You like chocolate," Joe observed, watching the waiter head for the kitchen.

"Yes. Hot chocolate, chocolate candy—dark preferred, and no creams. If there has to be something in the chocolate, let it be nuts, caramel, or cherries like they sell around Christmastime."

Joe pretended to pat his pocket in search of his memo pad then gave up and said, "I guess I can remember that."

"Forgetting part of it isn't a hanging offense, since I should be trying to quit splurging on chocolate anyway." She paused for breath—or maybe courage. "So, you and Marlene talked things over and parted friends?"

"I suppose that's about it. We didn't have anything to fight over. I had one cowboy shirt at the time. Some joker we didn't know very well gave it to me for Christmas. I came home one night and she was sewing sequins all over it. Red ones on the red, some kind of blue beads on the blue, and so on. She said I never wore it. I said she was welcome to it. Seems she and a friend had met this man who claimed to be some kind of agent, and she and her friend were going to Nashville to get into show business. They met him at some bar that had live music. She'd already talked to a lawyer."

"Already talked to a lawyer? Just like that with no warning? How awful . . ."

"No, it wasn't awful. She was all excited about it and I remember thinking I wouldn't have to listen to any more of that crap—pardon my Russian."

Marlene's an idiot! Maggie admired Joe's strong features in the candlelight as the waiter arrived with their coffee and dessert. She promised herself they would have a kiss tonight after all that rich dessert, one that would remove any doubt in his mind they were now dating.

CHAPTER ELEVEN

At home, Maggie got ready for bed and moved a lamp from the living room to her bedside table to read. Realizing she was getting adjusted to her own routine, she remembered the information Hank gave her on the house.

I know it's a pipe dream right now but maybe, some time, if the heap keeps running, and I keep working. She smiled to herself remembering how Aunt Myrtle had put the pressure on Hank to hire her. *At least, right now, I'm all right.*

She settled into her pillows to read the ad on her house. *My house! It doesn't cost anything as long as you just wish. The house does sound good, but that's what ads are for, to make what they're selling sound good.* She soon laid the flyer aside with a sigh and picked up her book. Horace appeared, glanced at the lamp she had moved, and left.

Unable to concentrate on the book, Maggie picked up the ad again.

It is a nice house, all right. She suddenly remembered the "Thou shalt not covet" commandment. But Hank didn't exactly own it; he was only trying to sell it. Her eyes devoured the good things in the ad. Three bedrooms; double bath and a half; fireplace in the family room. *All it needs is Wally and The Beaver,* she thought with a smile. *It says here it's got a separate triple garage with an apartment over it! Maybe I could rent it out?* She tried to ignore the flutter of hope the apartment caused. A glance farther down at the price shot down that hope. She laid it aside again, on the other side of the table this time, and picked up her book.

Since Joe had to work Friday night, he came to take Maggie to lunch. He arrived at the same time as the elusive Mr. Kranz. Hank heard their voices. He came out and beckoned to Josef Kranz.

Hank nodded to Joe and took Kranz's arm. "Mr. Kranz, I've been wanting to talk to you. Come on back with me."

Maggie exchanged a look with Joe as Kranz silently followed Hank. Kranz hadn't spoken except to ask for Hank.

"Fatima will be back in a few minutes and I can go," Maggie said. "Let's go fix us a cup of coffee and drink it while we're waiting."

"Good. I'd like some."

The coffee pot was on a table by the back door, and Joe glanced into Hank's office as they passed. Hank was talking and Mr. Kranz was listening. Kranz still sat silent, a glass of water in his hand.

Fatima came back and got settled at her reception desk as Hank walked Mr. Kranz to the door. Mr. Kranz laid a piece of paper on Maggie's desk without making any comment and left. Hank started for the back where he usually parked.

"Got to go pick up Grace for a luncheon meeting. Probably be back about three," he told Maggie without stopping.

Joe walked over to Fatima's desk where she was taking some lipstick and a paperback book out of a plastic sack. "May I have that sack?"

Fatima shot Maggie a grin, "What's it worth to you?"

"How long have I got to think it over?"

"Oh, well, if you're going to poor-mouth, you can have it."

"Thanks," Joe went back to Hank's office and came out with something inside the sack. "Playing detective again," he explained as he passed Fatima's reception desk. He held the door for Maggie.

Detective Alan Hill sat in his car down the street from the Gardners' house. When Jack Gardner came out and got in the car in the carport, he gave him a half block head start before pulling away from the curb to follow. He called in the license plate number as he drove. The result was about as he expected. The car was in the name of Jack's parents, no outstanding warrants or tickets.

Ahead of him Jack slowed and pulled into the back parking lot of an auto parts store. Alan followed and parked beside him, reaching for his badge as he got out.

"Detective Alan Hill." He flashed his badge.

Jack stopped. "I wasn't speeding or anything." He looked a little bit puzzled and a whole lot belligerent.

"No, you weren't. I just want to ask you a couple of questions." Alan glanced at the only other car parked nearby. "You working here?"

Jack nodded. "They have a management training program. I was lucky to get it. I'm not in any kind of trouble, am I?"

"No. I'm trying to locate a Michael Lewis and a Raymond Wilson. Do you know them?"

"Yes—I mean I did. I don't think they live here anymore. I haven't seen either one of them for a while. Is one of them in some kind of trouble?"

"It's only information I want. They were friends of another friend of yours, a Horace Murphy, isn't that right? He had a fatal accident on his motorcycle," Alan jogged his memory. "All of you had motorcycles. Was it some kind of club?"

"No, we just got together and rode sometimes. Mine's in the shop right now. I don't know whether it can be fixed or not."

"Oh, did you have an accident?"

"No, it's just old. Needs parts and some work. I may have to junk it. My mom and dad are letting me use their car to get to work right now."

"Do you know where Michael Lewis or Raymond Wilson live now, or do you have a phone number where you can reach them?"

"No, I don't know where either one of them is. I haven't seen Mickey or Raid since—" Gardner stopped, uncomfortable.

"Since Horace had his accident." Alan nodded, sympathetic. "That's why I'd like to talk to them. It seemed Horace Murphy ran off the road and hit a tree, but there were no witnesses to what happened."

"Probably wasn't any traffic is why there weren't any witnesses. He left us about nine or nine-thirty, I think."

"That's what the file says."

"Who told you that?" Jack narrowed his eyes. "His wife?"

Alan's eyes bored into his. "Was she there when he left?"

"No. No, she wasn't. I remember him saying his wife was expecting him at home." Jack looked uneasily toward the building. "It's time for me to go to work. I don't know where Mick or Raid are living now."

"All right. Congratulations on the job." Alan reached into his pocket and handed him a card. "If you hear from either of them, call me at this number."

A little after three o'clock Hank came in from the back and beckoned to Maggie. She got a couple of sheets of paper out of her desk drawer and followed him. She laid them on his desk, looking pleased with herself. "I've got everyone's name, address, DOB and a few other things, along with the phone number Kranz left, and I'm setting up a personnel file where you can find it when you want it."

"Why don't you put the information on the computer?"

"I might. Later, when I know more about it. But for right now, we've at least got it."

"Good. That's good. Needed to be done. Are you still thinking about the house?"

"I read it—the ad I mean, and it sounded good. All about the three bedroom, double bath and a half and the other good things, right down to the price." She paused. "That's where I got off." Her voice had the finality of a tombstone. She tried to soften it a little. "I'm sure the price is not too much, but it's too much for me."

"Grace asked me if I'd told you about it."

"Grace?"

"I've got a computer at home and she looks at the records and the new listings sometimes. She thinks it looks like a good investment. Did you notice it's got a garage apartment?"

"Yes, that got my hopes up, but the price brought them right back down."

"You still paying the same rent as when we were figuring up your salary?"

"Yes, it hasn't gone up, and I'm hoping it doesn't any time soon."

"Suppose we could refinance this house and get the payments down to what your rent is now?"

"Could we do that?" There was another fluttery flash of hope that died quickly. "But I don't have any down payment and it may need some repairs. No, I can't do it." Maggie shook her head. "Maybe later on."

"Bargains don't wait for later on. This man is in the military. When Uncle Sam beckons, he means now. That's why we got the listing. At least one of the reasons."

Maggie didn't like the "one of the reasons" things, but it didn't matter enough to ask questions about. She couldn't afford the house anyway.

"Why don't we go look at it?"

"You mean now?"

"Why not? This is business." Hank grinned, paying no attention to any of her protests.

"Okay." Maggie gave in. "I'll go tell Fatima we'll be back in a little while." *A very little while. Just a little excursion into Fantasyland. Has it been so long since Hank's been broke he's forgot what it's like not to have any money? Oh well, this won't take long; might as well enjoy the ride.*

She joined Hank in his car, eyeing the seatbelt. No doubt owning a Mercedes gives you a lot to live for. *Hank's right, sometimes I do sound like Aunt Myrtle.*

Hank's voice broke into her thoughts. "I haven't been out there. It was Grace that noticed the listing. If it needs cleaning and some minor repairs, we've got a crew to do that."

Maggie just nodded. She'd used up all her reasons this trip was a waste of time.

Hank pulled to the curb in front of a lot with trees and flowering shrubs in front that made it hard to see the house set back on a large lot. There was a gate in the fence that surrounded it.

"I like forsythia and whatever those other things are." Maggie admired the shrubbery as they got out. "Nice wide gate. Isn't this an extra large lot?"

"Its three big lots, and the previous owner still outgrew it before he got transferred. He's a colonel in the military."

Maggie smiled. "Outgrew? He had a lot of children?"

"Four and one on the way. And only three bedrooms and a small dining room. Sort of screwed himself out of a place to sit." Hank chortled.

"Hank!"

"Myrtle!" He laughed and made a face at her as he opened the walk-in gate.

Maggie noticed that the gate for the driveway was recessed about a car length and a half, the mailbox beside it.

The concrete walk was nice too, but Maggie didn't notice that. She was too busy falling in love with the house. It wasn't large, but it was pretty, with natural stone, white stucco, and big windows that made it Maggie's dream home before Hank opened the door.

She caught sight of furniture inside and peered at a window as they stood on the porch. "Is their furniture still in it?"

"Don't know." Hank held the door. "This is the first time I've been out here."

The drapes had been left. They were standing in a living room–dining room combination with a shelf that formed a half wall with glass doors on both sides. It separated the areas neatly, with a convenient place for books on one side and dishes on the other. The furniture she had glimpsed was dining room furniture that had been left behind, like the drapes. Maggie admired the china cabinet; graceful legs and caned seat backs on table and chairs caught her eye too.

She glanced down at the dark brown carpeting. "Practical to get dark carpeting with young children."

"Yeah, it still looks pretty good." He touched the dark wood of the dining room table. "Guess they outgrew this too. It seats six."

"It's beautiful. Does it go with the house?" *What am I saying? Not that I would be able to afford it.*

"Yeah, drapes and curtains and some things in the kitchen, too, from the info I've got on it." He moved on. "This hall must go to the bedrooms. There are three of them."

Maggie nodded. "I know. I read all the ad said about it before I had a reality attack and faced the fact I can't afford it." *But as long as I'm here and wishing I might as well go first class,* her optimist genes fired back at the mental brakes her practical side was trying to put on enjoying the tour.

"And they just left their drapes and the dining room furniture?"

"Yes. Why move it if you aren't going to use it?"

"I was just curious. There's no way I can buy a house, Hank. Not now."

"Don't give up so easily." He glanced in a bedroom door and went on. Maggie noticed the bedrooms and the hall all had the same dark carpeting. The first bedroom was beige, had drapes with a beige background and a large double closet with sliding doors. The next one was about the same; she admired the big closets and sliding doors.

The half bath across the hall was neat and larger than she expected, with built-in linen closets and some in the hall outside.

And there's room for a shower if you might want to add one. She thought of Horace, then thought of Joe and blushed. *This house is a better salesman than Hank. I've got to keep telling myself not to get attached to it. I can't afford it.*

"Hey," Hank called to her. "Come here and see this!"

She went to where he stood in the master bedroom and gaped. Much larger than the other bedrooms, it had a little sitting area near a gas log fireplace with glass doors. Hank was looking down at something. Frowning.

The something that had caught his eye was marks made by a chair. "Shampooing will probably get rid of these."

There was a floor lamp to the side and just behind the marks. "Someone sat here and read," Maggie said. "Does the lamp work?"

Hank turned it on, testing the three-way bulb, "Yep."

"The electricity is on?"

"The electric company probably got a cut-off notice, but the utility company is famous for not jumping very fast when someone says frog. They probably figure, where else are you going to get electricity?"

"Probably the understatement of the year," Maggie grinned. "Just ask Aunt Myrtle if you want to hear a speech on that and their other shortcomings and overcharges."

Hank was bending down beside the fireplace. "This opens in the family room, too. One of the salesmen said the family room goes all the way across the back of the house like the living and dining room goes all the way across the front. Go look at the master bath."

Maggie tore herself away from the picture of herself reading by the fireplace and investigated the master bath. It looked like *Better Homes and Gardens* to her. All it needed was a few plants her imagination was already supplying. Besides the usual wet and flushing furniture, closets and shelves near the conventional tub, there was a large tub across one corner with jets.

"What are you giggling about?" Hank stuck his head in then came to join her.

"I was picturing a great, big, overweight officer soaking away his problems. But I see it's really big enough for more than one."

"What other one do you have in mind?" Hank demanded.

"Me, myself and my tired remains, Aunt Myrtle."

"Oh. Okay." He never got embarrassed or apologized, only sidetracked once in a while. "Let's go look at the family room and the kitchen."

"No."

"No? What do you mean, no?"

"Oh, Hank, I've dragged my hopeless case in here and down the hall to see most of the goodies already. Don't make me go look at the other side of that fireplace and a kitchen I can't have, too."

"Yeah," he insisted. "I need you to see it."

"Why on earth? Are you some kind of sadist?"

"You can give me a woman's-eye view and opinion of the place. Come on." He took her arm. She didn't move. He pulled, "One foot, two foot—"

Maggie moved, giving him a dirty look.

She glanced around the family room, noting the other side of the fireplace with the glass doors intact. She stood in the middle of the kitchen waiting while he checked out other things. The stove, two ovens, and microwave were built in. She didn't bother trying them or the ice dispenser in the refrigerator door.

Big enough for a big family and meals at home. She pictured the colonel, his wife and their flock of little ones with their faces fogged out like some of the cereal commercials on television.

She was gazing down at a mark on the floor one of the children had probably made with a chair when Hank finished his look around the area.

"It's in good shape." He looked pleased. "What do you think?"

"Um-hum, good shape." She answered absently, looking out the glass back door.

"There's a deck out there. Let's go look."

"No. I mean it this time. I've seen enough."

"Oh," Hank grinned. "You're sold?"

"No, I'm not sold. I'm only impressed—not stupid."

"Meaning what? Come on out."

She went slowly. The yard was large and shady, the garage and apartment hardly making a dent in its roomy comfort. It dimly registered when Hank said he thought they had used the apartment for guest quarters. There were places visible where play equipment had been removed and swings on sturdy poles still remained.

"These are set in concrete," Hank explained as he sat down in one. "Have a seat." He gestured.

Maggie sat in the swing next to his.

"Well, how do you like it?"

"I can't afford it, Hank."

"Did I ask you that? How do you like it? If not, why not?"

"It's fine. Now that you've given me the grand tour, the only thing I can see wrong with it is it's not mine. And it's not going to be mine." She stopped her gentle swinging. "I can't afford it, Hank."

"I heard that. You don't have to keep telling me that." He looked at something beyond her. "Hey! We haven't looked at the apartment!"

"Do we have to do that, too?"

"Yeah. We're here, and I don't want to come back."

"Oh. Okay. That makes sense. I can do that."

"Good girl." Hank fingered through the tagged keys on the key ring.

The apartment was one that Maggie would have been glad to have. The garage had originally had room for four cars. The fourth space was now a long, narrow living room, dining room and kitchenette with a half bath and mud room added on the back, opening on a little patio. Above it were two bedrooms with ample closets and a full bath.

Maggie gave the house, yard and apartment her stamp of approval. "Can we go, now?" She pleaded, already taking a couple of steps toward the driveway.

"Yes. We've got to get back so I can officially leave work. How else am I going to get to gripe about the long hours I put in?"

"And Grace might be looking for you."

"Humph! And you had the gall to call me a sadist!"

CHAPTER TWELVE

After work, Maggie was glad to get home. *Maybe it's not native stone and stucco like that one Hank showed me a couple of weeks ago but it's comfortable and I can afford it.* She could already feel her body relaxing as she went inside.

She kicked off her shoes and set out leftover chicken for her supper. She put canned vegetables in a Pyrex bowl in the microwave and picked up the phone before running her bath water. It wasn't until the fifth or sixth ring that she remembered her Aunt Myrtle had a date with her retired teacher, Douglas Hawthorne.

Having satisfied her hunger and cleaned up the kitchen, Maggie climbed carefully into the high, old-fashioned tub and relaxed as she thought about that tub with the jets in it in her dream house. That's all it was, a dream. She shrugged off a brief stab of envy. The warm water felt good. She closed her eyes and lay back, breathing in the scent of the lavender bubble bath she'd splurged on.

Works just as well—who needs that other stuff?

Still, the tour of the house Hank showed her seemed to haunt her. After looking at the news, nothing else television had to offer looked as good as her book. She made sure all the doors were locked, as if she ever opened anything except the front one on her way to nightly food and comfort.

She got settled with her book and turned on the lamp on the bedside table. She scooted the lamp over a little to get the light just right and remembered the three-way light in the floor lamp the colonel had left beside the gas log fireplace.

Get over it! she muttered to herself, fluffing up her pillows.

About eleven o'clock she placed a bookmark at the end of a chapter and reached to turn off the lamp. The ring of the phone stopped her. She darted a surprised look at the clock and grinned.

Maybe it's a progress report from Aunt Myrtle! She dashed to answer the phone and beamed expectantly.

"Hello?"

Her face fell when a strange voice spoke.

"M—Mrs. Murphy?"

That gave her a chill. No one had called her that since Horace's accident.

"Yes?"

"Mrs. Murphy, this is Happy. Happy Harris. Do you remember me?"

"Oh. Yes, of course I remember you, Happy. How are you? Did you manage to get the motorcycle fixed?"

"Yes, ma'am. With the parts I had and the shop's help, I've got it fixed so I can ride it now." She could hear the smile in his voice. "I'm not doing any racing or anything, but I'm enjoying riding it." He sounded better talking about riding the motorcycle but still seemed a little worried or uncomfortable about something.

Maggie looked at the clock again and was sure of it. *There must be something wrong for him to call this late.*

"Happy, are you stuck somewhere without a ride?"

"No, no ma'am. And I'm sorry to call you so late. I'm at home, out in the carport with our cordless phone."

"What's wrong, Happy? Is it your parents? Are you all right? Are they all right?"

"Yes, ma'am. I just don't want to worry them. I—please,

Mrs. Murphy, don't say anything about me and Mick and Raid being with Horace the night he had the accident."

"I'm afraid it's a little late for that. I was with someone at the barbecue place and we ran into Jack Gardner. I asked him about his being there and who else was there. I just asked him what they talked about. You know, when he started home, things like that. I didn't think that was unusual. Anybody would want to know. But he wasn't very nice, come to think of it. He just said yes, you all were there talking and Horace left about nine or nine-thirty as you said he did."

"That's right. Jack came in after their disagreement about whatever it was. You didn't tell Jack what I said about the drink, did you?"

"No. Why? Are the others back in town now?"

"No, no. I just thought about it and I wondered. Please, Mrs. Murphy, don't tell anyone else about what I said."

"I won't. There isn't anyone else to tell. Are you sure you're all right?"

"Yes. I'm fine. I just got to thinking about it. You haven't heard anything from any of them, have you?"

"No. But as I said, it isn't very likely I would. The only one I've ever seen is Jack Gardner that time at the barbecue place, and I told you he wasn't very friendly. Acted like he didn't want to talk to me. So I don't expect to hear from any of them."

"And you won't say anything about what I told you? Jack wasn't there when they tried to talk Horse into whatever it was, but please don't say anything to Raid or Mickey or anyone about what I told you about the drink."

"But you said Jack wasn't there. Why would he act so unfriendly toward me when all I asked was about Horace and what time he left?"

"Guess Raid or Mickey told him not to talk to you. I don't know. I just don't want them to know I said anything about whatever they wanted Horse to do, or that they put something in his drink."

"No, I won't. Happy, there's no reason for you to worry about my telling Mickey or Raid or Jack Gardner anything. I'll probably never see any of them again."

"Yes, ma'am, you're probably right. I just got to thinking about it. Thank you. I'm sorry about calling so late, I didn't want my mom and dad to hear."

"That's all right, Happy. Goodbye."

Maggie sat with the phone in her hand picturing Happy's face when she had talked to him at the motorcycle shop.

Why would they care about my knowing when Horace started for home? Maggie shook her head. *Teenagers—the only time you can understand them is when you are one.* She went back to bed.

Happy stood by the back door with the phone in his hand. *I know I did the right thing telling Horace's wife he left early to go home. And about that stuff they put in his drink, too. Mick thinks he's so smart, but if he's smart he knows better than to come back here and cause me or her any trouble. I wish Horace knew I tried to help him, and that I told her he was coming home.*

Looking up at the stars, Happy said softly, "Horace, if you can hear me, please, if you can, let me know somehow I did right telling your wife you were trying to get home." He bowed his head. *I guess I'm a mental case, out here in the dark talking to myself.*

He reached to brush away a tear that tried to fall, and his hand stopped, arrested by a rustling in the tall bushes beside the carport.

Horace stepped out of the shadows of the shrubbery. Invisible to Happy, he reached toward the door and made a fist, drawing it back slowly. Nothing happened. He made two more tries before the door slowly opened. He held it there.

117

Happy sucked in a breath, feeling like a cold breeze was blowing through his middle as he looked at the open door, not daring to move. His eyes moved to examine the area around him. The carport was lit only by the distant streetlight and stars. Nothing he could see was holding that door open for him.

Slowly, he walked up the two back steps and went in. Horace let go of the door and Happy caught it, fighting tears.

Joe pulled his patrol car into the St. Olaf's parking lot.

"Thought we were going to stop for coffee." Charlie Coats looked up at the facade of the old church. He was a new patrolman and riding with Joe was part of his training.

"We are. We're going to have it in the soup kitchen."

"Oh." There was neither approval nor disapproval in the one-syllable comment.

Officer Coats got out on his side of the car and stretched, looking up at a particularly horrible grimace on one of the stone gargoyles. It had its mouth open, showing an awesome array of teeth. Coats pointed at it, evidently pained.

"That thing looks like what my mother used to tell me I'd freeze into if I didn't stop frowning and making faces."

Joe laughed, eyeing the thing. "Well, don't worry. I doubt there are any of those in the kitchen. And if there are, you don't have to have what he's having. Come on."

A few heads turned their way when they entered. Joe went to the end of the buffet line and laid his money down at the coffee urn by the cashier. He held up two fingers and handed Charlie a mug to fill.

The elderly cashier shook his head. "We're glad to have you stop by. It's all right." Joe didn't move. "You don't have to," the cashier repeated with a friendly look.

"Yes, I do." Joe returned his smile. He and Charlie got sugar for Joe and a couple of creams for Charlie as the register clanged, ringing up the sale.

"Do you, or did you by any chance, know Mr. Wartz?" Joe asked the cashier. "He used to come here once in a while. Worked at the *Herald*," he added.

"Yes, I remember him. Always had a smile for everybody. I was sorry to hear about what happened to him."

"Did you know him very well?"

"No." The cashier shook his head. "Just to speak to and pass the time of day sometimes."

Joe cast a cautious look around. "Anyone in here right now who was a particular friend of his or was with him much?"

The cashier tilted his head. "Try that red-headed lady and her friend over there."

"Okay, thanks." Joe sipped a little of his hot coffee and walked toward the ladies seated across the room. They both watched him approach with open curiosity. Charlie was close behind him, keeping an eye on his hot cup.

"Would you ladies mind if we join you?" Joe put on his best smile. "We don't like to drink alone."

The red-haired lady was over seventy, but her hair color and outlook were a lot younger. She smiled up at the handsome policeman and his partner. "Sit down. Being alone will drive you to drink."

"You got that right," her younger black friend readily agreed. "But being lonesome's not against the law, is it?" Her dark eyes were curious as well as friendly.

"Not that I know of. The jails probably wouldn't hold all the lonelys if it was. And how would you ever get a confession on something like that?"

Gales of delighted feminine laughter greeted that sally.

"My name is Millie and this is Pauline." The red-headed lady waved a hand at her friend, her bangs bouncing.

"I'm Joe and my partner here is Charlie." Joe sipped some

more of his coffee. "I asked when we got our coffee if there was anyone here who knew a Mr. Wartz. He worked at the *Herald* and he used to come in here."

"Yes, both of us knew him. Name was Fritz. Fritz for Frederich Wartz, Wartzy to his friends. He was a good man." Millie accompanied the information with a nod, looking more serious.

"He was liked and appreciated at the paper, too."

"Sorry to hear about what happened to him. We heard he was stabbed?"

Joe nodded. "Do you know of anyone he might have had trouble with or a disagreement with? Who would want to hurt him for some reason?"

"No. You handling this murder?"

"No, I'm not in charge. Just helping on the case."

Millie's face was solemn. "No, I never saw him have any trouble or heard any harsh words with anybody. You, Pauline?"

Pauline shook her head. "Somebody was here right after it happened, I heard. Asking about him and if anyone knew anything about it. But I wasn't here and didn't hear anything else." She hesitated, then said, "When I first heard about it, I thought somebody mugged him. Or they got the wrong man or something. He was kind, and he's been through so much—can't see why somebody would want to hurt him anymore."

Joe raised his eyebrows at that. "Hurt him anymore?"

"Auschwitz. His wife was Polish. She died there. He survived, made it to the end of the war and was rescued, then came here. He didn't like to talk about it."

"Oh." Joe's voice was soft. Charlie looked down at the dregs in his coffee cup, at a loss to express his feelings.

Then, as if he hurt as well, Joe looked up. His eyes met Millie's with an unspoken question in them.

"Yes, I was there too. We didn't have to talk about it. Don't look back except to remember the people we love." Joe noted the present tense.

"We put on a happy face and some Copper Penny hair color and look forward, glad to be alive. Wartzy was a kind man. If he was here when you sat down and you didn't have any coffee, he'd go get you some, because you're out there in your patrol car taking care of us. He was a good, kind, generous man."

Joe nodded. "That's what they say about him where he worked."

"I hope you find out who killed him," Pauline said.

"We're working on it." Joe took out a card and wrote Detective Alan Hill's name on it. "This is the detective who's in charge of the case. My name's Joe Driver and this number I'm writing on the back is my home phone number. If you hear anything, no matter how small, call me at work or at home and I'll either come talk to you or pass on the information you give me."

Millie and Pauline took the cards. "We will. Come back and have coffee again soon."

CHAPTER THIRTEEN

Maggie heard the phone as she opened her door and ran to answer it. "Hello," she got out breathlessly.

"Hi, is this a bad time?" Joe asked

"No, no. I just ran to get the phone. I just got in the door."

"I missed you at the office. How about I come by and get you? I've got to go out for some charcoal anyway, and we can have burgers at my apartment. Unless you've already got some kind of cordon bleu plans?"

Maggie laughed at the comparison of what she usually faced for dinner and anything cordon bleu. "I wouldn't know cordon bleu if it rolled up and bit me on the ankle. But I don't know much about cooking out, either. Are you going to need educated assistance of some kind?"

"No, just a cast-iron stomach. I'll be there in ten minutes."

"Don't hurt yourself or hit anything expensive." Maggie frowned at the phone as she hung up. *Oh, my God! Hank's right. I do sound like Aunt Myrtle!*

She used the ten minutes to put on fresh makeup and change into slides and pedal pushers. Watching, she went out before Joe had a chance to get out of the car.

"Did I mention how much I admire promptness?" He grinned as she got in beside him.

"Doesn't everybody? There's a great supermarket a couple of blocks down."

"That's where I was going. Need charcoal and a couple of things."

Maggie nodded. "Do you like cole slaw? I'll get us some and some ice cream."

"Yes, but this is my treat."

"Oh, cole slaw isn't much. Let me contribute something I like."

Joe got a good parking place near the store's entrance. "Okay. We're here without hitting anything expensive. Meet you back at the checkout."

Maggie picked up a large carton of cole slaw, green onions, crispy kosher pickles, ice cream, and two kinds of toppings.

"I forgot to ask about bread," she said when she saw Joe coming.

"Got buns. Why don't you put your stuff in here," he pushed the basket closer.

"Because this was my idea. I won't fuss at you if you want to bring something you like when I cook."

"Okay. That's a deal."

Joe's apartment was on the second floor of a three-story complex with limited parking in back.

"You're lucky with parking spaces." Maggie smiled as Joe pulled into one of the two places left.

"Sometimes. We'll go in the back. It's not far to the elevators." He put the sack of charcoal over his shoulder and Maggie got the groceries.

"If that's too heavy, I'll come back."

"No. It's okay and I need the exercise. Is it far?"

"No, I'm on the second floor close to the elevator. Which is great any time except when you're trying to sleep."

He braced the charcoal against the wall and opened the door, holding it for Maggie. She saw the elevator and went to push the up button.

"Must be a lot of people living here, with three floors."

"There are. It's usually full. They have a waiting list."

Joe did his balancing act with the charcoal again to unlock the door and hold it for Maggie. She went in and set the groceries on the bar between the kitchen and living areas.

"Have a look around while I get things started," Joe called.

She stuck the cole slaw in the refrigerator, the onions in a glass of cold water, and regarded the area where she stood.

Looking around isn't going to take much moving around, she mused to herself. *Small but adequate, as one of Hank's ads would say.*

Going to the bedroom door, she looked in and saw a bathroom that opened off of it. There was a small tub with a shower over it. She smiled to herself, betting Joe never closed the door, it was so small. The bedroom held a bed, a matching chest of drawers that looked like mahogany, and a whimsical bedside table with an elephant base. The only other thing in the room was an oval full-length mirror that matched the rest of the mahogany furniture. It was tilted back a little to reveal an oversized pair of boots.

She looked at the lovely lines of the mirror. *I'll bet there's a story behind you, but I'm not going to ask.*

"The tour didn't take long, did it?" Joe grinned when she joined him on the small balcony.

"No, but it looks new and you've got everything you need— except maybe more parking space."

The fire was going well and Joe carefully turned the burgers with a long-handled spatula. Foil-wrapped potatoes sat at the back of the grill. "Unless you'd rather go in, we'll eat out here."

"No, I'd much rather eat out here. I don't even remember the last time I got to do this. I'll go get the pickles and onions."

"You don't cook out?" Joe asked as she set the pickles and

onions beside the buns and mustard.

"I wouldn't know how to start, but you look like an expert."

Joe laughed. "You must not know much about it if I look like an expert to you. And I cheat."

"Cheat? Now, how would you do that?"

Joe pointed a fork at the potatoes. "Did these in the oven last night, then wrapped them in foil to finish up tonight."

"That's not cheating, that's a good idea."

"They seem to be trying to discourage company here, the way they manage to cram in everything that's classified essential in such a small space." He watched the burgers cook, pressing on the patties to get out the fat. Then, after looking them over critically, he put one on a plate and handed it to Maggie.

"Sit wherever you'll feel safe from not being stepped on. I'll get our drinks."

"I'll do that, but you've earned first chair choice." She giggled, eyeing the twin chairs with the table between them. She breathed in the scent from the burger on her plate. "This looks good."

She hurried inside before he could argue, and he was piling things on his burger when she got back. There was just enough room on the narrow table for what they needed, and Maggie looked with anticipation at what was on her plate.

"Here, let me do that." Joe reached over and gingerly handling the foil, opened her potato.

"Oh! My cup runneth over," she exclaimed. "Butter, cheese—and broccoli!" She got up, still holding her plate, and kissed him on the cheek.

"Hey, point getter! I'll make a note of that. Butter, cheese, broccoli. Got it. And how do you like the sunset I ordered?"

Maggie gave it a thumbs-up, her mouth full. The colors were running a gamut from pale pink to mauve to darker lavender.

Aside from a few trips inside to replenish their drinks, they spent the rest of the evening on the tiny balcony watching dusk and starlight take over as they talked. Joe was laughing at one of her problems with the computer she referred to as the arrogant monster machine when she slapped a mosquito on her neck.

"That was his last meal," she announced with satisfaction.

"Time to go in. He may not be alone." Joe stepped closer to give her a kiss on the cheek. "That's for being a good assistant chef."

Maggie looked up with a mischievous smirk. "I also brought ice cream and topping."

He grinned, moving closer. "All right, and a standing ovation for an award-winning dessert!" He pulled her up and put his arms around her. It was too dark for nosy neighbors to see them, not that Maggie cared at that point.

The kiss to confirm they were dating was nothing compared to this one. This one and the embrace that accompanied it staking a claim, was a real bell ringer. They stood there, arms around each other, her head on his chest. Another mosquito buzzed by and Maggie laughed. "We'd better gather things up and go in." Still neither of them moved.

His arms tightened around her and she stretched up to give him a brief kiss. "I know. Me too." She looked up at him, acknowledging the chemistry between them.

"We're dating, we're friends, we enjoy being together. Let's stay there a while. The chemistry won't go away."

"Not if it's the kind that lasts for fifty or sixty years."

"You're right." He raised both her hands to his lips and kissed them, then he quickly started getting things together to go in.

While he cleaned the grill, she put away food and washed dishes. She was finished by the time he came inside to wash his hands.

"I know you've got to work tomorrow, but it's only fifteen minutes till news time. Let's get a Coke and see what the rest of the world is doing." Maggie nodded.

Settled on the couch, Joe gestured at the living area, "Would you believe they've got smaller units than this?"

"Yes, I've seen some. Not here, but a friend of mine had one once. It didn't have a bedroom."

Joe nodded. "That's what the ones here are. I took a look at the two singles with a unit that doubled as a couch in the daytime and a bed at night and decided I had to have a good night's sleep."

"Wise move. I would have too."

Hating to leave the comfortable warmth of Joe's closeness, Maggie got up and retrieved her purse from the bar when the news was over.

Later in the week, Maggie and Fatima sat in the office sharing tuna sandwiches Maggie had brought from home.

"Your tuna and chicken salad are really good, Maggie. Maybe you should cater on the side."

"No, that would make it too much like work."

"That's what Momma says about her cuttings."

"Her what?"

"She likes house plants. She's always snipping off a piece of ivy or something and rooting it to make another plant."

"Sounds like Aunt Myrtle and her roses." Inspiration struck. "Say, why don't we start us a garden club?"

"You mean just a few of us to talk about plants and share cuttings when we want to? You know, I'd thought about getting a couple of Momma's cuttings to give to a friend later on. She's going to move out soon as she's been on her new job long enough to feel like she's going to make it all right."

"It would be fun, and I'm sure Hank would let us meet here after hours. It would be easy to get to for the others."

"Others. You mean us and Momma and your Aunt Myrtle—"

"And Aunt Myrtle's gentleman friend, and your brothers too, if they want to come."

"I guess so. But Shad, Shack, and Bed probably won't want to come unless they want to make points with a girlfriend," Fatima said doubtfully. "But this would be a good place to meet. We can meet the first Monday of the month. Nobody would want to stay on a Friday."

"Right. You talk to your momma and I'll talk to Aunt Myrtle, then I'll ask Hank about it."

"Okay, we'll do it!"

As soon as Maggie got home, she dialed her Aunt Myrtle's number. *I'll tell her about the garden club and get an update on her love life.* She smiled to herself, listening to the phone ringing. She wasn't disappointed in the reaction she got about the garden club.

"That's a great idea! Why don't you come on over now and we'll talk? You haven't eaten yet, have you?"

"No, I—"

"Well, just get in the car and come on. I want to show you something."

Maggie shook her head at the dial tone, locked the door again and left.

The *something* turned out to be a tiny little vine that had come up in the yard where some watermelon seeds had been dropped.

"Is that really a watermelon vine?"

"Yes. I'm as sure it is as I'm sure I can't have a watermelon vine there." Aunt Myrtle looked at it with compassion. "I can't stand the thought of running the lawn mower over it. It's such a healthy little runner."

"Don't. Don't even think about that. What would you call that, planticide?" Maggie chuckled. "I'll have to ask Joe. When we decide when our first meeting will be, dig it up and put it in a paper cup. Bring it to the meeting. Somebody will adopt it. If not, I'll put it in a planter on my desk till it gets so big I have to move it or somebody wants it."

"Good idea. I'll do that."

"And Fatima's momma will probably bring some ivy she's rooted."

"Momma? Sounds like two Ms the way you pronounce it."

"That's right. Her choice. The sign over her beauty salon says Momma's Sunday Best Beauty Salon."

"I guess that makes it official." Aunt Myrtle shrugged.

They dined happily, enjoying crock-pot chicken and plans for the garden club. Maggie floated home on happiness fueled by their plans and the healthy little melon vine.

All of that was completely overshadowed by her surprisingly comfortable but nonetheless heart-thumping relationship with Joe. Good, good-looking Joe.

The thought of him, the memory of his good-natured smile and the way her heart skipped a beat when he touched her, made her feel like her insides were full of butterflies. All of that made her mouth turn up at the corners, no matter when one of those memories or pictures flashed across her mind or where she was at the time.

The glow of well-being lasted until twelve-thirty A.M., when the phone rang.

"Hello?" She realized she sounded groggy.

There was no answer, but there was no dial tone either. She looked at the clock and after another hello, hung up muttering, "Dratted wrong number . . ."

At two-thirty, the phone rang again. Again, there was no one there.

Maggie stood listening, straining to hear. *I don't hear anything in the background and there's no one on the line.* Puzzled, she clutched the phone tighter, beginning to get frightened.

"Is anyone there?" Her voice shook a little as she asked.

There was still no answer. Maggie almost dropped the phone in her haste to hang up.

It must not be one of those "heavy breathing" calls. I sure didn't hear any heavy breathing. I didn't hear anything. Not anything at all . . .

She looked again at the clock. *Kids. It must be kids playing pranks. School is out and their parents are asleep. It must be kids.*

The floor felt cool on her bare feet as she walked back to bed. There were two more calls, but Maggie didn't answer them or look at the clock. She put her hand over the ear not pressed into a pillow and ignored them.

The next day Maggie knocked on the door facing to Hank's office. "Talk to you a few minutes, please?"

"You want to buy a house?"

"No."

"Do you want to place an ad?"

"No."

Hank raised his eyebrows. "How much of my time you talking about wasting?"

"Just a couple of minutes—or less."

"Okay." He gestured to the chair with the rebel spring hiding beneath the folded papers. *At least it looks neater now,* Maggie consoled herself.

She sat and leaned forward, a little afraid of being punched by the spring. "Do you mind if we, Fatima and I, stay after hours once a month and have a meeting? We want to start a garden club. A small one, of course. And we won't be here long or bother anything." She got it all out as quickly as she could, respecting Hank's time limit.

"A garden club . . ." Hank tapped his pen against his teeth and thought about it. "How many members do you have?"

"Not many. We may have a few more later, but right now

there's just Fatima, her mother, Aunt Myrtle and me. And we may swap plants and cuttings from time to time. I can probably get you a plant rooted for in here, if you'd like one."

She looked around and decided the top of the book case would be good. Hank's desk didn't look safe for a plant. She managed to keep a straight face as she pictured the watermelon vine climbing the wall behind him.

"I guess." Hank was cautiously grateful about the offer of a plant. "As long as whatever it is it grows slowly, doesn't take up too much room, doesn't talk, you water it and it doesn't eat flies or any of that other scary stuff."

Maggie laughed, picturing a vine's tendril reaching out for an unsuspecting Hank as he worked.

"I'll take care of it for you, and I'm going to get it free. All that scary stuff you mentioned, forget that, too. It would probably cost a lot of money."

Hank nodded. "Okay. First Monday of the month. Garden Club." He picked up his pen again, but Maggie was still sitting there.

"There's more?" Hank's eyebrows arched.

"I wanted to ask you if there's a place that sells answering machines close enough around here for me to get one on my lunch hour."

"Yeah." Hank's eyebrows got back to normal. "Wal-Mart sells them, they've got a big electronics department. Be careful crossing the street," he added as a gentle hint to hasten her on her way.

She went directly to Fatima with the good news that they could have their meetings beginning next month. "And I'm going to get him one of your momma's ivy cuttings or something from Aunt Myrtle for his office."

"You'd do that to a plant?" Fatima rolled her eyes heavenward.

"It'll be all right. I'll put it on the bookcase behind his desk and I'll take care of it."

Maggie bought the answering machine of her choice on her lunch hour, and when Hank left later on his, she quickly dialed her Aunt Myrtle.

"Are you going to see Douglas Hawthorne soon and does he know much about phone equipment?" Maggie jumped right into what she needed.

"Yes I am, and why do you ask?"

"I bought one of those answering things today, but I don't know how to put it on and I don't want to goof up anything. I know about as much about that as I do about what's lurking under the hood of the heap."

"Welcome to the club. The directions being on them, I'm sure Douglas could do it for you. There's just one hitch."

"What's that?"

"I don't want to talk to a machine!" Disapproval was loud and clear.

"You won't have to," Maggie soothed her. "I'm only going to turn it on when I go to bed, which is usually between ten-thirty and eleven o'clock."

"But why do you need it then? Not that it makes any difference, because I'm usually sawing logs by then," Aunt Myrtle conceded.

"Because I want to sleep. We've evidently got some little stinkers who play with the telephone now that school is out. And they've got nothing better to do than ring phones and wake people up. I got two or three calls last night."

"You did? How do you know it's kids? Did they say anything suggestive? Maybe it isn't kids." Suspicion and worry were audible.

"No, it's kids. It must be. It's nothing to worry about. They don't say anything. I crawled under a pillow at two-thirty this morning and didn't answer it again."

"And they didn't say anything?"

"No, no heavy breathing or anything like that. When they can't get anything but a recorded message instead of waking someone up in the middle of the night, it will take all the fun out of it."

"Hum. If they didn't say anything, did you hear any background noises or anything like that?"

"No. Not a thing. But they might think of something to say if I'm dumb enough to keep answering. Do you think Douglas will put the thing on my phone for me?"

"I'm sure he will. He's coming over for dinner tonight. We're going to eat about six-thirty. I'll ask him and we could come over about seven-thirty and still get home in time to look at a movie. And you can meet him," Aunt Myrtle added.

"Good. I'll get a cake on the way home and we can have cake and coffee for dessert while he looks the directions over. What kind of cake does he like?"

"Chocolate, same as we do. We'll see you tonight."

Later, Maggie was looking at the office clock, counting the minutes till she could leave and picturing all sorts of heavenly chocolate cake when her phone rang.

"Hi, this is Hank—"

"Oh, long distance—or have you sneaked out? I had no idea you were gone, or I might have considered sneaking out too." Maggie grinned into the phone.

"Didn't know I'm here, huh? You sure know how to hit a guy in his importance. Speaking of that, Grace wants to talk to you. She's on the line. I'm going back for my last cup of coffee, unless it's vile enough to bite back by now. I'll unplug the pot," he added. "Here's Grace."

Maggie," Grace trilled, sounding happy for some reason, which was an alert for caution among those who knew her, according to Hank. "Hank tells me you and Fatima are starting a garden club."

"Well, yes, if you could call it that. There's just me, Fatima, her mother and Aunt Myrtle. And of course Fatima's brothers and Aunt Myrtle's friend if he wants to come. I wouldn't take any bets on that, though."

"I wouldn't either, but you girls will enjoy it. I'm sure you know about my judging flower shows for some of the local organizations?"

"Yes, we've seen some of the write-ups." Maggie treaded softly, not wanting to get in over her head on anything. "We aren't doing anything like that or charging dues or anything that could cost us money, is what it boils down to." Maggie laughed at her self-described limitations.

"We haven't picked out a name yet either, but the Dirt Poor Piddlers would fit us just right."

Grace laughed with her. "I know what you mean. The main thing for any garden club to remember is its goal is to make the world a prettier place, not get our blooming faces in the paper."

"I knew you'd understand. And I'm going to get an ivy cutting or something and put it in Hank's office for him."

"Good luck finding a place for it." Grace got serious. "What I wanted to talk to you about is that next month some of our local garden clubs are going to be treated to one of those brief cruises down the river and back to have a show. It won't cost your group anything to go. I'll just tell them you're my guests. There will be the show and some punch and cookies or something, if you want to come. The *Herald* is one of the sponsors."

"Oh, how nice! Of course we would like to go. I'll tell them about it at our first meeting. We're meeting here at the *Herald* the first Monday of each month. Just let me know when. Hank hasn't said anything about it."

"He doesn't know yet."

Maggie's mouth dropped open.

"I'll let you know more later. Good luck with your first meeting. Goodbye, dear."

How do I get in the middle of these things? Open mouth—insert foot. Well, my money's on Grace. And she said the Herald *is only one of the sponsors, so it probably won't be too bad. I'm not going to worry about anything right now except getting the most gorgeous, delicious, sinfully rich chocolate cake I can. Black Forest, double chocolate, German chocolate . . .*

CHAPTER FOURTEEN

The cake Maggie chose was a large German chocolate triple layer with gobs of coconut on top, which naturally called for chocolate swirl ice cream. It would be an awful hardship to have to eat it without ice cream and chocolate fudge syrup dribbled over it.

Maggie's supper was simple, with a few dieter's rules in mind. *Chicken salad on a piece of toast to avoid using another piece of bread will at least partly make up for the chocolate orgy we'll have later.*

Maggie ate slowly, picturing all kinds of fat cells poised to jump on every bite of that cake to make yet more fat. She tried not to think about it. She thought about her Aunt Myrtle's gentleman friend.

I've been wanting to meet Douglas Hawthorne. I hope he's nice as Aunt Myrtle seems to think. She said he's a retired teacher, so he must be intelligent and the soul of patience. A teacher would have to be.

She recalled some recent headlines about violence in the schools. Some martial arts skills couldn't hurt either.

The sound of a car outside ended her speculation. She set down her diet cola, thinking what a joke on herself that was, and went to meet them.

Maggie's first impression of Douglas Hawthorne was good. From the smile wrinkles in his pleasant face to his casual clothes and comfortable shoes, she approved. He was about five foot ten, of average weight, hair mostly white, and he had a very nice smile.

And Aunt Myrtle obviously likes him, which is the most important thing of all, Maggie smiled at him.

"Maggie, this is my friend, Douglas Hawthorne. My niece, Margaret Murphy."

"I'm pleased to meet you, Douglas, if I may call you that?"

"Certainly, but Doug gets faster results."

"I'll remember that. And call me Maggie, please. Aunt Myrtle tells me you're a chocolate addict like us, so our dessert will be heavy on the chocolate. I keep powdered chocolate by the sugar bowl if you want to add it to your coffee."

"You really do like chocolate! Why don't we have a look at the answering device before we get comfortable with our dessert?"

"Yes, let's get it over with," Aunt Myrtle agreed, then turned to Maggie. "You'll have to record a message too, you know."

"I hadn't thought about that. I'll think of something."

Maggie went to get the device and Doug sat down beside the phone.

Maggie took her aunt to look at the cake and got a thumbs-up approval from her as she nodded back at Doug.

"It's good he's a chocoholic too." Maggie opened another envelope for the chocolate bowl as they waited.

"I think I've got the monster tamed," Doug called.

He showed Maggie how the device worked and had her practice a couple of messages.

After a good laugh at some of her efforts, and testing different ideas, Maggie decided on a message. It informed the caller, with a playful southern accent, they had reached her number but, "Rhett and I are out on the verandah having mint juleps. Leave your name and number, and we will get back to you."

Maggie listened and laughed, pleased with her message

choice. "I can't wait for Fatima to hear it. Come on, Doug, you've more than earned your dessert!"

When Maggie got back from lunch Friday, Fatima handed her a phone message. It was from Happy Harris.

"Just a phone number," Maggie observed. "How did he sound? Was he upset or anything?"

"No, just said to call when you have time and gave me that number."

"Thanks. I'll call him later."

Maggie had had a good week. Joe was coming to dinner, and hallelujah, it was Friday, she rejoiced silently. Small wonder she forgot the phone number tucked away in her purse.

At one minute to five o'clock, she and Fatima, giggling at each other, stood before the office door with their purses in their hands, waiting for the clock to tick one more time. They bolted like horses from the racetrack gate in Hot Springs as soon as the minute hand clicked.

Maggie had invited Joe over for spaghetti. She fixed the meat sauce the night before because the good spices and seasonings always tasted better after they'd "been married a while," as Aunt Myrtle called it. She stopped at the store for cole slaw and drinks and looked forward to the weekend.

She got the water on to boil for the pasta and went back to turn off the recorder on the phone.

Forgot to turn it off again. I'll have to get used to doing that. Don't want a lot of telemarketing on there.

The pasta had just reached the right degree of al dente when she heard Joe's car out front. She turned off the heat under the sauce and the pasta and went to meet him.

Joe stopped just inside the door and she reached out with both arms to give him an impulsive hug. She wore an expectant smile, thinking, *Maybe I don't cook out, but just you wait till you taste my spaghetti!*

The hug was abruptly aborted.

Joe reached out too, but not for a hug.

Maggie stared in surprise at the hands gripping her forearms, then raised her eyes to his face. Joe did not look happy.

Seeing her shocked expression, he dropped his arms to his side. "I—I'm sorry. I didn't mean to hurt you. Who the hell is Red?" He blurted it out.

"Red?" Maggie's face fell into puzzled lines. "I don't know any Red."

"Yes, you do. Red! He's the one you hold all calls for—I didn't know you had an answering machine."

"Oh, I see." Maggie exhaled with relief. "You called and got my recording. I forgot to turn it off. And I said Rhett, not Red."

"Rhett?" She waited for Joe's worry wrinkles to go away. They didn't. They only changed a little from worried to puzzled.

"You know, Scarlett and Rhett? In *Gone with the Wind*?"

"Oh, God! Am I going to get kicked off the verandah?"

"No, it could have been worse." She smiled up at him and a giggle slipped out. "You might not have cared who Red is!"

He reached out to pull her to him and his arms went around her. "It's too late for that, as if you don't know." He kissed the top of her head and let her go. "When did you get an answering machine?" He looked over at the little black intruder as if it didn't belong there.

"Last week. I only turn it on at night." She took his hand and led him into the kitchen.

"Um, smells good in here. What I called for was to ask if you wanted me to bring anything. I got so upset when I heard that message, I just rode my high horse on over here. But I can go back if there's something."

Maggie shook her head. "No, we've got everything we need. Cole slaw, French bread, and the spaghetti and meat sauce is ready. There's parmesan cheese on the table."

She put ice in their glasses and motioned for him to sit down.

Joe praised the spaghetti enough to make her feel good, even after she discounted a little of his praise as guilt and being hungry after a hard day.

"What made you decide you need an answering machine? And you said you only turn it on at night? Why is that? And did you put it on yourself or get someone to do it for you?"

The last question brought a little of the disgruntled expression back to his face.

"Do you want answers to all that in order or just at random?"

Joe smiled self-consciously. "Just start anywhere."

"Well, let's see. I only turn it on at night because I don't get that many calls during the day. Everyone I know is aware I'm at work, and I'm here to answer the phone myself during the weekends. Aunt Myrtle's gentleman friend, Douglas Hawthorne, put it on for me when they were over here having dessert and coffee. I also got to meet him. He's nice, I like him, and it didn't take him long to do it." She grinned. "I thought up the smart aleck message all by myself and I was proud of it. I didn't know it was going to be hazardous to my love life." She couldn't stop a little laugh from getting out. "And Red can get his own spaghetti, whoever he is. I'm particular who I fix spaghetti for."

"You are, are you? You left out why you thought you need the gizmo?"

"Oh, I did, didn't I? I got some nuisance calls from kids playing with phones now that school is out. So when I go to bed, I turn on the message and just don't let it disturb my sleep."

"Calls at night?" That brought back a couple of the worry lines. "Very many?"

"Not more than two or three. One about midnight, again at two-thirty, then one I didn't answer. Don't know what time that was. I put a pillow over my head and decided right then to get the answering thing."

"I can understand that." Joe smiled, relaxing a little. "And I guess I'm not jealous of Douglas Hawthorne, since he and Miss Myrtle are an item."

"An item, huh? She'd love that."

Joe was still not entirely happy. "How do you know the calls were kids? Did they say anything? Maybe it's one of those mental cases, a pervert who gets off on the sound of a strange woman's voice."

Maggie made a face. "I'm not a strange woman, and there wasn't any heavy breathing. Aunt Myrtle immediately thought it might be a *heavy breather,* as she calls it. But there wasn't any heavy breathing or any other sound. And if they decide they want to say ugly things to the recording, I'll erase them in the morning without losing any sleep over it. So no problem!" She nodded emphatically. "Oh, that reminds me of a call I've got to make."

"Right now?"

She blotted her lips with her napkin. "We're about ready for dessert anyway. It won't take long."

Joe clamped his teeth firmly over *who to,* but Maggie noticed the effort.

"Happy Harris called and left his number today, and I forgot to call him back. You remember, the boy I gave Horace's motorcycle to?"

"I remember." Joe recalled uneasily that Happy was the one who told her how the rohypnol got into Horace's drink. He listened to her side of the conversation as he finished his spaghetti.

"Happy?" Maggie's voice floated in to him. "I'm sorry I didn't answer your call sooner. We got kind of busy trying to get out of the office on time."

141

Joe saw eavesdropping as a necessary tool for gathering information and listened to everything he could hear without any pangs of conscience at all.

"Oh, that's all right, Mrs. Murphy—"

"Call me Maggie, Happy. How is the motorcycle doing?"

Horace appeared and listened, too.

"Just fine. I'm enjoying it. I appreciate your letting me have it. I just wanted to know how you're getting along. I—I'm sorry if I scared you telling you not to say anything about what I told you."

"You didn't scare me, and I was glad to know Horace was coming home early."

"Yes, ma'am. You haven't heard anything from Jack Gardner or any of the others since we talked, have you?"

"No, and I probably never will. As I said, Jack Gardner acted like he didn't want to talk to me at all, and I don't know the others."

"Well, thanks for calling me back and for giving me the motorcycle. And if I can help you, or cut your grass or there's anything else I can do to help you, you just let me know."

"Thank you, Happy. That's sweet of you. But I'm doing fine and I'm glad you're enjoying the motorcycle. I know Horace would be glad too. I've got company here for dinner, so I'll say goodbye for now."

"Goodbye. Take care, Mrs. M—Maggie."

Horace smiled, glanced at Joe's back in the kitchen, and disappeared.

Maggie went back to the kitchen and laid the memo on a counter before clearing away their plates.

"That his number?" Joe gestured at the memo.

"Yes." She paused to hand it to him.

Joe tore the memo in half, wrote the number on the bottom and gave her back the top of the memo.

"You need his number?"

"Probably not, but I'll have it if I do."

Maggie shrugged and set his ice cream bowl in front of him. Bottles of caramel and chocolate syrup followed. "I could write you an IOU for something baked, but it wouldn't be any good till fall. Late fall," Maggie warned. "Summer is hot enough without heating up an oven."

Joe laughed, "If your baking is as good as your spaghetti, I'll look forward to it." He got up and pulled her up and into his arms, holding her close. "If you're planning on letting me stay around till fall, I'm happy."

"Me too." She raised her face for a long, tender kiss.

CHAPTER FIFTEEN

Detective Alan Hill looked up as Joe stopped at his desk. "Hello, and how's Maggie?"

"That's Miss Maggie to you, and I guess she's fine."

"You guess? Explain that to me."

Joe told him about the answering machine and the Rhett Butler message.

"Who's Red?" Alan chortled, shaking with laughter at Joe's miserable face. "And she still fed you? After that?" He wiped his eyes. "Have no fear, son, that poor woman is in love." He pulled himself together. "You stop by here just to make my day?"

"No, I've got a phone number for Happy Harris, there being about two inches of Harrises in the phone book last time I looked."

"Okay, I'll check it out when I have time and see if I can find anything interesting."

"The way I got it, he called and left his number at Maggie's office and she didn't think to return the call till she got home. He called just to see how she was doing and she thought that was nice." Joe rolled his eyes heavenward. "She thinks everybody's nice."

Alan grinned. "And I hope nothing ever happens to make her think otherwise. But I can see why you worry about it." He stifled a chuckle, still picturing Joe shouting about some jerk named Red. "Maybe you could give her a distrust transfusion. Now, tell me what's really on your mind."

"I heard her say something about 'scare' and asked her about it. Happy said he hadn't meant to scare her by telling her not to say anything about what he told her. But she had already told him she didn't tell Jack Gardner anything and he didn't tell her anything, except he confirmed what time Horace left to go home."

Alan nodded, remembering the little he knew about the case.

"He asked her twice if she'd heard from any of them, the ones who were with Horace that night. It was just a friendly call on the surface, but it sounded like he was making sure she was all right and that she doesn't say anything about that doctored-up drink." His brows drew together. "To me it sounded like he might have thought they, Mickey Lewis and Raymond Wilson, would be some kind of threat to her."

Horace appeared beside the desk and peered at Alan.

"You think maybe these two nogoodniks were leaning on Happy not to say anything? If what they put in that drink did affect his reflexes, they could have caused the accident. Maybe that finally got through the fog in their brains."

"Also, Maggie has bought herself an answering device. She said it was because she's been getting some late-night calls."

He had Alan's attention and Horace's too. Horace touched his arm in gratitude, but Joe didn't feel it as he continued.

"She thinks it was just kids playing with the phone, but still a nuisance. She turns on the machine at night and just doesn't answer it. Whoever it is who calls doesn't ever say anything."

Alan sat deep in thought, Horace and Joe watching. "I don't think we've got grounds yet to put a tap on her phone. She could be right. It could be just kids. And you're going to stay pretty close around anyway, aren't you?"

"You better believe it."

Horace looked relieved and gave him a thumbs-up before fading out.

"I'll check out the records on that Harris number and the other one, too." He leaned forward to look at the plastic sack Joe had put down when he came in.

"What's this? You starting a hope chest?" Alan gestured at the glass he could see through the plastic.

"It's got fingerprints on it. Josef Kranz's prints. He's the man who helped Mr. Wartz deliver the *Herald* to their distribution boxes. He's a loner. Nobody even knew where to contact him, since Wartz just paid him himself to help him out. Don't think they ever got an address, but I think Maggie said she has a phone number now. I'll call and get it."

Alan pushed the phone toward him. "Didn't you say he knew Wartz was dead but they don't know how he knew?"

"Must have known, since he was worried about getting paid." He listened till Maggie picked up the phone.

"The *Herald,* Maggie Murphy."

"I'm impressed!"

"You should be." Maggie laughed.

"Can you get me that phone number for Josef Kranz without too much trouble?"

"Sure, hold on a minute." He heard a drawer open, then Maggie read him the number.

"That's all you've got? No address?"

"We probably wouldn't have got that much if he hadn't wanted to get paid. We don't know how he knew Wartz wasn't going to pay him either," she reminded him.

"That's what got my attention. I'm at Alan's desk and I'm going to leave this number with him. Maybe he can come up with something. I'll see you tonight."

"All right, tell him hello for me."

"Of course," Alan reminded Joe as he hung up, "Josef Kranz being as old as you guess him to be, he'll probably be dead before we get an ID on these prints."

"Yeah, I know. I just didn't want you to run out of something to do."

"You're all heart, Alan."

"Yeah, I know. And Maggie said to tell you hello."

"Thanks for finally remembering the message. What are you going to do the rest of the day?"

"Follow up on some nosy questions I didn't get answers to and have coffee with a redhead."

Alan's eyes nailed him. "Redhead?"

"This one's over seventy but the red is natural. She told me it says so on the bottle!"

"Out! Get out!"

Joe grinned as he left and closed the door.

Horace appeared as Alan turned away to type something, and the disturbed air from the closing door blew the memo with the phone number on it off the desk.

Horace held out his hand, raising it slowly. Behind Alan's back, the memo with the numbers on it obediently rose and settled gently beside the phone. Horace faded, looking pleased with himself.

Joe pulled up in front of the duplex Michael Lewis had once called home. There was now a car in one side of the garage. The *For Rent* sign was still in the window on the left side. A head wearing a wide straw hat appeared over the hedge at the side of the lot. Joe returned the friendly smile on the face beneath the hat and waved.

The man who opened the door looked suspiciously at Joe's uniform. "Yes? Being broke against the law now?" A burst of laughter came from beyond the hedge and the man shot a mean glare in that direction.

Joe smiled. "I'm trying to locate someone who used to live here. His name is Michael Lewis. Did he leave a forwarding address, or do you know of any way I can locate him?"

Art Dunkin stroked the white stubble on his chin thoughtfully. "No, I don't. Don't know anything about his family. Only talked to him a little, mostly when he paid the rent."

"You know of any friends he had who might know where he is?"

"Humpf! Only ones I saw were on motorcycles. They didn't come around much and I was glad of it."

"If you do hear from him, I'd appreciate it if you let me know. My number is on the back." Joe handed him a card, which was acknowledged by a nod. "Thank you."

At St. Olaf's midafternoon didn't seem to be a very busy time for the kitchen. Joe looked around before getting coffee, his eyes adjusting to the dimmer light indoors.

A movement caught his eye and his face brightened when he saw Millie waving to him. He took his coffee and asked politely if he could join her and Pauline.

"Sit!" The red bangs bounced, and Pauline smiled a welcome.

"You found out any more about what happened to Wartzy?"

"No, we're working on it. Haven't got much to go on. You said he used to come in here to eat sometimes and have coffee." Both women nodded. "Was he ever with a man named Josef Kranz?"

Their reaction to the name startled him.

Millie hissed, looking mean as an alley cat with its back up. Pauline spat, "Bigot! He a bigot! He don't even speak to black people."

"Won't speak to black people?"

"First time I saw him I said hello, friendly like, since we never saw him in here before. He don't say nothin'—just look at me like I'm dirt, and he don't say nothin'! Didn't make the mistake of speaking to him again. Not me."

"Neither one of us did. He wasn't around much anyway. Nobody liked him." Millie thought for a few seconds. "I think Wartzy was sorry for him. And as for Josef Kranz, I wouldn't bet on his having any feelings for anybody. I think the attraction there was Wartzy paid him a little bit. I never saw anything resembling friendship or goodwill on that bony, mean face of his."

"Do you have any idea where he lives?"

Millie shook her head.

Pauline volunteered, "John Bob, a friend of mine, told me he saw him once at that truck stop just before where you go up to get on the freeway. He was getting a towel and soap to take a shower like the truckers do."

"Taking a shower. You think he might be a street person then?"

Millie sipped coffee and put down her cup. "He wears the same clothes almost all the time, and he doesn't seem to have any income. No job except when Wartz let him help him. And that ugly, long military coat, if he's not got it on, it's over his arm. Why no pension then?"

"Humph! If he wasn't three years older than God, I'd think he was one of them runaway fathers duckin' child support. You can spot them a block away."

"No address, no friends, loner, no income," Joe added it up aloud.

"And he's a bigot and hates blacks," Pauline reminded him.

"I haven't seen any color he does like." Millie grinned, tired of being serious. "I'd hate to have to do his hair."

Joe laughed as he got up. "Thanks for the input, ladies. Have a good evening."

CHAPTER SIXTEEN

Hank appeared in the hall and beckoned to Maggie. Before she got up, she pulled a big sack out of her bottom desk drawer and took it with her.

"What's that?" Hank asked as he sat down at his desk.

"A surprise." She pulled a large, dark green pillow out of the sack, then threw the sack and the folded-up newspapers from the only other chair into the trash can beside his desk. She bent the spring over as far as she could, then replaced the papers with the new cushion and sat down in safety and comfort.

Hank cracked up. It took him a few seconds to get over it. He eyed Maggie's satisfied smile, as she sat there on the new cushion. "Talk about protecting your—backside!"

"Wal-Mart sells more than answering machines," was Maggie's complacent comment.

"So I see. It's good you're comfortable. I've got good news. Your house deal went through."

"My what?" Maggie was suddenly on the verge of panic. "What deal? What house? I don't have any deal going!"

"Yes, you do. You remember me asking how much rent you're paying?"

"I remember that, yes, but—"

"Do you also remember my telling you the house was a desperation sale? The man is in the military, his wife's pregnant, they'd outgrown the house anyway, the whole two-bit soap opera?"

"Yes, and what I remember best is I said no way! I can't buy a house or anything else right now." She leaned forward a little, keeping in mind the exact location of the butt-threatening wire. "You do remember that, don't you?"

"Don't be tedious. I've got you a house of your own at a figure you can pay. All you have to do is sign on the dotted line and you're a homeowner."

Maggie fought the urge to just get up and run. "I can't, Hank. I told you I can't. A thirty-year mortgage would be the last straw right now."

"It's not thirty years, it's fifteen. There wasn't all that much difference, and mortgage rates are low right now."

"But Hank, I can't pay for it!"

"Yes, you can." Hank sat there unflappable and positive. "The principle, interest and the rest of the escrow account are included in the monthly mortgage payment, and it's ten dollars a month less than you're paying in rent."

That stopped Maggie's panicked flow of denial. Her eyes grew wide and round. "Ten dollars less than I'm paying in rent? You're sure?" She paused, mentally going over Hank's exact words. "And that includes everything? Insurance and taxes and all those things that eat out of your pocket every month?"

"That's right. They're all included in the escrow account, and the payment is still ten dollars less than you're paying in rent right now. You'd have to have rocks in your head not to take it."

"It's beginning to look that way to me, too," Maggie said slowly, still not convinced. "How did you do it?"

"Trade secret. And besides, I'm smart."

"You must be. After all, Grace picked you, and she's smart, too." Maggie laughed. Nervously trying to take it all in, she was an eyelash away from hysterical in her excitement. Then she fell to earth in a pessimistic heap.

"Wait a minute. What about closing costs? And I've heard

somewhere about something that has to be paid in advance for the escrow account. What was it? And whoever heard of anyone buying a house with no money?"

"What you probably remember, incorrectly and at a heck of a time, is you need to pay the insurance in advance a few months, and of course there are closing costs."

"I knew it!" After such a roller-coaster high, she hated to give up entirely. "So, how much is all that? What would I have to have to get in there and start those payments that are ten dollars less than my rent?"

Hank glanced at the papers in front of him. "A little under thirty-two hundred dollars."

Maggie's body sat on her comfy green cushion, but her dreams went to renters' hell and sat on a pile of bills, looking stunned.

"Did you hear me?" Hank's voice broke into her gloom.

"What? No, what did you say?" *What else matters?*

"I said the costs were figured in with the financing, so you don't have to go out and beat the bushes trying to borrow the money."

"I don't? Figured in? I don't understand." *I don't believe it, either.*

"You asked me about the closing costs, et cetera. I said a little less than thirty-two hundred dollars. Are you with me?" Maggie nodded. "Read my lips. The closing costs were figured in the financing so you don't have to have any money. All you have to do is move in and start making payments."

Maggie realized her mouth was open. "Oh, my God! Oh, my God! I've bought a house!"

"Not yet, you haven't. Come over here and sign everywhere I've marked."

Maggie signed everything and sat back. "Thanks, Hank. Thank you. This is wonderful!"

"Wonderful for you," Hank grunted.

"What do you mean? What's bad about it for you?" She was still braced for some kind of a hang-up.

"To help get your credit through I had to say I'm not going to fire you for five years!"

"Oh. Wait a minute. Five years? Slavery's out, you know. Suppose I decide to quit?"

Hank grinned. "They didn't ask me that."

"I've got to tell Fatima!" She ran back toward the office and Fatima came to meet her. She put her arm around her shoulders. "What is it? Is it Joe? Is Joe hurt?"

"No, nothing's happened to Joe. This is good news. Hank found me a house I can buy! I'm just so happy! I didn't think I could get it!" She hugged Fatima and they danced from sheer happiness, Fatima laughing at Maggie's reaction and her dancing at the same time.

Hank stood at Fatima's reception desk answering the phone. It was Grace.

"Yes, I told her, Grace, and—can you talk a little louder? There's a dance or a native uprising or something going on in the hall. Yes. She's pleased about it. That's what the noise is all about. Yes, she's thrilled out of her gourd. I love you, too. Bye."

"Thanks for answering the phone, Hank." Fatima passed him going back to her desk.

"No problem. It was for you."

"It was?"

"Yeah, nothing important—said something about a lottery." Hank disappeared down the hall, laughing like a demon.

"I'm going to kill him," Fatima muttered.

"Not today," Maggie said dreamily. "Please. Not today . . ."

Before she left, Hank brought her the keys to the house and an envelope with some of the papers in it. "I suppose you'll go over and look at it again tonight or this weekend?"

153

"Both! Joe's coming over tonight and I want to show it to him. Hank, thank you for getting all this arranged. I wouldn't have even known where to start." She shook her head. "I had no idea I could ever get a house."

"I could tell." Hank grinned. "There's one more thing." He paused to wave goodnight to Fatima and Floyd. "I would have given you this when you signed the papers, but I was afraid you'd have a heart attack." He smiled as he handed her a check.

She held it in her hand, puzzled. "But—but—it's a check for eighteen hundred dollars! What is it for?"

"I asked for five thousand closing and related costs, and it only took thirty-two hundred. It's already figured in as I said, so this leftover money is to do whatever you want to with it."

Maggie gasped at the windfall and kissed him on the cheek. "Thanks. I'm still having trouble believing it. I really do appreciate this. It's like Christmas, only better." She laughed as a tear threatened to spill over.

"When the smoke clears, you'll realize all I did was sell you a house. The rest is up to you."

She put her arms around him and kissed him again anyway.

Maggie was waiting outside when Joe arrived, her purse and the papers in her hand. "I brought a pizza," he said uncertainly as she got in beside him.

"We can put it in the microwave later. Right now, we're going to twenty-four hundred Elmwood Drive."

"We're going visiting? Who lives there?"

"I'm going to."

"Oh." Joe assumed one of those "the mystery is solved" expressions. "They went up on the rent like you were afraid they would?"

"No. Hank found a house listed at a good price, and he got all the papers and legal work done so I can get it at the same as

I'm paying in rent."

"That's good luck! And it was good of him to do it for you. What do you know? I'm dating a woman of property." He smiled.

"I'm as surprised about it as you are. He made me look at it when he first listed it, but I didn't even consider it seriously. Then he told me he had got it all done, in spite of my saying no to it, and being as negative as—as a banker with loan papers in front of him."

Joe laughed. "That's generally pretty negative, all right. But owning is better than paying rent. I'm happy for you. When's the first payment due, or shouldn't I ask?"

"No, it's okay to ask. I just hadn't got around to telling you. It's deferred for sixty days, so that's like free rent for two months."

"Double good. You must have good credit."

Maggie laughed, clutching the papers to her heart to keep from dropping them.

"What's so funny?"

"Hank said to help me on my credit, poor old widow woman that I am . . ." She looked sideways at Joe. "He had to say he wouldn't fire me for the next five years!"

Joe laughed too, picturing Hank, then he slowed the car to look at house numbers.

Maggie stretched her neck, searching for the fence she remembered.

When they arrived, the electricity was still on for the grand tour of the house and yard, and Maggie showed him the garage apartment.

Standing on the little patio in back of the apartment, Joe asked, "Are you going to rent the apartment?"

"I had been thinking about it after Hank told me I could get the place, but I don't know. I think the only way I would rent it would be if . . ." She said it slowly, "If I could rent it to a good-looking policeman I know pretty well."

"I was afraid to ask, but I was more afraid not to. I don't think I want you to rent it to someone else."

"Someone like Red?" Maggie smirked, snuggling closer.

He put his other arm around her. "I guess I'm not ever going to live that down, am I?"

"Oh, sure, in twenty or thirty years maybe. Hey, the electricity's on. We can have our first meal here, if you would like to."

Joe's handsome face lit up. "I'll get the pizza. I got a six pack of Cokes, too. Meet you in the kitchen."

CHAPTER SEVENTEEN

Arthur Dunkin answered the phone, annoyed at being called during dinnertime.

"Who?"

"Mickey Lewis, Mr. Dunkin. I used to live there."

"Oh, yes. I remember you. What do you want?"

"Wanted to see if I had any mail, like a magazine with motorcycles on the front? I should have a couple more coming there to that address."

"No, ain't seen anything like that or any other mail either. But a policeman was here looking for you."

"A policeman? Looking for me?" Curiosity overcame panic. "What did he want?"

"Didn't say. Just wanted to know where you went. You ought to call and see what they want."

"Yeah, I'll do that."

Art Dunkin jumped when Mickey slammed down the receiver.

Monday afternoon after Floyd and Hank left, the new garden club had its first meeting. Attending were Maggie, Fatima, Fatima's momma and Aunt Myrtle.

"Before we get started, if anyone needs exercise bad enough to volunteer, I'm moving to my new house weekend after next, and all help is welcome. I think I can get Joe to grill us burgers when we finish, but I haven't asked him yet."

Aunt Myrtle shook her head. "It's not too early to start training him. He will grill burgers if you want him to."

Momma smiled, approving Aunt Myrtle's advice. "You see what they should do, what's best for them to do, what you want them to do, then you sees that they do it."

Aunt Myrtle nodded emphatically in complete agreement with Momma.

"Now, you girls know we're in the Deep South where man is the head of the house," Maggie said, giggling.

"Right." Fatima sneered. "If you don't believe it, just ask one of them!"

"Nobody is arguing with that. One would hope you'd choose one who's man enough to take on the responsibility. Man is the head of the house." Aunt Myrtle paused just long enough for Maggie to wonder if she'd heard right. "Woman is the neck, and if she's got bat brains she can turn the head any way he needs to go."

"Hear! Hear!" Fatima cheered for that.

"All right, suppose I suggest I do the burgers and let him take over and do it because he's so much better at it?"

Momma beamed at Maggie. "Now you got it, babe!"

"So much for marriage one-oh-one." Fatima glanced around the group. "Anybody got any ideas for a name for us?"

"Oh, wait, Fatima. There's something else. I need to tell about Grace's invitation."

"Invitation," somebody breathed. She had their attention.

Maggie told them about Grace's invitation to the flower show on the river cruise boat and the complimentary invitations she offered.

"That sounds like a nice time," Aunt Myrtle approved.

"Yes, something different."

"And we can see all the flower arrangements and how they're done," Momma Johnson reminded them.

"Doug and your sons are invited too, if they can come," Maggie looked around at her aunt and Fatima's momma.

"I think Doug might. Count on it, unless you hear different from me tomorrow—if it's RSVP?"

"Probably not, or Grace would have said so. What about your brothers, Fatima?"

"Probably got to practice, but I'll check."

"Well, that's five of us for sure. I think it will be fun. Now, for a name. What are we going to call ourselves?" Aunt Myrtle looked around the group.

There were lots of suggestions, including Dirty Digits and Green Thumbs.

"Green Thumbs is taken. There's one across town. I saw something about a show they were having in the paper about a month ago."

"I think I saw it too, in the calendar of meetings list."

"I guess Green Thumbs North is out too?"

They went through April Showers, Shady Ladies and several others before Momma came up with Eden Extended. It was an instant winner.

"That's a good one, Momma. Your Bible names came in handy this time," Fatima beamed at her.

"I like it better than anything I thought of, too."

"Eden Extended. We can make it official by acclamation. Everyone in favor say aye!"

Everyone said aye.

"We are now officially The Eden Extended Garden Club."

As everyone else left, Maggie called Grace to thank her for inviting them on the cruise and tell her their new name.

"So there will definitely be five of us for the river cruise show with a possibility of nine in our group."

At home, Maggie began cleaning out closets and throwing away things she didn't want to move. She firmly stacked

Horace's things in boxes for the Salvation Army to pick up and worked hard enough at home and at the *Herald* to sleep well. Her answering machine, which she referred to as her electric secretary, ensured her rest but still got an occasional hang-up call.

Art Dunkin called Joe to tell him about Mickey Lewis calling to check on his mail.

"He didn't give you a number or an address this time?"

"No, and when I told him to contact you I think he hung up on me. But he'll call again. He seems to want that magazine pretty bad. Said it's about motorcycles."

"Okay. Let me know if you learn anything that will tell us how to locate him or if he tells you when he's planning on being in town."

"I'll do that."

"Thank you, Mr. Dunkin."

Joe called to tell Alan about the call rather than make a note of it.

"I may have located Mickey Lewis," Alan said when he finished. "You remember that number for Happy Harris you gave me? Someone there accepted a collect call from Nashville. They don't get many long-distance calls, according to their bills, and this number belongs to an electronics equipment store in Nashville. It could have been Mickey Lewis calling Happy."

"That fits. Jack Gardner was impressed by his computer expertise and didn't think he'd have any trouble getting a job. You want me to go up there?"

"Not now. We'll see what develops. You working this weekend?"

"Yes. Maggie and her garden club are going to a flower show. Also, I'm moving some things for both of us as I have time, so it won't be such a hassle. We'll just have the heavy things left to move."

"Good idea. I finally got around to lifting the prints off that glass you brought in. It will take a while to identify them. I'll get back to you if and when I hear anything."

"Okay, I'll let you get your nose back to the grindstone. I'm going to call Maggie, since I won't see her till Sunday."

"Yeah. Tough." The word oozed sarcastic sympathy. "Bye."

The sarcasm didn't dampen Joe's joy at all as he listened to the phone ring.

"The *Herald*, Maggie Murphy," lilted into the phone.

"Well! You don't seem to be crying about not seeing me this weekend." Joe got as indignant as he could around his grin.

"I will see you too. I'll see you Sunday! What I'm in such a good humor about is I'm looking forward to the flower show on the cruise boat Saturday. And Hank gave the flower show cruise a half page ad on the back of the *Herald*. I'm sure it was Grace's idea. And it has our names in it."

"Your names?" Joe's tone was guarded.

"Let me read it to you. It tells about the cruise down the river and back and the people and clubs who have entered things in the contest, and listen to this: 'Special guests will be members of The Eden Extended Garden Club: Margaret Murphy; Fatima Johnson; Sharon Rose Johnson; and Myrtle Andrews.' Isn't that neat?"

"Yes, that's neat, but didn't you tell me Doug Hawthorne and Fatima's brothers had decided to go?"

"They did, but they won't mind not having their names on the guest list. They'd probably get ribbed unmercifully next time they go to practice."

"No doubt about that." Joe's grin was audible. "Have a good time."

The garden club met at the *Herald* to go to the river in a sixteen-passenger van Doug borrowed from Aunt Myrtle's church. The

161

trip in the van promised to be as much fun as the river boat as everyone got settled to look out windows and backseat drive.

"Haven't been able to catch you many times this week," Aunt Myrtle told Maggie, keeping one eye on Doug's driving.

Maggie nodded. "I know you don't like that machine, so I haven't turned it on except at night. Joe and I have been moving a bit at a time. We've got about everything done but the heavy things, and Joe's got a moving van coming to do that Sunday, tomorrow. It will cost, but it's worth it to go on and get it done. I'm leaving the curtains and drapes since the new house has the ones the previous owner left."

"Yes, I would too. And Joe is right to get the van. I was going to come help you but I was dreading it, to tell the truth."

"Goodness, everybody hates moving. But I'm too happy about my house to care. Joe is pleased about the apartment, too."

Aunt Myrtle didn't exactly frown, but she didn't look too happy. "That's ah, kind of close for someone dating, is all I sort of wonder about."

"No, it's not. He can go his way and I can go mine when we're working. I think it's a good thing for both of us."

"I guess so. I saw the nice publicity Hank put in the paper about the show, and Grace put our names in it, too. Doug laughed at how pleased with it I was." Aunt Myrtle leaned forward, stretching her neck. "Now, what's he doing? What's this he's turning in to?"

"It's a parking garage, Aunt Myrtle. It's not far down to the landing."

When the parking was done to Aunt Myrtle's satisfaction, they walked through a narrow alley to the street to go down to the landing. The late evening sun and the breeze off the water were pleasant as Aunt Myrtle, Momma and Doug led the way. Maggie and Fatima followed them and Shad, Shack and Bed brought up the rear.

Almost at the end of the alley, there was a loud cry from the back of the group.

Maggie and Fatima froze. They were suddenly seized and dragged backward as, unseen, Horace flew over to intercept a huge falling crate.

Hands extended, palms out, Horace hit the big crate as it fell. It split where it hit the concrete of the alley to reveal the metal inside it, missing Maggie and Fatima by about two feet. Horace hovered, making sure Maggie and Fatima were all right before fading quickly.

Shad and Shack let go of Fatima and Maggie to run swiftly after Bed, who was chasing someone down the alley.

The three of them returned, winded, as the others recovered enough to talk. They all talked at once, looking in horror at the crate and up at the roof it had fallen or was pushed from.

Momma reached out to hug her heroes amid thanks from Fatima and Maggie.

"We lost him," Bed told his mother.

"Did you get a good look at him?" Doug asked.

"Just good enough to know he's white, four or five inches shorter than we are, sort of thin. Had on some kind of cap, wearing it backwards. It fell off when he jumped off the fire escape." He turned to Shack as he joined them. "You get it?"

"Yeah, here it is." Shack pulled a rolled-up cap out of his pocket and handed it to him.

Shad came closer to look at it. "Black like his shirt. Harley Davidson logo."

"Hang on to it," Doug said. "We'll report this to the police. He could have hurt or killed someone."

Bed rolled up the cap and stuck it in his pocket.

"Yeah, that thing didn't move by itself, that's for sure." Bed looked up at the roof line.

A blast from the river boat stirred them into action and they hurried toward the street and the cobblestones leading down to the landing.

"We'll tell Hank when we get there. Hurry, Aunt Myrtle."

Shad and Shack took Momma's arms and Bed followed, turning to look back often enough to make sure no one was following them.

The cruise boat was gay with banners, balloons, flowers and people in a party mood. Grace smiled and waved to them, relieved to see them coming. She hugged Maggie as they came aboard. Hank was standing near the punch bowl. He turned and raised his cup of pink, frothy punch in greeting.

If he ever in his life was worried about anything, I'll bet a cookie it didn't show. Maggie envied him.

Her eyes tracked Aunt Myrtle as she quietly but relentlessly followed Hank from one conversation to another and finally trapped him against a rail on the other side of the boat. The hand gestures and emphatic bobs of Aunt Myrtle's head made it plain Hank was getting the whole report on their near fatal adventure, and with a few ninety-nine-cent adjectives thrown in for emphasis.

Near the front of the boat Grace smiled, enjoying her role as judge and hostess. Careful of her footing as the boat started down the river, she made her way to each of the Eden Extended members to see that they knew where the punch bowl, goodies and programs were and to give them name tags.

Maggie stood watching as Momma Johnson placed a name tag on Fatima at just precisely the right angle.

She didn't see the trio who were successfully eluding Grace and her handful of stackable posies. Then her eye fell on Douglas Hawthorne, her heart going out to that sweet, unfortunate man.

He was standing at the rear of the boat looking like he was in pain, clutching an empty punch cup. An overbearing woman with too much makeup on had him by the arm to prevent any thought of escape and was talking a mile a minute to him. She was about to be set straight by Aunt Myrtle, who was bearing down on them with a determined expression. She would be on them in seconds.

The cavalry's coming, Doug. Maggie stifled a laugh and someone behind her spoke.

"You're in an awfully good humor for someone who nearly got killed." He paused. "Or are you hysterical?" Hank peered at her.

"I'm fine. I just thought since I'm going to live I might as well have a good time."

"Very practical. How about some punch? It's Presbyterian," he warned as he steered her toward it.

"It looks good to me."

They took their cups of punch to the rear of the boat, and Maggie nibbled on a cucumber sandwich between answers as Hank asked her about the near miss in the alley.

"There's no way it could have been an accident, not with that joker jumping off the fire escape and running up the alley," Hank said. "As soon as we get back to the landing, I'll call it in. Which one of them's got that cap he dropped?" He nodded toward Shad, Shack and Bed.

"Bed, I think. Just ask."

"I will. Have a good time." He moved away and went to Grace, who was standing near the table with the arrangements on it.

No wonder they call her Princess Grace, Maggie thought. *She looks like a princess.*

Grace was beautiful, regal and her upswept blond hair was a natural crown. Her five-foot-eight fame in heels was just right for Hank's six-foot one to bend and kiss her on the back of her neck before he moved away again.

I can see who's the neck in that family.

The flower show mini-cruise was enjoyed by all, as the society pages say, and there were no more unpleasant happenings on the way back to the paper.

Doug pulled up at the *Herald* and let all of them out then waited till all of them had pulled out on their way home. This gave Aunt Myrtle time to ask Maggie if she wouldn't feel safer coming home to spend the night with her.

"Got plenty of snacks in the 'frig and would be glad of the company," she urged. "Also, a chocolate pie I just couldn't leave the store without." She gave a short laugh at their mutual weakness for chocolate.

Maggie had to insist that she would be more comfortable at home. "And the phone doesn't bother me anymore since I've got my electric secretary."

"But you and Fatima could have been killed!"

"I know, and that's certainly scary to think about. But I'm all right now. Thanks to God and Fatima's brothers, we're both all right. Nobody's out to get me, Aunt Myrtle." She worked affectionately at assuring her aunt.

"That guy was probably just trying to figure out how to steal that thing, and somehow pushed it off the roof. I'll be all right."

The others were safely on their way home and Maggie got out of the van, ready for a bath and bed. "Thanks for the ride, Doug. Good night, Aunt Myrtle."

CHAPTER EIGHTEEN

Maggie was tired. The day's activities, excitement, and the close call hit her all at once when she got safely behind her own door. She put a pimento cheese sandwich in on top of all the cookies and finger food she'd nibbled on the boat, and had no trouble falling asleep. In spite of the scare, it was a good night just as she assured Aunt Myrtle it would be. And it stayed good right up till one A.M.

At one o'clock the phone began ringing and rang until one-oh-three.

Nuts! I forgot to turn on my electronic secretary!

Maggie's feet hit the floor like she was mad at it and stomped to the phone. She picked the receiver up with a stranglehold on it as if it was a chicken slated for Sunday dinner and shouted, "Who is this?"

"Well!" Somebody just as mad as she was shouted, "I'll give you a clue, it's not Red!"

The voice sounded upset to the max, but she had no trouble recognizing it. "Joe? Do you know what time it is?"

"I know. I got off work at twelve o'clock and found out you nearly got killed! Why didn't you call?"

"There wasn't any reason to. You were at work, I'm all right, and Hank called and reported what happened."

"And you just went on home and went to bed?"

"Of course! What would you expect me to do?"

"You should have called, and you shouldn't be there alone."

167

"I'm fine, Joe. And looking forward to getting the rest of my things moved tomorrow. You should be getting some rest."

"I'm coming to get you."

"You're what?" She was talking to a dial tone.

Recovering from the stunning announcement, Maggie went into action. She threw her gown into the clothes hamper and pulled on some clothes, muttering angrily to herself. *I probably couldn't sleep now even if I wasn't halfway engaged to a paranoid policeman.*

Too soon for him to have been safe on the street, she heard Joe's car pull up in front of the house. A truck following him pulled into the driveway and two policemen in uniform got out.

Joe opened the door for them and pointed to the bedroom. Maggie stood there with her mouth open.

She started sputtering when they came out of the bedroom carrying her mattress and crowded past her. "What the heck do you think you're doing?" she demanded as Joe headed into the kitchen.

He got a hammer from a drawer and said, "Get whatever you need for tomorrow into an overnight case."

"Why?"

"Because you're moving now."

She had to follow him to talk to him. He started breaking down the bed. The noise of the hammer on the steel frame rang between her ears. Between blows, Joe ordered, "Get your things."

Looking at him as if he was a mental case, Maggie stood there with her hands on her hips. When she didn't move, he looked up. "Do you want to go with the case or without the case?"

Maggie snorted, dragging her overnight case out of the closet. She started grabbing things. Underwear, toothbrush, makeup . . . Where the hell are all those axes no murderer ever has any trouble getting hold of in the damned movies?

At twenty-four hundred Elmwood, Maggie didn't trust herself to speak. Joe went out and thanked his friends for their help. She stood there looking down at her bed—or rather her mattress and box springs with the linens tumbled on top of the heap. She felt the sting of tears starting as Joe came up behind her and put his arms around her.

"What makes you think you deserve a hug?" she managed to get out.

"I'm not stealing a hug, I'm pinning your arms so you can't hit me."

The dam burst. Tears and laughter tumbled out together as she turned in his arms.

"Are you laughing or crying?"

"I swear, I don't know. I was looking forward to moving tomorrow, but just look at my bed. And it's the middle of the night! Joe, what possessed you?"

"Love, I guess. I couldn't leave you over there by yourself." He looked away, all of a sudden uncertain. "My bed's out in the apartment. I can go out there, but I'd rather—I'll go now."

"No," she took his hand. "No, stay. I'll feel better too. Grab hold of that yellow thing. It's the bottom sheet. Come on, let's get this bed together."

"Yes, ma'am."

The next day the rest of their furniture was moved, Maggie's to the house and Joe's to the apartment. Their work week started on time in spite of the clutter, as if the guardian angels in charge of work had arranged the whole thing.

Joe glanced at his copy of the report about the crate, waiting for Alan to answer his phone. When he answered, Joe told him his plans. "I'm going to interview some of our eyewitnesses on this crate thing and I'll see you later today, unless there's something you need me to do first."

"No, go on. You are going to get me that hat, aren't you?"

"Cap. Yes, sir."

"Okay. See you later."

Joe managed to catch Shad, Shack and Bed between classes at school and added his thanks to everyone else's about their swift reactions when that crate fell.

"Was too quick to take any credit for," Shad said modestly.

Shack and Bed smiled. "Momma's got us trained. That's why we were in back of them."

"She did a good job and so did you. Did you get a good look at the man who must have pushed the thing off the roof?"

Three heads shook in unison. "Never saw his face." Bed spoke for all of them. "He was white, four or five inches shorter than we are, dark t-shirt, cap on backwards. Dark brown hair. The cap fell off when he jumped from the last rung of that fire escape. I gave it to Mr. Hanover." Bed anticipated Joe's next question. "Gave it to him soon as we got to the river boat."

"Anybody know what was in the crate or have any other ideas about it?"

"No." Bed looked at the others, who shook their heads too. "All we know is it looked heavy, split a little at the end and there was something metal inside it. Somebody said it must be something to do with the air-conditioning."

"Okay, you're good witnesses. Thanks. I'm going over to the *Herald* now to talk to Hank and Fatima, and I'll pick up the cap."

At the *Herald,* Joe talked to Fatima and Maggie in the front. They didn't have much to add except to be grateful for the couple of feet between them and that crate. He went back to talk to Hank.

Joe noticed the green cushion Maggie had told him about.

He sat on it when Hank motioned him to sit. He refused coffee and got to the point.

"I know you weren't an eyewitness, but do you have any ideas about what happened? And I want to pick up that cap the perp dropped."

Hank gestured at a paper sack on his desk. "There's the cap. I put it in that sack, hoping there might be fingerprints on the brim or something, I don't know much about police work."

"Good idea. Thank you." Joe reached for the sack and set it on his knee.

"The only thing I feel sure of is that crate didn't fall by itself. Whoever it was who ran away gave it a nudge. Fatima's brothers didn't see his face. Too bad."

"You don't have any idea who might do such a thing, do you?"

"No. There doesn't seem to be any reason that makes sense. But the papers are usually full of things that don't make sense. There may not be any reason but being mad at the world or looking for excitement. I don't know how you'll ever be able to catch him, but I sure hope you do."

"We'll get him sooner or later. Maybe not for this, but for something else. But," Joe said, smiling, "being an optimist, I'm hoping to get him for this."

Hank rolled his eyes. "Optimist too, huh? If you and Maggie have children, I'll have to give them mean lessons!"

"Oh?" Joe gave him an impish smirk. "Who told you my intentions are honorable?"

"Have you met her Aunt Myrtle?"

Joe left laughing.

Maggie walked out to his car with him. He raised the hand he was holding to his lips for a kiss, "See you tonight."

See you tonight. That has a nice ring to it . . .

★　★　★　★　★

Alan beckoned Joe in when he knocked on the door facing. He tossed the cap on the desk, still in its sack.

"This is all we've got. The girls only know they missed being crushed by less than two feet, and the boys got a pretty good general description but didn't see the running man's face. All of them saw the cap fall off though, when he jumped off the fire escape." He sat down. "That and we're agreed it was an attempt to do bodily harm." Sarcasm didn't suit Joe.

"Yeah. Turns out it was air-conditioning equipment in the crate. I talked to the owners of the building. Here's a call I got for you this morning."

Joe picked up the memo. "Art Dunkin. Did he say what he wanted?"

"No, just his name and left the number."

"Do you mind? This won't take long." Joe picked up the phone as Alan nodded.

"Mr. Dunkin." Joe was all polite business. "This is Patrolman Joe Driver. I'm returning your call." He paused to listen. "He did?" Joe's eyebrows went up. "Saturday afternoon, you're sure it was Saturday afternoon." He listened. "Yes, it will probably help a whole lot. We may need you to testify to the time he was there. I'm not sure, but we'll let you know if we do need you. Thank you."

"Michael Lewis?"

"Yes. He came and got that motorcycle magazine he's been looking for. He wouldn't give Mr. Dunkin his current address. Said he'd sent in an address change. But he was here in town Saturday."

"I'll follow up with the electronics store and see what the lab can get from this cap, too. That motorcycle magazine may trip Michael Lewis up when it's added in with the other things we've got."

Joe glanced at the files on the side of Alan's desk. A picture of Mr. Wartz was on the top of one of them. He touched the grisly red star on the victim's forehead. "We're not going to have to wade through witchcraft too, are we?"

"No," Alan answered solemnly. "But something just as old. That's a star of David."

CHAPTER NINETEEN

Maggie called her aunt. As she touched the numbers, she mentally went over her progress report on moving. *Guess I can censor as I go along; won't take much brain power to know what to leave out.*

She felt her neck and cheeks grow warm at a scene she was definitely going to delete as Aunt Myrtle answered.

"Oh, Maggie. I was just thinking about you and feeling guilty. How did the move go?"

"Just fine. No need to feel guilty. That's what I called to tell you—"

"You haven't eaten yet, have you?"

"No. Joe's not coming over and I'll probably just snack out of the refrigerator."

"Forget that. Come on over here—"

"Douglas not coming over?"

"No. I talked to him a few minutes ago. He's going to help somebody catalogue something that sounds boring enough to put you to sleep on the way over there—"

"Ugh! What are you having to eat, not that it wouldn't beat—"

"Leftover roast beef and homegrown snap beans that were on sale—"

"I'm coming! Bye!"

Maggie locked the door again and chuckled, remembering how few finished sentences there were in their conversation.

Dinner was on the table when she got there and tea was in the glasses.

"Yum, sliced roast, warm beans and corn cakes! I wouldn't even wash first if I didn't know Mama might come back and slap me!"

Aunt Myrtle laughed. "Yeah, she did a good job of training you, and you won't starve."

As they ate, Maggie filled her in on the move to the new house. The flight through the dark night en caravan with Joe's policeman friends carrying the bed the night before their scheduled move had Aunt Myrtle in stitches. Maggie sat with her fingers crossed in her lap and stopped her story right after saying Joe's bed was already in the apartment.

Aunt Myrtle reached for Maggie's empty plate and stacked it with hers in the sink. "Let's get some tea and go out to the swing. We can have ice cream or something later."

"I think I need to digest some of that good food before there will be any room for ice cream." Maggie followed her favorite relative outside.

"Well." Maggie got settled. "How are you and Doug getting along, and does he like his job?"

"Given the limited choices of part-time jobs for our age group, he likes it pretty well. And we enjoy the same things." She smiled affectionately. "He's good company."

"I know what you mean about enjoying the same things. That's one of the troubles that led to Joe's divorce."

"He's divorced?" Alerts flashed across Aunt Myrtle's forehead like news bulletins across the bottom of a television screen.

"Yes, a couple of years ago. I thought I told you."

"I don't know. Maybe you did and it just didn't register."

"They weren't married very long." She saw the worry lines getting ready to deepen on her aunt's forehead and quickly added, "He's not an abusive monster. They had nothing in common; and she's the one who asked for a divorce. Any questions?"

"There probably will be after I've digested all that and have time to think."

Maggie told her about Joe coming home to find Marlene sewing sequins on his cowboy shirt.

"So he doesn't miss her or the shirt either," Aunt Myrtle said sympathetically as she pictured the scene. "That's a relief. I can tell by the look in your eyes he must be pretty special to you. And he must be one of the good guys, since he's been a policeman for a while. I sort of had mixed feelings about his moving into your apartment, though, being so close—." The worry lines were threatening to come back.

Maggie abruptly changed the subject. "What about Doug's family? Any children to object? To just generally rain on your parade, or hopefully, to wish you well?"

Settling comfortably again, Aunt Myrtle answered. "He had just one son who's grown and living a couple of hundred miles away." She smiled confidentially about that. "Which is just right for visiting when you want to. I've seen pictures of him and his wife and the little grandson."

"But you haven't met them?"

"No. Talked with them on the phone once, and I think peace has broken out between us. There's no reason for any objections since Doug has his papers and his will in order to leave his money and the little house he owns to them."

"You've been discussing money?" Maggie tilted her head, studying her aunt's face. "That does sound serious."

"Serious? At our age, it's grim. He's got a pension and the interest from some investments. That's what he lives on, along with his part-time work salary."

"And you've got the pension as Uncle Clarence's widow and your house."

"That's something I need to find out about. I'll have to check and see if the pension will be cut off, and my insurance too, if I decide to marry. My own Social Security won't start coming in for about two years. With my house and the pension and my insurance coverage, I don't know how I'd manage if I lost any of that. And my Social Security check probably won't be much."

"There's an eight hundred number, I think, where you can call and ask about it. I hadn't thought about that and the insurance coverage."

"I had. If I want a companion in my feeble old age, it looks like living in sin is my best bet."

"Living in sin? What are you talking about?"

"Doug could rent out his house and move in here with me. We'd have the rent, our pensions and my Social Security check to look forward to in a couple of years."

Maggie sat listening in dumb surprise, unaware her mouth was open.

"He could keep his money and his will just the way they are and I could do the same. We would only use the interest on his investments, like he's doing now, and my accounts could stay the way they are, too. Money may be the root of all evil, but not having any is just as bad."

"And causes a lot more temptation," Maggie pointed out. She shook her head. "But for him to move in here—" She contemplated the ice melting in her glass. "You were worried about Joe being too close to me in the apartment, but you're considering living in sin—just like that?"

"It's one of those 'don't do as I do, do as I tell you to do' situations. That's what it boils down to, doesn't it?" Aunt Myrtle was a realist.

Maggie laughed. "Yeah, classic example. Well, I'll still love you no matter what you decide. But I'd give it a lot more thought and not be in any hurry."

"As I said, Doug and I haven't talked about it yet. Not all of it, anyway. I'm just thinking about it because I know we will. It's one of the things that will have to be talked about if things work out between us. And about Joe, I'm glad he's going to be around for protection. He still thinks that accident with the crate was aimed at you, doesn't he?"

"He didn't say so in so many words but it's not hard to figure it out, the way he acts and the things he does. I don't think he loves me for my brains. If I don't get myself killed before Christmas, he'll probably get me a boot with instructions on the heel—"

"Maggie, he couldn't be that bad."

"He's close. But he means well. And it's hard to see any other reason behind it. The crate that nearly crushed us, I mean. The thing was too big and heavy for it to have been an accident." She paused. "And there's something else I haven't told you about Horace's accident. I didn't tell you because it seemed so far out. I only told you Horace had started home a long time before the accident was discovered."

Aunt Myrtle sat listening to what Happy Harris had told Maggie about the doctored-up drink that spilled and the report Joe told her about that included the wounded dog on the road.

"Humm, I see."

Shaken up about the possibility someone had tried to stop Maggie from finding out more about Horace's death, Aunt Myrtle drew a deep breath. "What was that drug they found a trace of?"

"Rohypnol. They call it the 'date rape drug.' I know you've read about it in the papers."

"Yes. I'd forgot what it was, but I remember someone going to jail for putting it in some woman's drink. She didn't even know what happened to her until she was shown pictures he took. It must be really strong stuff."

Maggie nodded. "It is. They couldn't figure out why someone would do that to Horace. And thanks to Happy, there was only a trace of it found in his blood."

Aunt Myrtle patted her hand. "Well, now Joe will be close to watch over you, but you can't be too careful. And what about that man you found at the dumpster? Have they found out any more about that?"

"Not much. Joe and the detective in charge of the case have been talking to people and following up on everything they have so far."

"He was stabbed in the chest and had something carved on his forehead. You said it was a star?"

Maggie nodded. "Joe said it was a Jewish symbol, a star of David."

"A hate crime, maybe," Aunt Myrtle said thoughtfully.

The prospect of hate, murder and living in sin had taken all the sweet out of Maggie's tea.

Detective Alan Hill entered Computer Magic in Nashville and located the elevators to the credit department. He asked for the manager's office and was shown into a small office with a wet bar and a coffee machine in the corner.

"Mr. Ward." He stuck out his hand. "Thank you for seeing me. I won't take much of your time."

"Detective Hill." The manager's handshake was firm as he looked at the badge in Alan's other hand. "I wasn't too surprised to get your call about Michael Lewis. Please, sit down."

"He been giving you trouble?" Taking the chair he was gestured to, Alan opened a folder and held it on his knees. He drew out a picture. "This is not very good but you should be able to recognize him if that's your employee. He hasn't been in much trouble . . . that he got caught at." Alan watched as Mr.

Ward looked at the picture. "Is this Michael Lewis the one you hired?"

"Yes, that's Michael. It's not that he gave us all that much trouble. He just didn't give us anything else—like a decent day's work or half his mind on his job when he did show up."

"And you told me he didn't show up for work this particular Saturday?" He made notes in the file.

"No. He called in sick the Friday before, then just didn't show up Saturday."

"Did he come back at all? Is he here in the store now?"

Mr. Ward shook his head. "Whether he plans on coming back at all is anybody's guess. If and when he does show up, his termination papers are waiting for him. Along with a check minus charges for a couple of long-distance calls he placed when he was here at night without anyone to watch him closely."

"Long-distance calls. Could I get those numbers?"

Mr. Ward read off the number, which was the one Alan had for Happy Harris. "Both to the same place. Don't have a home address for him. He was always going to bring it in, that and a phone number where he could be reached. But he never got around to it."

"That's all right. What I'd like right now is a copy of what you've got in that personnel folder showing he was not here on the date I asked about and the phone calls he placed."

"All right. I'll have copies made for you."

CHAPTER TWENTY

Maggie was in Hank's office watering the ivy plant the Eden Extended Garden Club had given him when Hank came in with a cup of coffee. The phone rang as he sat down.

"How does it know?" He frowned at the inconsiderate phone before picking it up. "The *Herald,* Hank Hanover."

He listened, then turned to Maggie, a strange look on his face. "It's for you."

Maggie set the pitcher down and started to wipe her hands on her skirt, wondering at Hank's expression. He handed her a handkerchief.

"This is Maggie Murphy."

"Maggie," a serious, masculine voice said. "This is Alan Hill."

Maggie's throat closed in panic. "J-Joe?"

"No, no. Joe's all right. This is not about him. Did you see or talk to Happy Harris after you moved? Did he know you moved?"

"No, I don't think so." She pictured Happy lying in some street beside his motorcycle. "I haven't talked to him and I don't know any of his friends. The only way I knew him is he happened to be with Horace the night he had the accident." She ran on as if talking would prevent hearing any bad news. Alan Hill broke in.

"So, as far as you know, he didn't know you moved."

"No."

"What about your phone? Is the number the same?"

181

"Yes, I asked for it. It's the same number. We hadn't had the phone long and I wanted to keep the number the same. What is this about? Has something happened to Happy? Or can you tell me?"

"No, it's not about Happy Harris, and I might as well tell you. You'll know soon anyway. Someone drove by last night and threw a couple of Molotov cocktails through the front window of the house where you used to live."

Maggie gasped, her eyes finding Hank's. He looked like she felt.

"My house where I used to live? I can't believe it! It's a wonder I wasn't there. If it hadn't been for Joe, I would have been there! I'm going over there and just look at it." She hastened to add, "I won't touch anything."

"When you get there, don't go any closer than the sidewalk. Joe went too."

"Oh, is he looking into it?"

"No," Alan said through his teeth. "He's there because it would have taken too many of his friends away from their jobs to stop him." He was obviously not happy about it.

Maggie was at a loss for words, afraid that any that came out would be the wrong ones. Open mouth–insert foot, she warned herself.

"Joe happened to be here when I heard about it. My orders from him were to make sure you were all right and tell you to stay there till he comes to drive home with you."

"Your orders," Maggie smiled. "I don't want to get either one of us in trouble. But I am going." She looked again at Hank. "Hank will go with me." Hank nodded, finishing his coffee.

"All right, good. I'm sure Joe will still be there, since he doesn't know right now where to go and kick ass, which is what he wants to do."

Maggie hung up the phone. Hank was already at the back door.

When Maggie and Hank got to her former house, they could see all the activity from the end of the block. Hank parked several doors down from the house. He and Maggie walked up to stand on the sidewalk outside the yellow police line.

Joe saw them coming and met them in front of the house. He shook Hank's hand and gave Maggie a brief hug.

"It's a mess, isn't it?" Maggie's eyes took in the damaged wood, broken glass and the charred wood between the picture window and the door.

"Any witnesses?" Hank asked.

"No. The men have knocked on doors and covered the area, but no one saw anything and only a few heard it."

Hank had his digital camera with him and moved away, taking pictures and listening while he was at it.

Joe stood close to Maggie and spoke softly. "I'm glad you're here, since Hank came with you. I don't want you to talk to Happy Harris again." He shook his head when Maggie started to speak. "Even if he had nothing to do with this. He probably didn't. But he will call when he hears about it."

"But—"

"No buts. I don't think he had a hand in it, but I think he suspected something like this might happen. And the one or ones who did it will be talking to him."

"What do you want me to say if he calls?"

"Nothing. Tell your Aunt Myrtle what's going on and call her often enough to keep her off the panic button. But leave the answering machine on. Don't answer any calls at all. The machine will record the messages, so you won't miss anything important."

"All right. I'll call her when I get back to the office. But, I don't think Happy—"

"I don't want him to know where you are." Joe held up a hand to stop any more protests. "It's not because I don't trust him, but what he doesn't know, he can't tell."

Hank had quietly joined them and nodded, agreeing with Joe.

"Does he know you work at the *Herald*?"

"No, I never told him." She thought it over. "No." She sounded positive now. "No, he doesn't know. Hey, wait! The article about the flower show!"

Hank was dubious about that. "All that said was the Eden Extended Garden Club would attend the river cruise flower show." He looked at Joe. "That's probably how the Cat in the Hat knew to go down there and wait on that roof for them. That alley is as good as one of those ambush valleys in an old cowboy movie."

"Yeah, that's the way I had it figured. You're sure there wasn't anything about her working at the *Herald* in the article?" He thought back to Maggie reading part of the article to him.

"No, not a thing. I remember now. I read it to you and Fatima, too." Maggie shook her head, relieved.

Joe's eyes went to Hank's. "So, what are you and Fatima going to say if someone calls and asks if Maggie works there?"

Hank squinted. "Who?"

One of the calls Maggie played back the following Friday when she got home sounded urgent. It was from Aunt Myrtle, and she returned it immediately. She had brought Aunt Myrtle up to date, and she really hated having to talk to a machine. It must be something important.

"Maggie." Aunt Myrtle got started breathlessly. "I know it's Friday, but is it too late to invite you and Joe to dinner Saturday night?" She rushed on, "Do you have any plans that won't wait?"

"No, Aunt Myrtle. Are you all right? Is something wrong? If

you need something, I'll come right now—"

"No, no. Everything's all right. Doug is going to be here Saturday and I want to meet Joe. I've talked to him on the phone, but I want to meet him. And he hasn't met Doug either. We need to get together."

"Yes, we do. We'll be there unless something happens and Joe has to work. I'll call you immediately if he does. But as of right now, we'll be there. I want us to get to know each other, too. I'm looking forward to it. Do you want me to bring anything?"

"No, just yourself and Joe."

"All right, you call me if you think of anything."

What Maggie called the Fickle Finger of Fate must have been unaware of their plans, because their luck held and Joe didn't have to work. He showered in his apartment and picked Maggie up at the back door in his car Saturday evening to go to dinner at Aunt Myrtle's. He had the usual jitters that come with meeting in-laws or other ogres unknown to him.

A hug, kiss and compliment later, they were settled in the car with their seatbelts fastened. But Joe didn't start the car; he sat there looking worried.

"This is a happy occasion, isn't it?"

"Certainly." Maggie's word was reassuring; her expression was not.

"I know there's something on your mind, Maggie. It's all over your face. Has your Aunt Myrtle taken a dislike to me? Doug eats soup that clots?" Horror dawned in his eyes in spite of his grin. "They're cannibals?"

"I'm going to take away your library card," Maggie scolded. "Where do you get such far-out ideas? We're going to have a nice meal with people we're already—or almost—family to. What could be bad about it?"

"Then why don't you look glad about it?"

"I am! I am glad about it."

"Then what's wrong with your grin? Is it not working? Got a glitch in it like that monster computer you gripe about?"

"No." A small smile finally appeared. "It's got nothing to do with tonight. It's just . . . I haven't been answering the phone—"

"Good girl." There was nothing wrong with Joe's grin. "So what's wrong? You can't weasel out of marrying me. I haven't proposed yet."

"You mean, like, 'You can't fire me, I don't work here'?" Maggie laughed.

"That's more like it. Now, what is it that's bothering you?"

"Happy is what's wrong. He's called several times and left messages. The last time, I nearly picked up the phone." Joe's brows drew together. "I didn't, though."

Joe relaxed. "What did he say?"

"It wasn't what he said. The first couple of times he just said hello and left his number. The third time he said it was important. And this last time, Joe, he sounded like he was going to cry. He said he had to talk to me."

"He didn't say why or what about?"

"No, just that he has to talk to me."

"Maggie, you did right." Joe picked up her hand and kissed it. "You get an A in blind obedience. Don't pick up the phone, no matter how he sounds. If it is important, he will give you some idea of what it's about. If he does, still don't answer or call him back. Call me and tell me what he says and we'll go from there."

"That wild move in the middle of the night and the Molotov cocktails convinced me to pay attention, all right. But Joe, he just sounded so miserable."

"We can't let him or anyone who may be threatening him or listening to him know where you are. Don't answer. Don't answer. Just call me. Promise?"

Maggie nodded, looking resigned. "All right. I promise."

Joe started the car. "What is Aunt Myrtle having besides company?"

"She didn't say and it doesn't matter. She can cook an old boot and make you wish you had the other one. I asked her if I could bring anything, but that didn't give me any clues. She said just bring you."

"Right." Joe stifled another grin. "But if I see a bonfire and cauldron in the front yard, I'll just dump you and run."

"That's twenty-one," Doug observed.

"What?" Aunt Myrtle turned, raising one eyebrow.

"That's twenty-one times you've made an excuse to get close enough to that window to see if they're here yet."

"It's just that I've got everything ready, and I don't know yet what foods Joe likes. What his favorites are."

"If he doesn't like what you fixed, there's something wrong with him, not the menu."

"That's what my mother always said about one of my cousins. She'd shake her head at him and say, 'That child's not right.' " She laughed. "But we don't really know each other yet. What if when we finally all get together, we rub each other the wrong way or say something that may be remembered for the next twenty years?"

"We'll nip that in the bud. We'll all take big bites of your good food and cram them in on top of any unfortunate remarks." He came to kiss her on the forehead. "You're almost as good a worrier as you are a cook." He looked over her shoulder. "They're here."

Hugs, handshakes and general joy were permeated by delicious aromas from the kitchen.

"Ham and sweet potato casserole," Maggie exclaimed with delight.

Joe's appreciation was evident by the way he ate. Aunt Myrtle beamed approval of his hearty appetite and smiled to herself at his puppy love glances at Maggie. No one took a violent dislike to anybody else and *Joe likes ham and sweet potato casserole* was logged in Aunt Myrtle's mental files under kinfolks' preferences.

CHAPTER TWENTY-ONE

Monday Aunt Myrtle called Maggie, sounding mysterious, and invited her to lunch. "We can eat somewhere close enough to get you back to work on time," she promised.

"I guess I'm going to have to get a social secretary," Maggie said. "Joe called a few minutes ago and is coming to take me to lunch today. What is it you want to talk to me about?"

"It will wait. I want to show you something, too. What about tomorrow?"

"Tomorrow's fine. Do you want me to come over tonight? Joe's working tonight is why he's able to have lunch with me."

"No, it will keep till tomorrow. Have a good lunch and tell Joe hello for me. And Joe was no disappointment, while we're on the subject. He's even better looking than I thought he'd be, and appreciates good food. I'll see you tomorrow." She sounded excited. Excited and happy about something.

She hung up, leaving Maggie curious. Maggie was still wondering if Aunt Myrtle had decided to take the plunge and live in sin after all when Joe showed up. Joe also looked suspiciously happy.

"I'm going back to see Hank a minute, if he's back there."

"He's there." Maggie clamped her mouth shut on any questions, and he was soon back. He opened the office door, held the car door for her and was still too pleased with himself to be trusted as far as she could throw him.

"What's your favorite jewelry store? I'm going to buy you

189

something."

"Excuse me, Senator, I was expecting a policeman by the name of Joe Driver—"

"Just tell me. We've only got an hour."

He's lost his mind. Thank goodness it's something he won't miss. "Is this a trick question?"

"No, where would you go if you were going to buy jewelry?"

"Straight to the nearest asylum, since everybody I know is aware of my financial condition. And I've just bought a house. Me and the finance company."

"Maggie." Joe sat with his hands on the steering wheel. "You're going to marry me, aren't you?"

"I haven't been invited, I mean, proposed to yet." She was a little disappointed, if this was his idea of a proposal. "Are you asking me to marry you?"

"No. I mean, I'm asking you to be engaged to me. There are a lot of things to clear up and work out, but I love you and I want to—to—" He struggled to find words. "—to walk all the way to the Pearly Gates with you."

"I love you, too." *What things to clear up? These cases? Something about Marlene?* "I guess I would like to be engaged to you, but I don't think this parking lot is a very romantic place for a proposal."

Joe's smile wrinkles showed his relief. "When the time comes for a proposal, I'll do it right and throw in dinner and candlelight. Now, where are we going?"

"Let's go to the jewelry shop in the mall. It's a branch of one that's been in business here for years, and I can get back to work on time."

At about the time Joe and Maggie went in search of a jewelry store, Alan Hill had visitors. He looked up from his desk at the two men in dark suits who had stopped in his door. He rose as they came in, flashing FBI badges for him to see. The second one closed the door behind him.

Alan motioned them to chairs and braced himself.

At her desk the next day, Maggie reached for her ringing phone. "The *Herald*, Maggie Murphy . . ." she answered with one eye on the clock.

"Hi," Aunt Myrtle's voice sang. "I just called to tell you I'm on my way, if you can go to lunch now?"

"I can. Come on. I've got something to tell you, too."

She hung up and moved the phone out of the way to stack some of the necessary debris on her desk more neatly. Her mind went back to the three rats' nests she saw on the desk when she had come to work there.

Looking up, she saw Fatima coming in. She smiled to herself as she touched the zippered section in her purse. *I want to tell Aunt Myrtle before I tell anyone else.*

"Hi, I'm back!" Fatima came in like a fresh breeze and put her big purse down on her desk. "I'm going to have to get rid of some stuff or put wheels on this thing, and soon."

Aunt Myrtle appeared in the door before Fatima could make up her mind about what had to go.

"There's my aunt. See you in an hour." Maggie hurried out before her phone could ring again.

"Let's go to the cafeteria. It's the fastest and we're early enough the line won't be too long."

"Suits me." She didn't see any ring on Aunt Myrtle's hand, and wondered if you were supposed to get a ring for living in sin.

The line was not very long in the cafeteria, but it seemed too crowded and public for any swapping of secrets, much less the emotional bombshells they wanted to share.

They got through the line quickly and found a booth near

191

the hallway leading to the restrooms. There were no other booths around and no one at the two tables close enough to overhear their conversation.

"This is just right. I don't want anyone hearing my news except blood kin!" Aunt Myrtle's secret seemed about to burst out.

"Me either. What is it you wanted to tell me?" *Oh, Lord, maybe she really has decided on living in sin!*

"About Doug and me. I did all that worrying for nothing."

"Oh." Maggie risked a relieved grin. "He doesn't want to live in sin?"

"We'll never know. I didn't get a chance to ask!"

"He turned you down?" Shocked, Maggie looked ready to go to war with her steak knife.

"No, no. Just listen. I think we were both trying to get up the nerve to talk about money. He brought up the subject and we talked, laid all our little marbles out in the ring, so to speak. His pension is enough for us to live on, to make a long story short. And there are other good things, too. The house I told you about, he's already talked to his son about what he wants to do, not that he needed permission—"

"But it's better if everyone approves. I did some of your worrying for you about that."

"Thank you. Every little bit helps, and prayers too. But what he wants to do is sell the house. He's already had a couple of offers on it. And he's going to put the money in his investment fund. That way, we will have more interest coming in for us to live on, and the principle is still there for his son."

"That's great, a wise move." Maggie approved.

"And I can be covered on his insurance if mine is cut off. I found out I won't get the pension anymore and that was such a blow, I forgot to ask about the insurance there, but I assume that will be gone too. Anyway, Doug and I, we'll have enough to live on, more when my Social Security starts coming in, and everybody is happy about it."

"That's wonderful, I'm glad for you, both of you."

"And Maggie, this is what I wanted to show you." She opened a compartment in her purse, drew out a jeweler's box, and opened it.

"Oh, Aunt Myrtle, It's beautiful!" The ring she saw was a heavy gold band with five diamonds across the top.

"This is the wedding ring we picked out. And he gave me this one. It has to be sized. It was his mother's." She unwrapped another ring she had stuck in beside it, wrapped in tissue paper. She held it out.

Maggie took the other ring in her hand. It was an emerald surrounded by diamonds.

"It's beautiful, and probably very old. Emeralds are so costly now. It's really beautiful, Aunt Myrtle. A precious antique, I'll bet!"

"It must be old. I thought so too, just by looking at it. And he told me it was his grandmother's. He doesn't know whether it was bought for her or passed down to her or what, but it's such a pretty thing, and it's been in his family at least that long."

"This pretty thing will go up in value every year. It won't get crow's feet or wrinkles or middle-age spread," Maggie said dreamily.

"Don't dwell on old age. Haven't I warned you about that?" Aunt Myrtle lowered her voice a little, though there was still no one close enough to hear. "And I have already asked him if I can leave it to you!"

"Oh, maybe you shouldn't have done that," Maggie worried.

"No, it's all right. The son has his mother's wedding set, so he doesn't mind. Let's see, now." Aunt Myrtle didn't want to leave out any of her good news. "So, we have enough pension to live on, the interest on top of that, and we will both have insurance. That reminds me, Doug's investments will go to his son, but on his insurance I will be the beneficiary. It's not very much, but it will pay any outstanding bills and tide me over since I will have his pension and, of course, will still have insurance if, heaven forbid, anything happens to him."

"Heaven forbid is right. Amen." Maggie smiled.

"So everything's all worked out from food to funerals." Aunt Myrtle laughed. "We're going to get married soon. Neither one of us sees any point in waiting. What is it you want to tell me?"

"Joe wants to be engaged." Maggie grinned like a four-year-old turned loose in an ice cream parlor. "I'm not sure if he's afraid someone will propose before he thinks he can afford to, or he just doesn't think I've got sense enough to take care of myself. But, I'm now engaged to Patrolman Joe Driver!" She showed the ring to her aunt and waited. "Well, aren't you going to say something? Good luck? Good Gawd! Any comments at all?"

"Yes, it's just too much change for me to take in all at once, I guess. You know I like Joe."

"What is it you're not saying?" Maggie's brows drew together; she knew her aunt.

"You said he asked to be engaged. Seems to me he's dragging his feet a little. Or am I just looking for calamity? I've been accused of that."

"I don't know. Sometimes it seems that way to me, too. But I know he loves me, and I know he's a good man. You know, we met under sort of strange circumstances when he came out on Wartzy's case with Detective Hill, and Horace had just had that accident."

"And you said he had been divorced."

Maggie sighed, "I'm sure I don't have to worry about any feelings for that dumb woman who left him. If you had that on your mind, you can cross it off. But Aunt Myrtle, maybe it damaged his self-confidence a little. I'm going to do my best to fix that. The woman must have been an idiot. And another thing. I just kicked over the traces and went in debt when I got a chance at that house Hank helped me buy. Maybe Joe's a little afraid of all this debt."

"But he watches over you—"

"Too well, sometimes. I'm a big girl, Aunt Myrtle."

"And kin to me, judging from that look on your face. But that's all right. I wouldn't want him not to worry about you. And you're sure of him, sure he loves you? Sure he's all of that, and gentleman enough to see you to your grave?"

"Yes. I'm sure." She put the ring back in her purse. "This is a set. The wedding ring has diamonds, and the solitaire fits into the curve." She laughed. "I hope this isn't part of his worry about debt."

"If he says anything about it, tell him what a bargain he's getting. Divide the price by fifty years and heck, you'll probably be working cheap." Aunt Myrtle and Maggie laughed together, fighting tears of happiness.

"I've got to get back to work. I'll show the ring to Hank and Fatima. I wanted to tell you first."

"I'll let you know when we get into the plans for the wedding. It will be simple, and soon. And I want you to be my matron of honor."

CHAPTER TWENTY-TWO

Happy Harris heard the phone and ran to pick it up before it woke his parents. "Hello," he said softly into the phone.

"Happy? Happy, is that you?"

"Yes, Raid? Raid Wilson?"

"Yeah, it's me. Hope I didn't wake everybody up."

"No, I ran to get the phone. Mom and Dad are still asleep. I, have you, do you know where Mickey is?"

"No! And I don't want to know. He's paranoid, thinking someone's going to link us up with that trouble we got into."

"What trouble?"

"Oh, you didn't know about it? We, me and Mickey, planned on stealing a truckload of computers and laptops and things from a warehouse. That's what we wanted Horse to help us with."

"You mean the night we were having barbecue? When Horace left early and had his accident? Is that what you and Mickey wanted him to do with you, this warehouse thing? I didn't hear what it was you had in mind. Just that he didn't want to do whatever it was, and he left to go home."

"Yeah, he was smarter than me. I wish to God I'd gone too."

"What are you talking about? What happened?"

"There wasn't anybody we could trust, so Mickey talked me into going with him without anybody else. The load of stuff he wanted to get was coming in too soon for us to get somebody else anyway, according to the messages he intercepted from their shipping department."

"You mean he got the e-mail messages about the shipment? I knew he did a lot of fooling around with computers."

"Yeah, he had been getting into their system and got lucky, heard about this shipment that was coming in. We had to go on and do it, just the two of us. He said that was good in a way, because it would all be over before Horse could tell anyone about it."

"Oh, then he told Horse about what you had planned?"

"Not me. What Mickey had planned. He told him enough that he was afraid he'd tell someone. Horse knew what he was going to steal. He was afraid someone would figure out where and when he meant to steal the stuff, I guess is what worried him."

"I didn't know what was going on. I was asleep part of the time—"

"I know. He only told him enough that Horse knew we were going to steal something from a warehouse, not what warehouse. Not any of the details, only that it was electronic gear. And he didn't know what kind or what company."

"To hold up a warehouse." Happy was puzzled. "Wouldn't think you'd find any money in a warehouse."

"No, no. Not cash money. Just all this equipment he could turn into money real fast. He broke into some kind of company computer system the warehouse has, like I said, and he knew there was a truckload of expensive equipment coming in that would 'move real fast,' as he called it. That's what he thought anyway. He wanted to steal it while he had a chance and sell it. Said it should be worth a lot of money, even hot. He claimed to know where to sell it. He said it would be quick and easy. I didn't think anybody would get hurt. Anyway, I went with him to get him off my back about it."

"Raid, is he trying to cause Maggie, Horse's wife, any trouble?

He's called me trying to find out about her and what I told her, as if I could tell her anything. Like you said, he sounds paranoid. I'm afraid of him, too. Someone threw a couple of Molotov cocktails into Maggie's house, and I know it was him. I can't prove it, but I know it was. And he's been calling me, trying to find out things about her. What is he afraid she could do, for heaven's sake?"

"I don't know. Thinks she could tell that we tried to get Horse to go with us on that warehouse thing, I guess. Happy, he—he killed one of the watchmen there."

"Oh, no!" Happy collapsed into a chair, horrified. "What happened?"

"We went there and we watched when the truck rolled in right after dark. Mickey had seen the records and knew it would be in, like I said. He thought he was so smart. He'd got a diagram of the electric fence and gate somewhere, and we got in all right. We waited till the driver left to go check his papers or something. And he walked up just like he belonged there, to the watchman who was waiting. He pulled out a gun. I didn't know he had one! Then he made the watchman break the seal on the back of the truck, and Mickey was standing there look-ing at all those boxes and crates inside the trailer. He looked at them like they were gold or something. A lot of boxes. The trailer was full. They had writing on them that might as well be Greek to me, and pictures of electronic stuff. He was practically drooling over it. Then another man came up—"

"Another watchman, you mean?"

"Yeah. He didn't know there were two watchmen. Mickey jumped and his gun went off and the bullet hit the second watchman. I don't know if he meant to shoot or he was just scared and the gun went off. It scared the living juice out of me. We ran like scalded dogs and got out of there—took off in the car and been scared of our shadows ever since."

"That's enough to make anybody paranoid. But, what makes him think Maggie would know anything about it?"

"He talked to Jack Gardner not long after Horace's accident. Jack told him Maggie—that's her name, isn't it?"

"Yes, that's her name."

"Anyway, Jack Gardner said she came up to him there at that barbecue place and asked him about that night we were with Horace. She was with a policeman."

"That doesn't mean she knew anything—"

"Jack also told him you told her Horse left early to go home that night. He thinks she must know something."

"That would be downright funny if he wasn't such a mental case. Maggie doesn't know anything, and I didn't know anything to tell her."

"He also said the police had come to the place where he used to live and were asking questions about him."

"Then he must be the one who threw those Molotov cocktails into her house. Raid, you tell him—"

"I'm not telling him nothin'! He's so nutty. Now he's got the idea there shouldn't be any witnesses, that it's the only way he can be safe. He doesn't know where I am and he's not going to find out."

"But you can tell me, and what are you going to do?"

"Never mind where I am. What I called you for is, there's very few places I can pick up any money doing odd jobs. As soon as I can get my hands on enough money to buy food, I'm going to get a bus ticket, hitchhike or walk to Mexico and put this behind me. Have you got any cash you can let me have?"

"No. My mother takes my check and puts it in my college fund and gives me lunch money. I don't have any loose cash."

"Aw, dang—I'm snake-bit for sure."

"I'm sorry, Raid. Listen, but don't try to go to Mexico. Go to another state or something until Mickey calms down. Don't try to go to Mexico, man."

"I don't know. I don't know what I'm going to do. Maybe I'll talk to you again or get a ride on a truck or something. But stay the heck away from Mickey. He's flipped."

"I will. I knew there was something wrong, and I'm sure he was the one that threw those Molotov cocktails too. Maybe the police will get him for that and we can quit worrying about him. Good luck, man."

Happy put the phone down carefully and listened. Not a sound in the house. Then the phone rang again and he grabbed it. He just held it a minute, his heart beating wildly.

"Happy?" It was Mickey's voice.

Happy's chest ached and his mouth was too dry to speak. "Y-yeah," he managed to get out the word.

"You must be sleeping with the phone."

"No, I was—I was just going by on the way to the bathroom."

"You heard anything from Raid?"

"Who?"

"Raid! Our old bike buddy. You remember Raid?" Sarcasm dripped off the words.

"Oh. Yeah. Why would I hear from him?"

"Just tell me. You heard from him lately?"

"Haven't seen him, no."

"If you do, I'm looking for him. You tell him that."

"Okay, but I don't know if I'll be seeing him. I haven't seen him since Horse's accident."

"You heard from Horse's wife?"

"Horse's wife?"

"You don't hear too well early in the morning?"

"Sleepy, I guess."

"Have—you—heard—from—Horse's—wife?"

"No. No reason to, I guess."

"You tell her Raid and I and you were with him that night?"

"Told her I was. Jack Gardner told her you and Raid were. Why?"

"What else did you tell her?"

"Only what time Horse started home. She wanted to know that."

"If you hear from Raid, you tell him that I'm looking for him."

"Okay."

"You got a phone number for Maggie Murphy?"

"No. Did have. Guess I lost it. Don't need it now."

"She's moved."

"She's what?"

"Moved—moved, like packed up and went."

"Oh. How do you know?"

"You're not only deaf and dumb, you can't read either. There was a little thing in the police news about an explosion at her house. It said she was the last tenant, but the house was empty."

"Empty?"

"Yeah, empty. So she must have moved. If you hear from her, ask her where she lives."

"Why?"

"Just ask her, you hear? And if you hear from Raid, you tell him I'm looking for him. You might as well go back to bed for all the help you are. You just remember what I said."

The dial tone came on and Happy sat there until his heart stopped beating so hard, listening to the silence surrounding him. Then, knowing it was probably a useless gesture, he reached for the phone and punched in Maggie's number. He let it ring three times, then gave up and went to bed, feeling helpless. He hoped that policeman Jack Gardner had said Maggie was with at the barbecue place was still around to take care of her.

Happy's call to Maggie was noted if not answered. Joe

thought he heard the phone ring but didn't get up. In the morning, he checked the answering machine. Whoever it was had hung up without leaving a message. He didn't mention it to Maggie.

CHAPTER TWENTY-THREE

Doug and Aunt Myrtle's wedding was planned in record time, and nothing but the picture of the happy couple was slated for the paper a week after the ceremony. Aunt Myrtle and Doug didn't want any help making plans, and simply called on the people they wanted for certain assigned tasks.

The one exception was when Fatima and Maggie shanghaied Aunt Myrtle in the middle of her busy day and took her to Momma's Sunday Best Beauty Salon to get the works and relax a little before the last-minute chaos.

The ceremony and the reception were mostly family and took place at the neighborhood CNNC, Christian Neighborhood Nondenominational Church Chapel. Grace and some of her friends in various garden clubs had decorated the little chapel to enchanted fairy-tale pretty with a bower for the minister, Myrtle, and Doug to stand in while they said their vows.

Maggie stood with her aunt as her matron of honor and Doug's son was his best man. A tiny cousin, a blond cherub looking like an angel in her fluffy pink dress, was the flower girl, and the only other attendants were various other cousins and friends, including Fatima's brothers.

The reception was typical of weddings and funeral reunions, which were the only occasions for which most of the family were able to drop their daily responsibilities and get together. In addition to Doug's son, his wife and child, sister-in-law and her husband, there were about twenty of Aunt Myrtle's family who could get there on short notice. Hank and Grace were there; some of the garden clubs were represented; and friends of Joe's came, some of them still in uniform.

"Good boy!" Aunt Myrtle's head bent close to Maggie's to whisper. "Joe's keeping watch like a hawk on a chicken house."

Maggie smiled proudly. "I was too busy admiring how nice he looks to notice that, but it does make me feel good to have some of his friends here. Are you and Doug all ready to leave?"

"Yes, we've got everything in the car. I haven't told anybody where we're going, but we're going to spend the first two nights at Gatlinburg, then just take our time looking around as we drive back. We'll be back by about midweek."

"Sounds wonderful." Maggie squeezed her hand. "Joe's slipped out and parked the car off the church lot for a quick getaway. You'll have to deal with the few cans somebody insisted on tying to the bumper. You call if you have an emergency—and be careful so you don't have one!"

Grace and some of the flower club members, including the members of Eden Extended, saw that the finger food trays and platters were kept filled, and a rather slip-shod watch was put on the punch bowl. The consensus seemed to be that anyone with the nerve to spike the punch with Grace presiding deserved his booze.

Hank contributed compliments on the flowers and apprecia-tion of the buffet as he ate and mixed with the crowd. He brought out his whole repertoire of old W. C. Fields jokes, all of which Grace had heard till she knew them by heart.

Fatima surreptitiously kept an eye on Maggie. When they took Aunt Myrtle to the beauty salon, she and Maggie had slipped away to the herb shop as she was being shampooed. Glancing at Maggie through a connecting door, Fatima bent to talk to Evil Elvira.

"Last time we came, you said my friend had company." Her

eyes slid back to Maggie, a bit worried.

"Still got company." The old woman stated it flatly.

"You see some company around my friend now?" Fatima's eyes widened.

"No." Elvira's sparse white hair floated around as she shook her head.

Before Fatima could feel relieved, Elvira added, "He out there lookin' in the window."

"He is?" An icy little finger of fear ran down Fatima's back and she held her breath a second before speaking again. She finally managed, "What's he look like?"

"He white. Young but older'n her. Black hide jacket—whoo! I bet that cost somethin'!"

"Is he—evil?"

"No. Not evil. He good. Ain't nothing bad there. He tryin' to help her—but he daid! Don't want no daid folks around—be daid myself, by'm bye . . ."

Elvira sighed, laying her head back against her chair. She dropped off to sleep before it occurred to Fatima to ask what the visitor was trying to help Maggie with.

After glancing down a few seconds longer at the peaceful old face, Fatima had quietly gone back to join Maggie. *She told me true, or what she thinks is true. And at least she said there's no danger. Maggie's company doesn't mean her any harm.*

She put the matter out of her mind. Coming back to the present and the recent problems, Fatima saw Maggie close the back door behind her Aunt Myrtle.

Slipping out. Good, and nobody sees. Fatima smiled to herself. *I'll go have some punch before Hank drinks it all.*

Grace was doing a good job watching the punch bowl and keeping it Presbyterian, but she needn't have worried. Hank had brought only enough Irish Cream to lace his own coffee and punch and had no intentions of sharing it.

Maggie joined him just as he was fixing his coffee, his back turned to Grace and most of the others.

"Don't worry. I'm more for moderation than prohibition," she assured him when he jumped at a step behind him.

"I knew you were one of the few smart ones in the family." Hank looked around at the crowd. "Nice ceremony, wasn't it? I'm glad for them. Everybody should be happily married four or five times a week."

"Married four or five times a week?"

"No, happy four or five times a week. Five days out of seven isn't bad."

Maggie laughed. "I agree. It beats living in sin."

Hank studied her face. "Don't tell me she considered it? Myrtle?"

"You didn't hear it from me. And they're married now, so we can both cross it off our worry lists."

"Speaking of that and related things," Hank said, hastily changing the subject. "I figured out by the ring you're wearing and the noise Fatima made when you showed it to her—Joe proposed?"

Maggie tilted her head. She started to nod, but didn't. "Not exactly. Not marriage anyway. At least not now."

Hank's expression struggled between shock and admiration. "Don't tell me. I don't want to know."

Maggie left him trying to drown his curiosity in Irish Cream.

Chapter Twenty-Four

Maggie used several lunch hours in the next week to shop for showers and talk to ceramic tile salesmen.

I can't see Joe being uncomfortable the rest of his life in a tiny space like that. "That" was the small space in the ready-to-install shower she was looking at. She finally decided on building in a shower twice the size of the ready-to-install ones and got estimates on the costs.

Maggie decided to put eighteen hundred dollars she had from the closing costs on the house in an IRA and pay out the balance on the new shower. *It will only take a year and a half, and Aunt Myrtle seems to think it will take him that long to propose to me. I'll tell him about it tonight. Maybe it'll encourage him a little, or maybe he'll only see it as more debt. Who knows?*

Joe's reaction about the shower was mixed, not wholly approving or disapproving. "A shower? I thought you liked bubble baths and that hot tub?"

"I do. I'm going to put it in the smaller bathroom since there's plenty of room there for it. I don't want to lose all that linen storage in the other one. Come on, I'll show you where it will be."

He looked at the corner and the big space she indicated. "More than enough room here. The ones I've seen in home supply stores aren't very big."

"No. I looked at them too. They're not, and certainly not as well built. I've got some estimates on the plumbing and tile. It will be twice as big as those you can buy and just set in."

"Sounds pretty expensive," Joe commented cautiously.

"I'll use some of my savings." She remembered saving every penny she could of the retirement money Horace had left her. "With a good down payment, I can get a loan to pay the rest of it out. It will only take a year and a half and it will be worth it." She smiled. "This must be what they mean when people who own a house say the house owns them."

Joe extended his arms from side to side of the anticipated shower and raised his eyebrows. "You must have some big guy in mind?"

"Yeah, about this high." She put a hand on his head. "Who did you think I want it for—Red?"

"I guess I'm never going to live that down, am I?"

"Oh, maybe in twenty or thirty years."

He put his arms around her, holding her close. "This is sweet, and I love you for it. But I can't let you do it."

"I didn't ask permission. I want to do this, and it's sure not going to get any cheaper. Better do it now, while I can."

"Are you sure you can handle the extra debt? I can, if you've got your heart set on it. But we can add the shower later, you know."

"No, the time is now. I've got estimates and arranged for the loan, and I can manage it. It will be paid off in eighteen months, and you remember Hank had to say he wasn't going to fire me for five years." She giggled, remembering Hank's face.

Joe laughed with her and gave up, his arms tightening around her.

The next day, before Joe reported for work, he knocked on the facing of Alan Hill's door. Alan motioned him in.

"I guess you know Maggie and I are engaged."

"I guess I know you ought to be."

"Yeah. Well. She's working at a job she likes and can handle. That's good. And I've been here seven years—"

"Six and ten months. Is this going where I think it is?"

"Yes. What are my chances?" Joe's handsome face was troubled.

"I'd think, pretty good. There's the test and waiting for an opening and a few other stumbling blocks. But you'll get there. I feel sure of that."

"I'm going to do my best to make it as soon as possible. We'll survive in the meantime, but I hate to see the house and everything on Maggie's back. And she needs a car. At least the rent I'm paying on the apartment is helping some." Joe smiled self-consciously. "If her Aunt Myrtle wasn't so glad I'm around for protection and pay the rent on time, she'd be accusing us of 'living in sin,' as she calls it."

"Are you?"

"If I didn't tell Aunt Myrtle, what makes you think I'd tell you?" Joe laughed as he got up to go to work.

"Wait a minute." Alan scrambled around for scratch paper. "What were the names of those two women you talked to at St. Olaf's?"

"Millie and Pauline. They're usually around. The cashier will point them out if you want to talk to them. Why?"

"I had a visit from a couple of FBI agents."

Joe's jaw dropped, and he drew in a surprised breath. "FBI agents?"

"Yeah, I got them instead of answers on the prints. I'll fill you in later. On that other thing, I found out a lot about Michael Lewis, but he's under some rock I haven't turned over yet. Raymond Wilson is completely invisible, and I put an alert out on him in case he tries to leave the country."

"A warrant as a witness?"

"That, and I have a few friends."

"Always helps."

"Yeah. Have a quiet night."

Maggie waved to Carl Peabody, the part-timer, as he came into the office. "You're here early today."

"Yeah, Hank let's me come in whenever I can and I can use the money."

"Welcome to the human race," Maggie said. "Oh, that reminds me." She took her wallet out of her purse and went to Fatima's desk. "Here's the two dollars I owe you. Thanks."

"You're welcome." Fatima smiled as she picked up the money. "I wasn't holding my breath."

"I like to keep my credit good."

Fatima looked at the picture she could see in Maggie's billfold. "Is that Horace?"

"Yes, Horace and his motorcycle. I'm going to put it in our album when I get around to it. I haven't got one yet of Joe."

Fatima studied the picture, remembering Evil Elvira's words. *White, young, older than she is. That hide jacket, bet that cost—*

In the picture, Horace was wearing a black leather jacket. A little troubled, Fatima didn't say anything, and Carl came up to Maggie.

"I'm emptying my trash. Want me to get yours? I'm going anyway. I might stop and get Hank's and make a few points . . ."

"Brown nose." Fatima made a face at him.

"Thanks, Carl." Maggie watched him go down the hall balancing the trash cans. "He's a nice boy."

"Yes, he is. Smart, too. Too bad he can't go to school."

"What? He's a senior this year, isn't he? But what do you mean, he can't go to school?"

"His dad died a couple of years ago and there was mortgage insurance on their house. So they've got the house and enough for them to live on since his mother's working. But no school money. And he's got to work."

"Oh. Maybe he can take some courses like you're doing."

"You don't know how much it costs. Just one item, books, is expensive. I buy mine secondhand, and they still cost an arm and a leg."

"Hank hasn't got anyone for circulation yet, maybe—"

Fatima shook her head. "Don't think it would work. He'd have to work on Friday and the weekend, not when Hank would want him."

"Well, Hank's got his own presses. Maybe they could get together?"

"And maybe pigs will fly!" Fatima rolled her eyes and reached for her ringing phone.

Maggie smiled at Carl and said thanks again as he came back. She couldn't get her mind off possible ways to help him.

Joe would ask me how I know he even wants to go to school. And I doubt Hank would change his routine. Maybe I did grow up to be Aunt Myrtle like Hank accuses me of. Right now, I've got to turn off my worrier and get to work on my column.

At that moment Joe was hurrying down the hall at the police station, passing Alan's office. The door was open and Alan reached out and touched his arm.

"Come in here a minute."

Joe looked at the clock on the wall. "I'm nearly on the dot here—"

"Come in anyway." He looked serious.

Joe closed the door behind him, his hand staying on the knob. "What is it? I already know there's no hope, or nearly none."

"There may be."

"May be? How?"

"This is privileged information, and it may not happen."

Joe nodded.

211

"Captain Thomas is thinking about taking early retirement."

Joe took a deep breath, listening, one eye still on the time.

"Thomas's wife's got cancer. He's got arthritis himself so he could probably get the medical. He is seriously considering it. He told me this morning. I think he can get it. I'm hoping if he does it will be good for both of us, and him and his wife too."

"Thanks." Joe opened the door—one minute to get twenty feet down the hall.

Alan jerked his head toward the hall. "Keep your mouth shut and your fingers crossed."

Maggie had beat Joe home and was in the yard clipping some crepe myrtle blooms to take in the house when his car pulled in and stopped beside her. He got out and came to give her a hug and a kiss on the cheek.

"What was that for? I might want to do it again." She hugged him back.

"Just glad to get home. Is there anything you want me to go out and get before I get comfortable?"

"No. I've got the crockpot full of stuff. And Doug and Aunt Myrtle got back today. Just hurry and come on in."

Fresh from his shower and full of hope from Alan's news, Joe enjoyed the good dinner Maggie had fixed them in the crockpot. He listened and laughed with Maggie about the good times Aunt Myrtle told her she and Doug had.

"She said she'd have pictures to show us soon as she gets them developed," Maggie finished up.

"I'm glad they're back safely. And I'm glad they have each other now. I like Doug."

"You seem to like everything tonight. Are you going to tell me what brought on all this good humor?" When he didn't answer immediately, she eyed him suspiciously. "Marlene didn't send that shirt back, did she?"

"No, Ms. Smart. I'd lost interest in that shirt before I saw the sequins she put on it. And her too—can't you tell?"

"I hope. I'd decided to take that on faith until you tell me different."

Joe got up and pulled her up into his arms, holding her close and resting his head on her hair. "I'm never going to do that."

He let go of her and looked down at the table. "I'll dry dishes for you." She nodded, picking up a plate.

Taking some dishes and glasses to the sink, he said, "You know, you could have got a couple of dishwashers for what that shower is going to cost."

"A dishwasher? For two people? And Aunt Myrtle won't put her good china in one of the monsters. No sale. My favorite tool in here is the disposal, so forget about it." She changed the subject. "Have you heard anything new about Mr. Wartz?"

"Yes and no, which means no. I'm just guessing at some things. I don't think Alan knows anything either. I do know it's a much bigger case than we thought it was going to be, with two government agencies involved. I couldn't tell you about it anyway."

"Two government agencies?"

"I gave my notes and the little I'd found out to Alan. Wasn't all that much. The people's names I talked to, everything I'd learned, though it was mostly hearsay, and where to contact the people I'd talked to. Alan gave them what he and I both had."

"But, Mr. Wartz was so well liked. I can't picture anyone who let his friends call him Wartzy being some national-level criminal."

"No," Joe agreed. "He probably isn't. Just don't worry about it. They're working on it, and the local case will be closed soon, they say."

They. Maggie nodded, putting her curiosity on hold.

★ ★ ★ ★ ★

Michael called Happy twice more, getting more demanding each time. Happy steadfastly denied he had Maggie's number, saying he'd lost it and didn't remember it. Then it got through Michael's thick head and self-centered attitude that Happy would be happier if he never heard from Michael again. He was no friend of his and didn't want to be.

"You're sure you didn't tell that woman—"

"Maggie. Her name's Maggie."

"You didn't tell Maggie anything? The police must have come looking for me for some reason."

"I don't know anything about that. Nobody asked me anything. I-I can't help you, Mickey. And the last time you called, it woke up my dad."

"Woke up your dad? Who gives a crap about that? I've been calling at night when there won't be anybody answering but you. Have you heard anything from Raid?"

"No. No, I haven't seen him at all. I don't know where he is."

"Well, go on back to sleep then, you brain-dead little nerd!"

Happy sat in the chair shaking, looking at the phone as if it might bite. *Mickey's as desperate as Raid said he was. There's no telling what he might do.*

Michael was thinking about Happy, about the potential damage he could do to him. It was not a comforting thought. He remembered the night of Horse's accident. *Horse said he had just had the phone put in. Wish I'd asked for the number then. I wonder . . .*

Michael dialed information. No listing. He tried asking about a new listing. Bingo! Mickey's smirk was downright diabolical as some machine told him the number would be in the next issue of the phone book. He quickly wrote down the number the nasal voice told him twice.

He studied the prefix on the scrap of paper. He didn't know

where it was. Maybe the old place? He laid the paper down beside the phone and punched in the number. He sat tense and listening until the answering device came on. He listened to the message, relieved when it confirmed the number. He hung up after the dumb thing about the mint julep, wondering what the face with that laughing voice looked like.

Mint juleps, huh? I'm going to mint julep Happy! I'm none too sure he was asleep as long as we thought he was. I don't know what he told her, but he's not going to tell anyone else. I'll fix him.

CHAPTER TWENTY-FIVE

Maggie knocked on Hank's office door. He looked up. "Certainly not!"

"Certainly not what?"

"Every time someone knocks like that, they want something."

"Oh. Well, I guess you're right."

"You going to tell me what it is or do I have to guess?"

Maggie struggled to find an answer.

"Is it bigger than a bread box?"

"I don't know—is the bread box full of money?"

"Ma'am, you've made a wrong turn. The bank is four blocks down that way." He pointed helpfully, even hopefully. Maggie didn't move.

"Would you just listen to me five minutes and maybe we can figure out something?"

"This thing, if we get it figured out, will it be of any possible use or benefit to me and the paper at all?"

"Yes!" Maggie's smile lit the room and Hank smiled in spite of himself. "Yes, it just might be."

Hank was not convinced that whatever this was would be good for him, but he could tell Maggie honestly thought it might be.

"Okay." He gestured to the chair with the spring. "Possible benefit. Hope springs eternal. Sit down. Five minutes."

Maggie talked fast with the time limit in mind. She outlined Carl Peabody's problems, the circulation problems, and offered a few ideas to help both.

Hank used up one of the remaining minutes sitting there with his mouth open, looking stunned.

Words tumbled out to sum up what he'd heard. "Change the press day so Carl Peabody can work and go to school?"

"I guess that's what it boils down to, yes. I don't know much about printing and presses and such—"

"God knows, you've proved that! Did he put you up to this?"

"No! No one knows. Please don't tell him. I only thought since he needs to work and you need someone for circulation—"

"Maggie, first, I won't tell anyone your idea. Second, thank God nobody else out there is so causal about the press. Third, there's got to be some businesses looking for a college student for a part-time job. And four, I'll look around for some places he can try." He glanced at his watch. "And you just made it."

"That's great and thanks." She stopped at the door. "But you took the last minute, so you still owe me one."

Hank was a fair man. He wet his finger on his tongue and drew an invisible one in the air. "Payable when I've got time and the building's not on fire."

"Thanks, Hank."

She left and didn't hear him mutter, "If I didn't know better, I'd swear Grace is giving her lessons!"

Joe kept mum about his possible promotion, not wanting to disappoint Maggie if it didn't happen. He concentrated on studying, Alan's tips and sincerely wishing the best for Captain Thomas and his wife. Maggie blamed his preoccupation on the hours he was putting in at work and visited with Aunt Myrtle and Doug.

It seemed like an eternity until the announcement came out about Captain Thomas's retirement for health reasons and another eon or two until they got the news Lieutenant Alan Hill was promoted to Captain Alan Hill and Patrolman Joe Driver was promoted to Lieutenant Joe Driver.

The building couldn't hold Joe when he got off work. He went to a pay phone and called Maggie from the privacy of its little glass cubicle.

"The *Herald*, Maggie Murphy."

"I love you, Maggie Murphy at the *Herald*!"

"That's great. Did you think I'd forgot you?" Maggie laughed. "Wait a minute." The words oozed disappointment. "Are you about to tell me you've got to work tonight and our date is off?"

"No, it's on. I want to splurge. Let's go to the Italian place I took you to the first time we splurged, if that's all right with you. We could go somewhere else."

"No, no. That's great. I'd love to. Are we celebrating something? Should I be remembering something? First date that's called a date, not first kiss? What could it be? Drat! I may be headed for the doghouse!"

"Yes, we're celebrating. I'll tell you about it tonight."

"All right." Maggie let go a relieved breath. "Sounds great. See you tonight."

Maggie eyed the phone before going back to work. *Wonder what he means? I'm just glad he didn't call to cancel because he had to work. Wonder how that rates on the pitiful scale of one to ten?*

She looked up as Carl Peabody came in with a box in his hand and a strange grin on his face.

"Hi, Carl. What's the big grin for?"

"It's a combination glad school's out and a 'whoopee I got work' kind of thingy."

Fatima came over to hear better. "You got a job?"

"I've got two!" Carl chortled with glee just thinking about it.

Fatima and Maggie's eyes met. "Two? We're going to have to run his runty body through the copy machine!" Fatima raised her hands, curved like claws to grab him.

"Hands loose. It's all fixed so I can handle it."

"Where?"

"Yeah, tell us about it."

"Mr. Hanover must have been afraid I was going to put the touch on him for a loan. He called me in Saturday to talk to him. He said you mentioned I need a job so I can go to school." He nodded at Maggie. "Thanks! Anyway, he was looking around, and Mrs. Hanover has some influence with that big flower company branch here—"

"Heaven Scents!" Maggie and Fatima screeched together.

"Yeah, that's the one. This is their district hub, whatever that is. They do a lot of their data processing at night. Soon as I'm trained, and they say it won't take long, I'll be working from five to ten o'clock four nights a week."

"What about Saturday mornings?" Fatima frowned.

"That's what I was about to say. Then I'll still be here Saturday morning like I always am. I can go to classes in the daytime the rest of the week. Isn't that great?"

"Since it won't involve me and Maggie having to take turns coming in on Saturday mornings, yeah, that's great!" Fatima high-fived him and he grabbed her hand, happy as she was. They danced a few steps as Maggie watched. Then her eyes fell on the box he was holding. He stopped and Fatima went back to her desk.

"That's the best news I've heard all week, Carl. I'm glad for you. What's in the box?"

He held it out, still looking pleased. "It's a surprise for you."

"For me?"

"Yeah. Besides answering the phone, generally de-trashing the place, and polishing up the handles on the big front door—" He danced a couple more steps. "I see to any name plates, desk titles and so forth."

Maggie watched as he drew out an elongated strip wrapped

in plastic. "You got me a name plate?"

Carl carefully unwrapped it as he talked. "I know you're engaged, so I just got the plate to stick on the front of the desk for now." He looked up and saw Hank had come in and stood watching them. "What do you think?"

"I like it. It's pretty. Maggie Murphy." She smiled at it.

"I thought about getting one to set on the desk too. But what do you want? Just Helena, maybe? Help from Helena is kinda long, but just Helena . . . I don't know."

"It would look sort of lost, wouldn't it?"

"You want a last name, pick you out one." Hank teased her, coming forward to admire the name plate.

"The name Hand Basket did occur to me." Maggie grinned. "Aunt Myrtle would love it!"

"It's not Aunt Myrtle's desk," Hank pointed out. "You can think about it, since you'll have to change the plate anyway if Joe ever gets up the nerve to set the date."

Maggie narrowed her eyes. "You've been talking to Aunt Myrtle," she accused.

"Nobody talks to her. Might have listened a little," he admitted.

He left for his office and Maggie admired the name plate that declared to the world this beat-up desk belonged to Maggie Murphy.

Carl was gone too, tossing his cap onto a desk near the door to the pressroom. She followed Hank to his office.

"Thanks," she said and sat down on the edge of the chair. "It's great for Carl to have a job and be able to go to school."

"You're welcome. But my best effort was getting Grace interested. She's the one who set up the interview with Heaven Scents."

"Tell her thanks, and I'll thank her too as soon as I get a chance." She got up to leave.

"I guess you and Joe are getting along like a racehorse on speed?"

"Oh, yes. In fact, we're celebrating something tonight."

"Really? What?"

A brief, pained expression crossed Maggie's face. "He didn't say and I've got no earthly idea. I hope it's not some little anniversary I'm supposed to remember." Her smile came back. "I'm just going to celebrate having something to celebrate." She grinned and left him chuckling at having company in his misery. Hank was famous for forgetting anniversaries.

Across town, Mickey Lewis was not celebrating; he was making plans. *Maggie Murphy isn't going anywhere, and I've got her phone number now, no thanks to that sleaze, Happy. Raid is long gone to no telling where. He's too scared to be a threat. That leaves Happy, and I'll take care of him.*

A BMW went by fast enough to get his attention. *Nice. Maybe I'll borrow one like that to use. He pictured the big parking lot at the all-night mall not far from Happy's house.*

I'll wait till twelve or one o'clock to call him, pick up a car to use. It'll be no problem at all. He glanced down at the little sack in his hand. It held a pair of cheap gardening gloves. No, no problem at all.

Maggie had her clothes laid out on the bed and was just stepping out of a lavender-scented bubble bath when she heard Joe's car in the drive. She pulled on a terry robe and met him at the back door.

Joe eyed the robe. "You're way ahead of me." He pulled her into his arms and kissed her. "Um, you smell good."

"Thanks. I splurged on some new bubble bath. Fatima brought it to me from her cousin's shop."

He let her go. "I won't be too long. Our reservations are for seven o'clock."

When Joe stopped his car at the back door again she was ready. She wore a new sequined blouse and carried a tiny, more fashionable than useful, evening bag to match.

"You look great. New blouse?"

"Yes, thank the Lord for plain black skirts. I bought my evening ensembles half at a time." A parody of pride, Maggie stuck her nose up in the air. "Both of them!"

They entered the restaurant and Maggie again admired the decor. It looked like an outdoor patio in the moonlight.

The Italians sure know how to decorate for romance and celebrations, Maggie thought as she followed the waiter to their table. *And I know how to pick a handsome escort. Eat your heart out.* She aimed the thought at a life-size statue of David standing near a small fountain.

She shook her head, refusing wine, and looked at the appetizers on the menu, not meeting Joe's eyes. He was so handsome in the candlelight, her heart skipped a beat when he took her hand.

"Maggie," he said seriously. "My beautiful, sweet, Maggie." His smile, his eyes, held hers.

I'm going to melt and run right down in my shoes! For God's sake, what was it I was supposed to remember?

His voice broke into her panic. "About this engagement of ours—"

She paled. *Oh, my God! He's leaving me! He's letting me down easy! Right into the spaghetti sauce!*

"Maggie, I love you. I'll always love you. I want to spend the rest of my life with you. Will you marry me?"

Maggie fought tears. "Yes. I will. I love you, too."

Joe put both his hands over hers. "I've wanted to say that for a long time, but I wanted to be able to provide for you too, to take care of you." He took a deep breath. "You're doing pretty well by yourself. What would you need me for with nothing to contribute?"

"Well, really!" Maggie would have been more indignant had her temper not been saturated with pure happiness. "What about to love and to cherish for better or worse, in sickness and in health?"

"I know the words," he chuckled. "And I know money isn't everything."

"I can't believe you think I want you for your money!"

Joe laughed loud enough to attract the attention of a nearby older couple, who smiled at them.

"For my money! Now that's the joke of the week." He picked up Maggie's hand and kissed it several times between words. "There's more."

"More? More to celebrate? What are you talking about?"

"You're now having dinner with Lieutenant Joe Driver!"

"Oh!" Maggie gasped. "That's wonderful! Congratulations! I'm so proud of you and I know Alan is too."

"He's Captain Alan Hill now." Joe told her about the promotions and the things that had led up to them.

"So now I've got the job I've always wanted, a little more money and I can propose to my dream girl," he finished up.

"Dream girl? That's a lot to live up to. Me, Maggie Murphy, somebody's dream girl?"

"Yes, my dream girl," Joe smiled into her eyes. A movement caught his eye and he glanced at the waiter. "I guess I'd better wait till we get home to try and convince you."

Chapter Twenty-Six

Aunt Myrtle's reaction to the news about Joe's proposal of marriage was as joyous as Maggie had pictured it.

"And do I hear a little relief mixed in with all that glee?" Maggie asked.

"Well, maybe a little. I never heard of anybody proposing to get engaged. It made me wonder. He must want it to be soon then, to be making his proposal official. Have you set a date yet?"

"Joe wants it to be in two weeks, which is the best we can do, I think, and get the arrangements made and get invitations sent out. The printer said he could get them for us in seven or eight days if we chose from the ones he showed us."

"And where? In the chapel where Doug's and mine was?"

"Yes. It's easy to get to and there won't be all that many of us."

"I'll get hold of Grace. Most of those flowers we used were silk, and I'll get the reception set up and ready too. About the same as mine except for Hank's Irish Cream." She laughed.

"I didn't know you knew about that, he was being so careful. It sounds wonderful. And what I don't write a check for when you need it, make a list of so I can pay you back before the ceremony. I don't want to start out in debt, or any farther in debt than I already am. Except, that is, for the love and help you've always given me, and I'll never be able to pay that back."

"Maggie, don't you dare start crying or I will too! And don't

worry about anything. I'll take care of it. All my life felt like I
could handle anything, and with Grace in on this too, it will be
a snap." She laughed happily.

"And I've always known I've got the best family in the world,"
Maggie said. "I guess we'll have to give Hank credit for choos-
ing Grace."

"We don't have to bring it up all that often, though. You said
there aren't going to be very many to attend?"

"Mostly just family. I'll make out a list to send invitations to
and you do the same so we won't forget anybody. Joe's parents
and a cousin and his wife are coming, and some of his friends.
Oh! And I nearly forgot! Joe would never forgive me. He got a
promotion, Aunt Myrtle. He's Lieutenant Joe Driver now."

"That's wonderful news. Tell him congratulations. I'll tell
him too, next time I see him."

"That's why he was dragging his feet, as you called it. He
told me he felt he needed the money and security before we got
married."

"That's good old-fashioned horse sense. Makes me feel even
better. You won't snitch on me about my doubts, will you?"

"Never, ever."

Maggie crossed her heart as if Aunt Myrtle could see her,
and Fatima laughed at her from her desk.

"I couldn't help hearing about the proposal, not that I tried.
Congratulations. Am I on that invitation list?"

"Right at the top, and so are momma and the rest of the
family. You'll have to give me Aunt Elvira's last name."

"That's been known to change according to who you're talking to. Just put Auntie Elvira on the invitation and don't mail it.
I'll give it to her."

Mickey Lewis was spending his time stocking in a small mom-
and-pop grocery store. The job didn't pay much, but he got his

money in cash and didn't have to fill out any paperwork. He got paid from the cash drawer and was planning on cleaning it out when he got ready to leave. He bided his time, doing enough to qualify for stocking without hurting himself. He did his work silently, keeping his thoughts and his plans to himself.

When I'm ready, I'll make Happy pay for this delay. The little sleaze! I've called twice now and got that woman. Blessed me out good the second time. Must be Happy's mother. Well, he can't stay gone forever. I'll get to him . . .

Raymond Wilson had let the water fountain run till it got as cool as it was going to get in order to quench his thirst. He was in a small rest area park in Texas, sitting on the grass lawn in the shade. His hopes rose when he saw a semi coming, but it went on by.

There aren't any likely candidates here to bum a ride with. I feel like I've been walking all my life.

It felt good to sit and rest. His eyes wandered over the scene around him, taking in everything from the late evening sky to the people coming and going out of the park.

I don't see how that couple and all those kids got in that car they piled out of. That older couple is looking at me like they wonder if I'm an escapee from somewhere, and that's a mean-looking boxer they've got on a leash. I'll wait until it gets a little cooler to start walking on, maybe somebody else will come in, or a trucker will stop and give me a lift.

Joe listened to Maggie and Aunt Myrtle's plans, supplying needed names and addresses.

His own plans for their wedding were decidedly less upbeat and flowery than Maggie's. Captain Alan Hill and other friends took their roles as seriously as Joe did when he laid out his security plans.

Hank didn't know about Joe's security plans, but he was a long way from being as optimistic as Maggie. He conferred with Joe as soon as he learned about the wedding.

Hank's equivalent of calling out the militia consisted of making himself, Floyd Graves, Tim Thompson and Carl Peabody available, along with an offer to round up more troops if needed.

Joe thanked him. "I've already got some volunteers for outside surveillance and inside, too. But since all of you will be at the wedding ceremony and reception anyway, you stand by in case we need you."

"Good. Good. I'm glad you've got that covered, and by some professionals, too. We'll be at the ready."

After their talk, Joe hung up with affectionate gratitude and other mixed feelings. *God,* he prayed, *don't let us ever get that hard up for help.*

Grace took Maggie to lunch a few days before the wedding. They talked of general bridal registry items, and necessary as opposed to snob appeal gifts. Also some voice of experience, pearls of wisdom from Grace were thrown in as she gathered information on her own without appearing too nosy. Maggie, having heard most of the advice already from her Aunt Myrtle, smiled affectionately and answered patiently.

"Yes, I have an IRA, probably the smallest one in the history of banking." Maggie made gentle fun of her financial progress and told Grace about the eighteen hundred dollars left over from the closing costs.

"I opened the IRA for two thousand dollars with a little help from my savings account I had from Horace's job, and I can add to it over the years. I guess what's left of my savings will be about wiped out by the time Joe and I get back from our honeymoon. But with both of us working, I'm going to put all I can into an investment account like a friend of mine had where

I used to work."

"An investment account. I was going to suggest that." Grace nodded approval.

"My friend doesn't take any of her interest unless she has some sort of emergency. It looked like a good idea to me."

"It is," Grace agreed. "It's marvelous. It would be a financial safety net. You can have a little of the interest if you need it and not have to touch your principle. Wait a minute."

She searched in her purse and handed Maggie an envelope. "This woman has handled my investment account for years, and she's really nice and helpful if you want to ask questions."

"Thank you. I'll keep it. It will be a little while until I can get started. I have a bill that I will pay off in a year and a half. I'll start on it then."

Grace was delighted. "I'm so glad you've come to work for Hank. I know he needs you, too. And Maggie, I hope you won't think I'm prying—"

Maggie's heart warmed at Grace's troubled expression. "There's a big difference between prying and caring. What do you want to know?"

"I just, I wondered—your Aunt Myrtle told me a little about your Joe's suspicions about those fire bombs or whatever they were." Grace's brow showed some unaccustomed worry wrinkles as she tried to find the right words.

"They're called Molotov cocktails, and he's afraid someone who might know something about Horace's accident threw them. But, we don't know for sure who did that or why, and I had already moved. So, we may never know."

"But Joe will have some of his friends there at the wedding and reception, won't he?"

"Of course. There will be quite a few." Maggie smiled, patting Grace's hand. "There's nothing to worry about, Grace."

"Well, good." Grace relaxed a little. "Hank seemed worried

about it, though he didn't say anything about it to me. But, I saw him get out his gun and check it."

"Gun?" Maggie looked up in surprise as they rose to leave. "I didn't know he had one."

Grace nodded. "He bought it about two years ago, and once in a while he goes to a practice range to shoot it. Then he makes a big deal out of cleaning it and taking care of it." Grace's amusement smoothed out her worry lines.

"If he does that, at least he knows how to use it."

"Oh, yes. They had some kind of a discount deal on training or something when he got it. He'd have dropped it and shot himself in the foot before now if it hadn't been for that."

Both of them laughed on the way out. "Thanks for lunch, Grace."

The day before the wedding, Fatima and Maggie went to Momma's Sunday Best Beauty Salon to get their hair done.

"Since I'm going to deliver Aunt Elvira's invitation, I'll splurge on a couple of bottles of that lavender bubble bath for our honeymoon." Maggie hugged Momma on the way out. "See you tomorrow!"

Aunt Elvira was napping when they entered the shop. Fatima and Maggie knelt down beside her and she opened her eyes.

"You remember Maggie, don't you, Aunt Elvira?"

"Course I do. I just forget the stuff I don't want to remember so there's more room for the good stuff in here." She tapped her forehead with her finger and smiled at Maggie. "What that you got?"

"It's an invitation to my wedding." Maggie put the envelope in her hand.

"Your wedding? You getting married? Now see there, Fatima, you needs to find you a man and settle down too."

"She's got plenty of time. She's a lot younger than I am."

"He good lookin,' this man you got?" Auntie Elvira narrowed her eyes.

"Oh, yes. He's very good looking. And he's a good man too. So you don't have to worry about that." She laughed with Aunt Elvira.

"I wishes you bon chance." Auntie Elvira held up her thin arms and Maggie hugged her back.

"Thank you. Will you come to see me married?"

"No, no, child. I don't got the strength anymore. Fatima and Rose of Sharon goin' to see you married?"

"Yes, they're coming."

"They can tell me about it. I be thinkin' about you. And wishin' you love and bon chance."

At the car, Fatima stopped. "Wait, I think I'll get some of that lavender bubble bath too."

She hurried back in and bent down to the old woman. "Auntie Elvira, you see any company with Maggie this time?"

"No." Aunt Elvira cackled, "Maybe that good lookin' one done run him off!" She laughed, thin shoulders heaving, happy as the bride-to-be as Fatima hugged her again and kissed her goodbye.

CHAPTER TWENTY-SEVEN

Maggie drummed her fingers on the phone, waiting for her aunt to answer. She said "Hi," and stopped, uncertain what to say.

"Is this your nervous system calling?" Aunt Myrtle read her mind.

"I guess it is. Did I catch you in time to ask you to come over and help me clean out the refrigerator for supper? Joe had to work," she explained.

"I haven't started anything yet and don't really want to. I have to be inspired to cook. What kind of stuff is this we need to rescue from the disposal?"

"I've got chicken, and I stopped on the way home and got some potato salad. I was thinking chicken pie, potato salad and about half of a really scrumptious chocolate cake."

"Sold! We're coming." Maggie heard her call Doug before the line went dead.

Casual and comfortable when they arrived, Doug made a tour of the place while Maggie and her aunt talked about the wedding and saved a couple of pieces of cake for Joe and Maggie to have with coffee when he got home.

"I'm so glad it's all over but the ceremony." Maggie sighed, feeling guilty. "Even though you and Grace and the garden club ladies did all the work."

"You and Joe just stay married so we won't have to do it again. The biggest job was getting everyone invited. I called the ones out of town and told them the invitations were on the way, to give them as much time as possible."

"The ones out of town? There weren't many, were there? I mean, the distant ones—"

"The ones in the hills are kin of mine and your mother's, even if we haven't got together in years. But I doubt if they will come. There was some kind of reason they couldn't come when I called about my own wedding, but I really think it was just too far for them to make arrangements for the children and come on short notice."

"Don't some of them . . ." Maggie began uneasily.

"Yes, some of them make moonshine. They're not going to take off and leave the roads unguarded and lose any of their stills. And I told Hattie your husband is a policeman and a lot of his friends will be here."

"That was a good idea. I don't want to be put in a spot between my family and what's legal. But how did you tell them? I remember Mother saying once there aren't any phone lines up in the Tennessee hills where they live, because a couple of shots across the front of an installation truck can be very discouraging and it wouldn't pay the company to run lines up there anyway."

Aunt Myrtle nodded. "There is a computer server in town, and Hattie can get e-mail at the library. Their two children are doing well in school and have computer skills, too. Of course, she may not get the news about the wedding until it's over."

Maggie was trying hard to say "That's a shame" without grinning when Aunt Myrtle continued.

"The ones closer to town may get their invitations in time to make it."

"You mean . . . you don't mean the s-s—"

"Yes, but I don't know if they still go to that church that handles snakes or not. Anyway, I doubt they will come, since they didn't come to mine."

Maggie sat, trying not to see the pictures forming in her imagination—or worse than that, Joe's reaction to them.

"Where are you going for four days?"

"Joe wanted to surprise me, but my guess is Hot Springs. Maybe on the Ouachita or maybe here in Tennessee. Up to Gatlinburg where you and Doug went." *If he still wants to get married when all the guests get here.*

The day of the wedding, the little chapel was a flowery tribute to the artistry of Eden Extended and the other garden club members who helped Grace decorate it.

Before the ceremony, Maggie took advantage of Grace and Aunt Myrtle being engrossed in their conversation, and ducked out to look at the reception area and the chapel. She stood gazing at it in awe.

There it is, and thanks to Grace, it's beautiful. The altar where I'm going to become Mrs. Joe Driver. I mean Mrs. Lieutenant Joe Driver. She smiled to herself. *But I'd better get back before Grace and Aunt Myrtle put out an APB on me.* As she turned, a loud but happy voice stopped her in her tracks.

"You got to be Cousin Maggie!"

She turned to see a man about Aunt Myrtle's age holding a snapshot in his hand. He was a little taller than Aunt Myrtle, but not as tall as Joe. His hair was mostly white, and there was a woman, a young girl and a boy with him.

These are my cousins, the snake handlers. Key phrase there being my cousins. "Well, if I've got to be." Maggie smiled at all of them and got a grip on her manners.

Feminine laughter joined the big man's glee at her response, and the two women came to hug Maggie and kiss her on the cheek.

"I'm your cousin, Jacob Amos Dunn. This is your Cousin

Lorena, my wife." He put his arm around his wife and turned to the others. "And our daughter Matilda and our son Johnny."

Feeling a little weak, Maggie said, "I'm so glad you could come. Aunt Myrtle and I didn't have much hope," she added lamely, but smiled at the youngsters as she spoke to their parents.

"Nearly didn't make it," Lorena confirmed gravely.

"That's right." Jacob poked Johnny in the ribs. "Wasn't for our computer expert here, we might not have."

"I saw Cousin Myrtle's e-mail to Cousin Hattie at the library," Johnny explained.

"That was lucky. And it's good you're learning about computers, too," Maggie told him.

She turned to Jacob Amos and Lorena. "All of you make yourselves at home. It won't be long before the ceremony. I just came out for a minute—"

"Slipped your leg chain, did you?" Jacob Amos beamed at her. "You go on, we'll be fine."

When she reappeared to check her hair and the blue suit she had so carefully chosen to wed and travel in, worried questions greeted her.

"Where did you get off to?" Grace demanded, looking relieved enough to make Maggie wonder how much Hank and Aunt Myrtle had told her about the obvious security arrangements. She remembered how worried Grace looked as she told her about Hank checking his gun.

"I just turned around and you were gone. Where'd you go?" Aunt Myrtle chimed in.

"I wanted to look at the chapel, is all, and I stopped to hug some guests." Her eyes met her aunt's. "Cousins Jacob Amos, Lorena, Matilda and Johnny."

"They came?"

"Johnny saw the e-mail to Cousin Hattie at the library.

Matilda and Johnny are really nice, bright children."

"Well, they're family. I'm glad they managed to come. Did you see Joe's parents while you were out there?"

"No, but he says they and his brother and his wife will be here."

"I'll go make a last-minute check and see if anything else needs to be done." Grace left. The picture of efficiency on the march.

"I'm glad she's gone! She's a dear, but quick—did Jacob and the family bring any of those snakes with them."

"Goodness, Aunt Myrtle, I don't know. I didn't see any and they didn't say. But I'm glad they came, too. Jacob Amos had an old picture of Mama and me, is how he recognized me. And the children are nice, and nice looking, and well behaved. And Aunt Myrtle, I'll bet a cookie their boy Johnny already knows more about computers than I'll ever learn."

"Well, good for them. We'd better get ready."

Maggie and Joe stood before the minister in the beautiful arbor the garden clubs had created and spoke their wedding vows to the accompaniment of sniffles, tears of joy and a few allergic sneezes—all the flowers and greenery not being silk.

It was not till the ceremony was over, the pictures taken and their eyes got back to normal from the flashbulbs that Joe and Maggie could see well enough to greet their guests, much less make guesses about who some of them were.

Maggie met and got hugs from Joe's parents, Gill and Martha Driver. Also his younger brother Ken and his wife Carol. Then it seemed everyone talked at once, until a booming voice demanded, "Where's the bride? That lass brave enough to take on the Driver clan?"

"Uncle Chance!" Joe covered the distance between them as if he had wings and threw his arms around a big, burly man with a short, bushy beard. He looked capable of challenging the house, and was wearing a strange-looking hat with its brim turned up on one side.

Maggie tore her eyes away from the alligator claw on the man's hatband to see there were tears in Joe's eyes.

This must be someone special, she thought as Joe reached out to draw her close to him.

"Maggie, I can't believe he's really come from Australia, but this is Chauncey Castleberry, Esquire. My Uncle Chance. This is my bride Maggie, Uncle Chance."

Chance hugged Maggie carefully, as if afraid she might break, and kissed her on the cheek.

"So." He closed one eye and squinted at Joe with the other. "Ye've made it legal then? Would it make any difference if it wasn't?"

"Not a bit," Joe vowed without hesitation.

"Good. Ye'll make it, then. Where is the food? I just made it here, and my poor sister here . . ." He put an arm around Martha Driver's ample waist. "Mere skin and bones, she is—"

"I love you, Chance." Martha beamed. "All one hundred seventy pounds of me."

"We've got plenty to eat. Go with Maggie and her Aunt Myrtle here. I've got to check on something."

Joe went to the front of the chapel to speak to Alan Hill, who stood there with a radio in his hand. "Nothing suspicious," he reported. "Couple of punks in a car cruised by. Probably were looking for something loose and not locked up in the cars, but they went on."

"Better to be safe than sorry. Come in and eat."

"We will. We'll go in shifts."

Joe and Maggie were about ready to steal away when a commotion was heard outside.

"Stay here," Joe told her, eyes on the door.

"I promised to love, honor and cherish, not obey." Maggie

set her cup of punch down.

"Please?"

"Okay." Maggie's resistance melted in Joe's concern. "Be careful!"

Outside the chapel, the first thing Joe noticed was that Uncle Chance's rental car door was open. A surprised-looking youngster quickly turned loose of it and melted back in among his relatives, trying to look as if he didn't know how the thing got open. He stared down the street like everybody else.

Farther down the block beside Jacob Amos and Lorena's dusty station wagon, people had cleared the sidewalk, some stumbling in their haste to get out of the others' way. People and children cleared the path of what was on the sidewalk. Two snakes had the concrete to themselves and were slithering as fast as they could, accompanied by shrieks from the onlookers.

"Are they poisonous?" some lady inquired with loud horror.

No one bothered to answer. Most of the attention was on Captain Alan Hill, who was running down the sidewalk. He was in pursuit of an animal that was in pursuit of the snakes. There was a chain attached to its collar, not that it was slowing the furry little hunter down any.

Alan's big foot came down on the chain. The sudden stomp brought to a halt the aggressive little beast that looked like a ferret on steroids. Not too far in front of it, the two snakes were still slithering as fast as they could. Both of them were large rattlers.

Jacob Amos and Johnny appeared and went into action as if they'd done this before. They quickly captured the snakes with something that looked like nets on long sticks and put them in the box Lorena got from their car and handed to them.

She was obviously telling them what a good job they did as Uncle Chance burst from the building and his eyes fell on the little furry hunter who was standing on his hind legs. The dark, beady eyes glared indignantly at the humans who had stolen his prey.

Uncle Chance shouted, "Punjab!"

The poisonous snakes out of sight, Chauncey Castleberry picked up his furry friend and comforted him, scratching his neck and between his ears to calm him.

Alan Hill still had his foot on the leash and eyed Punjab warily. "Is that what I think it is?"

"He's going by the title of ferret, temporarily." Chance sized up Alan Hill as he stroked his pet.

"But usually he's a mongoose?" Alan demanded confirmation.

After a brief look around, Chance gave an imperceptible nod. "That's what he's called when he's at home." His eyes pleaded as Joe joined Alan. "I'd no one to leave the poor beastie with. He lost his first master, and I promised I'd take him in."

"They are an illegal import," Alan said without looking at Joe.

"When are you going back, Uncle Chance?"

"Tonight. I'll go back with my sister and spend tomorrow with her and her husband. Then I'll be going back to Australia. I have my tickets." With one hand, he managed to get them from his pocket and held them up for Alan Hill to see as Joe's father joined them.

"Can I be of help? Is there some kind of trouble?"

"No, just a couple of pets got loose. No problem now," Alan assured him. "Mr. Driver, if you'll help your brother-in-law with his ferret here, I'll see Joe gets on his way all right."

Gill Driver looked at the mongoose and smiled at Chance. "Sure will. Drive safe." He hugged Joe.

"Thank you, Captain Hill, and all the rest of you, too." Joe shook his hand, his eyes and his grateful smile taking in all his friends in uniform he could see at the moment. Alan followed him as he turned to go.

Maggie was witness to part of what happened and was waiting at the back door for Joe.

Alan Hill spoke to the policeman standing beside the car.

"No bombs, tracking devices—"

"No problems," Alan finished for him as he held the door for Joe. "Come back safely." Seeming to look at everything in the vicinity at once, he slammed the door. Maggie and Joe were on their way.

Joe had removed the cans from the back of the car, and the car's engine purred as it picked up speed going up the ramp to the freeway. Joe relaxed, watching traffic.

"You still haven't told me where we're going, not that it could possibly be as exciting as here." Maggie giggled.

"We'll see," Joe grinned.

"So—where? Where are we going?"

"New Orleans!"

CHAPTER TWENTY-EIGHT

"New Orleans! I started to say I've never been there, but I was once. It was a long time ago. My dad took Mother and me there for a couple of days. I guess it was a weekend. I don't remember much except some candy with nuts my mother really liked when my daddy bought it for her, and puffy doughnuts. I loved those doughnuts!"

"Beignets?"

"I don't know. I just remember how good they were, and I got sugar all over me."

Joe nodded with a smile. "Beignets. We'll get you all you want, I promise you."

They only took one organized tour of the French Quarter, preferring to explore on their own. But they always wound up there, no matter where they went. As promised, Maggie had her fill of beignets and bought boxes of the candy mix to take back to Aunt Myrtle, Grace and Fatima and her mother. Making love and shopping and exploring ate up their days until it was time to leave.

Joe went to a public phone on one of their shopping trips and called his Uncle Chance's number. Maggie could have told by Joe's face whom he was calling, but she could also hear the merry, booming voice she recognized.

"I won't insult you by asking are you all right, but I worried about Punjab." Joe winked at Maggie.

She went to look again at souvenirs in a nearby shop, giving him as much privacy as he could find out there.

When they started packing to leave that night, Joe patted his stomach. "When I begin to slosh when I walk, I know it's time to go home and let someone else have a go at the cafe au lait."

"Good thing I had enough beignets to soak mine up." Maggie gave her own tummy a pat. "Of course, I won't go near the scales for a couple of weeks."

"As Uncle Chance would say, if it kills us, we'll die happy, right?" Joe held out his arms.

"Delirious!" Maggie gave him an enthusiastic hug back. "Joe, I love you. And I hate to leave. This has been fabulous, but I'll be glad to get home, too."

"We'll come back. Or go play somewhere else," he promised. "It's a big world."

"I guess your uncle got home all right with his . . . ferret?" She smiled.

"That must have been embarrassing for him, since Punjab's a mongoose worthy of his name. But they made it fine with no trouble."

"I'm taking some beignet mix for souvenirs."

"We'll stop on the way out of town and have some more and some cafe au lait for the road."

Sunday night Maggie called to let her Aunt Myrtle know they were home. "I feel like I've been in another world. Anything exciting happen?"

"You mean has that nut been up to any more of his Molotov bombing mischief, don't you? No, everything's been quiet except Hank. He called to see if I'd heard from you." Her grin was audible. "I don't think Fatima can read his writing."

"I'll catch him up on his correspondence as soon as I get back. We haven't been gone all that long. Joe and I had beignets and cafe au lait every day we were there, and I brought you some mix so you can make some for you and Doug. Do you know alligator meat sells in the French Market for eight dollars and ninety-five cents a pound? Good thing I didn't want any."

"Ugh! Me either. I'll tell Doug. It'll make the leftovers I'm going to feed him tonight look a lot better." She laughed.

"I'll talk to you soon. Joe wants to call and tell Alan we made it back safe and sound and, what's more to the point, he's ready to go back to work."

"Fine. We'll have lunch in a couple of days. Bye!"

Joe finished his own calls and came into the kitchen where Maggie was microwaving snacks for them. "Anything new on either one of his cases?"

"As a matter of fact, there is. He's closing the one on Mr. Wartz tomorrow."

"He is? Coffee's ready. Sit down and tell me about it. If you can."

"There isn't going to be much in the local file. I know I told you the FBI had contacted Alan about it. They were watching the man who killed Wartz, but hadn't arrested him yet. Then Alan asked for help on our local case and sent in those prints we hadn't been able to find a match on."

"You mean the ones from that glass you took from the *Herald*?"

"Yes. To make a long story short, the prints confirmed who he is and that Josef Kranz killed Wartz."

"His friend killed him?"

"He wasn't his friend. He's not even Josef Kranz. That's an alias."

"Who—who—"

"I don't think they told Alan his real name. So much of that is classified, and the FBI is not the only agency that was working on it. But they gave him enough on things to close his local file. He said he'd fill me in on it when I get to work tomorrow."

Maggie didn't comment. She could still see the cruel features of Josef Kranz and the way he looked when she and Floyd took the papers to him.

"They still haven't located Mickey Lewis or Raid Wilson. Alan had located Mickey Lewis, but he left the place he was working and they don't know where he went."

But they will, they will find them, Maggie hoped, trying not to worry or feel depressed.

Monday morning Maggie entered the office with a wave for Floyd and stopped to hug Fatima. She had a sack full of souvenir boxes of beignet mix with her and set it down to talk.

"Joe and I had some French doughnuts in New Orleans—"

"You went to New Orleans?"

"Oh, that's right, you didn't know. I didn't know where we were going either till we got on the freeway. Joe surprised me. But, these little puffy doughnuts were so good, I brought you and Aunt Myrtle a box of their mix so you can have some too. And I brought a box for Grace."

"Grace?"

Maggie turned at the sound of Hank's voice.

"He's been standing there listening," Fatima told on him.

"I'm sorry, Hank. You need me?"

"He sure does!"

Hank shot a squinted-up frown at Fatima. "My trash can's not on fire or anything, but come back in a few minutes." He turned and left.

Floyd joined them. "I've been listening, too. I'm not going to ask if you enjoyed New Orleans since, being normal, you should have, but how's the price of alligator meat?"

"It's up to eight dollars and ninety-five cents a pound. We didn't have any."

"We don't eat anything that bites back at our house. But Momma will be tickled with the mix."

Maggie got three boxes of beignet mix from the sack and left two of them with Fatima before she went back to Hank's office.

"Sorry it took a little while. I brought some souvenirs," Maggie explained. She set the box on his desk. "We thought Grace might like to try these."

"Beignets." Hank smiled. "She will, thank you." He waved at the papers and folders covering his desk. "There's good news and bad news."

"Give me the bad news first so I can feel like I'm making progress."

"This stack is correspondence ready to type up, and the files have things in them that will be ready soon. The good news is our wedding present from Grace and me will be mailed to you and Joe sometime in the next thirty days."

"Thank you, Hank, but with all the work Grace and Aunt Myrtle did on the wedding and reception, that was a tremendous present. We weren't expecting any more presents."

"They enjoyed it so much, you probably should have charged to let them do it."

"Shame on you, Hank. And by the way, thank you too, for helping Joe and his friend keep an eye on things."

"I'm sure Joe has checked in with Captain Hill. Have they found those two yet, Lewis and Wilson?"

"No. No sign of them. But they'll turn up somewhere, unless they've left the state entirely. Maggie, you're kin to me, and my luck doesn't run that way." Hank looked like he was the one sitting on the chair with the loose spring in it when he mentioned his luck.

"I know, but I've got enough bad luck of my own without blaming it on anybody else. They will catch them, though. Joe said Alan told him they are also watching in case they try to leave the country, so they're working on it."

"Speaking of leaving the country, did Joe's Uncle Chance get home all right?" Hank's good humor was back as he remembered Punjab.

"Yes, he's fine. Joe called him from New Orleans, and they made it home all right."

"I checked with one of the pet shops, and they said you can't get a mongoose here. I'll bet they come in handy where there are lots of snakes." He added two more memos to the correspondence stack. "Carl Peabody called to see if you'd be back today. I think he's got a new name plate for you. Wasn't hard to figure out, since he asked how to spell Driver."

"Dead giveaway," Maggie grinned.

"Lately he's been handier than an octopus in work gloves. He's taking training on his new job already and helping with circulation until he goes to work. Josef Kranz disappeared on us again."

"I wouldn't depend on him ever showing up again." Maggie's dislike showed.

"I remember you saying he looked like the Gestapo to you." Hank laughed.

And I was right, Maggie thought without sharing as much. "If you have anything else," Maggie picked up the correspondence without any further comment on Josef Kranz, "let me know or give it to me when I bring this back."

Alan gestured Joe to a chair. "How was New Orleans?"

"Fantastic as ever. We nearly drowned ourselves in cafe au lait. It was good to know nobody would be throwing anything in our windows, too. Heard anything from Mickey Lewis or Raymond Wilson?"

"Not a peep. But they'll surface. We'll find them. Here's the little the agency let go of so we could close the Wartz case." He handed Joe a folder.

Joe read quickly. "He was at the war crime trials?"

Alan nodded. "He was at the concentration camp where Wartz's wife died. He also helped Dr. Mengele get some of his victims, but they haven't got the proof on that."

"Sweet Jesus!" Horror at what he read showed on Joe's face. "Is the rest of this stuff official?"

"Yes, he was convicted of war crimes. It's still not certain how he managed to get away. My guess is they've got a good idea and are still working on that. Josef Kranz is not his name, and there are organizations that help find these monsters. They were watching this Josef Kranz when I asked for help on the fingerprints we couldn't identify."

"So, they're sure Josef Kranz is their man?"

"Right. He killed Wartz because he made some kind of a slip, and Wartz knew he was at Auschwitz—and not as a prisoner. Once he found out, he may even have recognized him. Anyway, Kranz not only killed him, he carved that Star of David in his forehead to show his contempt."

Joe bowed his head a few seconds at such pure evil hate.

"He may not live long enough for them to execute him, but they've got him, and the world is rid of him."

"He's a monster. This is unbelievable." Joe got up and laid the file back on Alan's desk.

"Case closed."

Carl Peabody came in that afternoon with a sack in his hand and a grin on his face. "Welcome home, Maggie Driver!"

"Thank you. You're the first one who's called me that. I brought you and Floyd and Hank alligator claw key chains but I forgot them. I'll bring them tomorrow."

"Alligator claw? That's rad! I'll be by to get it before I go to Heaven Scents."

"Hank told me you're in training. How do you like it?"

"I like it and the people there. I might even go to work there when I get my degree."

"That's wonderful. Is this my new name?"

"This is it. Voila!" Carl pulled the name plate out of the sack.

He held it up for her to admire. It had a black background and had her name on it in gold caps.

He removed the old plate for her to keep and put the new one on. "And that's not all." He paused. "But, you may not want this one, and it's okay if you don't—"

"Carl, stop holding out. What is it?"

He pulled out the name to set on the desk, but held it against his chest. "Help from Helena was too long, and you've already got Maggie Driver on the front here, so—"

He turned it around, watching her expression.

"Oh, I love it! Fatima, look!"

Fatima's perfect teeth gleamed in a grin. She gave Carl a thumbs-up.

The colors were the same as the one on the front of the desk, but the one sitting on top was longer. Between two miniature baskets it read: Helena Handbasket.

The next day Carl came by and got his alligator key chain, and Maggie gave the others theirs. That night she and Joe went to dinner with Aunt Myrtle and Doug, taking the last of their souvenirs with them.

Over dinner Aunt Myrtle demanded, "I've got to know. Did your Uncle Chance have any more trouble getting home with his—Punjab, wasn't it?"

"Yes. He's a mongoose and his name's Punjab." Joe grinned. "I've never known of anything Uncle Chance couldn't handle. And if he had any sort of trouble, he didn't admit it when I talked to him. I called him from New Orleans and they were both fine. I was knocked for a loop that he could get here for the wedding."

"I'm glad we got to meet him." Doug winked at Aunt Myrtle. "After it was all over, I was glad he was there in case no one else could round up those snakes."

CHAPTER TWENTY-NINE

Raid's head jerked up; he'd dozed off again. Apprehensively, without moving, he let his eyes examine the area. He relaxed a little; the night security was nowhere in sight.

He'd been run out of the rest parks before. *Where do they think you're going to sleep, with no traffic moving? There she comes. I woke up just in time. I'll go over there like I'm going to get a Coke and get a drink of water.*

A swarthy-skinned woman in a park security service uniform glanced at him as she passed, her attention on a pickup truck that was pulling in.

A larger truck followed the pickup and the drivers got out to talk. The second truck was covered with a tarp. There was only the driver in the larger truck and two in the pickup. Raid watched them as he drank from the paper cup.

They're speaking Spanish. At least, I think that's what it is, he thought as he turned away, keeping a lookout for park security.

Gradually he became aware the men from the two trucks were talking more softly, and once or twice they looked over at him.

If you're looking for something to steal, you may as well forget it. Raid almost smiled at the idea. But there was only one man in the second, larger truck. Maybe he could get a ride with them. Wouldn't hurt to see where they were headed.

All three men turned to face him when Raid started walking

toward them, almost as if they were expecting him to give them some kind of trouble. He knew that feeling well.

Maybe they're here illegally. They were all speaking Spanish. That's not my problem. All I'm interested in is maybe getting a ride.

There was complete silence when he stopped in front of them. Surely one of them speaks English?

"*Buenas noches.*" Raid hoped that was right. "I, I don't speak much Spanish, but I'm looking for a ride." He tried to appear friendly instead of just dog tired. "Trying to get to Mexico. I'll appreciate a ride, if only to the next truck stop."

Nobody spoke at first.

"Where are you headed?" Raid tried again.

The man who got out of the larger truck spoke. "We go to the border with some produce."

"Oh, I've heard about that trade plan. Other truckers take it on and distribute it?" Raid looked up at the tarp-covered load. "Produce from the valley? The Rio Grande Valley?"

"Cantaloupes," one of the others answered.

"Can you drive a truck?" The driver of the big truck looked him over as if thinking he might be too young.

"I sure can. I drove a semi once, but just a short distance. I don't have a truck driving license." He looked closer at the truck. It was not a diesel and it was a Ford. "I could drive this one. Do you need someone to help drive?" He studied the man's face, getting his hopes up.

One of the others shook his head. "We talk about it," the driver of the big truck said. He beckoned the other two, and they retreated to the back of the truck with the tarp.

Sounds like the one who doesn't like me is losing, Raid thought. The security guard was nowhere in sight when the three men came back.

"We take you with us." Short and sweet to Raid's ears. "We

go to *los hombres* and get a drink, then we go."

"Fine. Thanks. I'll get my pack."

Joe saw Alan come in and went to talk to him. "I thought only us peasants worked nights and days too."

"All of us peasants work whenever we're told to and the job demands it."

"Yeah, I figured that out. What brings you out this time?"

"We've had a smattering of petty hold-ups. I just came from the scene of one of them. Perp was a young white man in a ski mask. Just grabbed what he could from the cash register and ran. The camera was useless, even if he hadn't had a ski mask on. Medium height, and the little sprig of hair the cashier saw was dark brown, she thinks."

"Ran. He was on foot?"

"That's what she said. There was no one else in there, but she didn't see him get in a car and didn't hear one."

"Did he have a gun or just tell her he did?"

"He had one, and showed it to her. Can't tell what it was from the description. It looked like a cannon to her."

Joe nodded. "He didn't shoot at her or threaten her?"

"Just laid a candy bar on the counter and when she opened the cash drawer, he showed her the gun and asked for the money. She backed up and let him take it himself. Then he just turned and ran."

"And there's been a few other jobs?"

"Four to date. All convenience stores, at night, deserted, but nobody hurt. The description, such as it is, is the same."

"And he's got a gun." Joe chewed thoughtfully on his lower lip. "You heard anything more on Mickey Lewis?"

"No, nothing. It crossed my mind he might be the one picking up a little change with these robberies if he's afraid to go to work."

"Afraid?"

"He must be afraid to have thrown those Molotov cocktails into the house where he thought Maggie lived."

"I've been trying to convince myself he's given up and left the area." Joe took a deep breath. "He's waiting for her, isn't he?"

"As far as we know, he doesn't know where she lives or where she works. And you've fixed it so that Happy Harris can't help him find her. He'll either move on or do something stupid, and we'll get him."

Joe's worry lines met above his eyes. "I didn't know he had a gun."

Maggie picked up her phone, glancing at her Helena Handbasket sign. "The *Herald*, Maggie Driver."

"Hi, Maggie." Aunt Myrtle sounded excited. "I've found something I want to get you and Joe for a wedding present, but I want you to see it first to see if you like it."

Maggie laughed, "I like it! But, you and Grace are already way ahead on giving. I don't expect any more."

"Remember those pretty dishes of your mother's? The china with the blue flowers?"

"Yes, I remember them. She had the teapot and things, too. Why?"

"I've found a soup tureen that matches the blue perfectly and a covered serving bowl too. But I want you to see it before I buy it, and if you'd rather have something else, we'll look around. Can you go to lunch today?"

"Sure, and looking around is the thing I like best. The soup tureen sounds great, or I'd like the covered serving bowl. Whatever you think. I'll be ready whenever you get here. Just make sure it's after twelve-thirty so Fatima will be back."

★ ★ ★ ★ ★

Maggie fell in love with the covered serving bowl. "If you're going to get the tureen, I'll get the serving bowl. The lid fits both of them. I'm going to get these blue napkin rings, too."

"I'll get them all." Aunt Myrtle put her hand over Maggie's purse to keep her from getting to her billfold. "Those dishes will be beautiful in the hutch that came with your house. I can just picture it."

"But the dishes are yours."

"No, they're not. Your mother told me a long time ago to take care of those dishes for you if she wasn't around to do it. I was going to give them to you as soon as you and Horace got a place and a china cabinet to put them in."

"No, I wouldn't feel right taking them. She was your sister as well as my mother. I want you to have them."

"I promised her, and you're going to have them. End of discussion." Aunt Myrtle picked up the tureen. "Bring the serving dish and napkin rings."

Maggie saw Joe's car in the garage when she turned in the driveway. He met her at the back door.

"Hi." She stood in his arms and hugged him back. "Hope you had a good day. You've seemed to have cases follow you home the last few days. Is there one that's really bugging you?"

"Just the usual good guy–bad guy daily struggle. And you got this in the mail." He smiled and kissed her again.

"What is it? More junk mail? I may already be a winner? Heck, I am already a winner. Why didn't you open it?"

"It's addressed to you."

"You are hereby granted permission to open any of our mail regardless of which one of us it's addressed to, and I will do the same unless told not to. Or Marlene mails that shirt back." She giggled.

"We'll take it one day at a time. But you can open the shirt if you want to, or it can go directly to the can out back." Joe pronounced the rule carefully, as if pointing out this was more important than the dratted shirt subject deserved.

Maggie looked up from the pages in her hand. "Joe, I think you better look at this."

What Maggie held in her hand was a statement from the investment company Grace had recommended. The pages showed investments and an amount in money market funds.

"Looks like investments," Joe said, taking it to look closer.

"It's Hank and Grace's wedding present. He told me they were mailing it. This is the investment company she recommended when I told her about the IRA."

"What IRA?"

Maggie told him about the closing money she had invested instead of spending it on the shower. "I told Grace about it. I forget why she asked. Anyway, she suggested a fund like this. A financial safety net, she called it. We can put money in it and in the IRA too. The IRA is a long-term thing, but this one we can use the interest for emergencies." She grinned in anticipation. "Or if we don't have any of those, we could go back to New Orleans for a couple of days."

"I married a wealthy woman!" Joe exclaimed, pulling her to him with his free hand. "Maggie, this is for twenty-one thousand dollars! Twenty in investments and one in money market funds."

"I've already sent thank-you notes to Hank and Grace and Aunt Myrtle and Doug too, but this calls for hugs and kisses, wouldn't you think?"

"I'd think," Joe agreed, and promptly hugged her and kissed her, laughing with her.

"Oh, and Joe?"

"There's not more? There couldn't be more."

"My mother's dishes. Her pretty china. Aunt Myrtle saved it

for me. She hasn't even used it. I tried to get her to keep it, but she insists I have it and says it will be pretty in our china cabinet." Tears started, and one rolled down her cheek.

Joe led her to the sofa and cradled her in his arms. "Everything has moved so fast, hasn't it? Then sometimes, it just hits you right between the eyes how damned lucky you are. I love you, Maggie."

"I love you, too. And am I imagining you've had something on your mind the last few days?"

"Yes, I have." He kissed the hand he was holding. "I think you deserve to know, and I have to remind myself to let you do your own thinking. That was a pretty smart move to start that IRA instead of blowing the money or spending it on the shower. I worried about that debt before I knew you had a brain under all that cuteness."

"Flattery will get you everywhere." Maggie snuggled closer. "But what is it that's bothering you?"

"That no-good friend of Happy's who's leaning on him to find out where you are. He's more than likely still around. I know he's the one who pushed that crate in the alley, even if they didn't find anything but his hat. And he's the one who threw the Molotov cocktails into the house where you used to live."

"Happy hasn't called lately. Maybe those two have left town or something."

Joe shook his head. "I don't think so. He and that other one, Raymond Lewis, must have been up to something that Horace turned down the night they met, and it must have been serious for him to try and shut up anyone who knew about it."

"But I don't know anything about it, whatever it was."

"Mickey Lewis and Raymond Wilson don't know that. They may think Happy told you something that can incriminate them some way. That crate and the drive-by bombing were serious things."

"There's more, isn't there?" She studied his face.

"Yes. I ran into Alan Hill a couple of nights ago, and they've had a rash of petty hold-ups. Most of them convenience stores. There is no description good enough to identify anybody, but the general description could be this Mickey Lewis or Raymond Wilson. We don't know what either one of them looks like except the general descriptions Happy gave us and an old picture Alan dug up on Michael's record sheet."

"You really think they might be still around?"

"Yes, I do. Be very careful, Maggie. They don't know where you live or work, but I wouldn't stray very far from work for lunch, and never go far without letting me know."

Maggie frowned, knowing he was right, but still hating it.

"Alan says it won't be long until this Michael, if that's who's been doing these petty hold-ups, gives up and moves on. Or does something really dumb, and we'll nab him. Alan's right. We've just got to watch out till we do get him."

"I know you're right. I'll be careful." She brightened. "But don't let us be too depressed to enjoy the good stuff. Next time you have to work at night, come by and take me to lunch. You haven't seen my Helena Handbasket desk plate."

CHAPTER THIRTY

Happy struck his foot on a chair leg and crammed his fist in his mouth to keep from yelling.

Could have broken it, the way my toe feels. He hobbled fast and grabbed the ringing phone in the dark den.

"Hello?" he whispered into the phone, knowing who it must be.

"Where in the name of holy hell have you been the past week or so? I called three times and hung up. Then I let it ring one night and some woman blessed me out like I was trying to sell magazines!"

"That must have been my mother."

"Your mother? Leave home, kid."

"She told us about it the next morning. She thinks it was students out of school and playing with the phone."

"That's good. At least she's not nagging you about who it was."

"You managed to find a job anywhere?"

"No. I think what I'll do is go somewhere else. No use taking a chance on Horse's wife putting two and two together. You sure you didn't tell her anything?"

"There was nothing to tell. What are you talking about?"

"Don't hand me that dumb-innocent crap. I know Raid called you when he was trying to find some money to leave on. What did he tell you?"

"He told me he needed money."

"Smart ass! I mean about the job Horse turned down."

"What job?"

"Oh, you're cool. Well, whatever. What I'm calling for is now that I've decided to leave, I need money too. How much can you let me have? And it has to be in cash—no checks or anything. And I need it now."

"Mickey, I don't have any money. I didn't have any when Raid called, and I still don't have any. Do you know for sure if he left?"

"Must have. I haven't heard anything from him and I can't find him. The little jerk. Forget him. What about the money?"

"I don't have any."

"You've got a job." Mickey didn't buy the excuse.

"My mother takes my money and puts it in my college fund and gives me a little for lunch and things."

"That's a lot of bull."

"It's the truth."

"When do you get paid?"

"Couple of days ago."

"How much you got on you?"

"I think about thirty-five dollars."

"You're kidding."

"No. She gave me forty, and I went out for barbecue. That's it."

"Okay, okay. Roll your bike out where they won't hear you leave and bring it to me."

"You mean now? I can't do that."

"The hell you can't! Or would you rather I called Horace's wife and got the money from her?"

He heard the rapid intake of Happy's breath.

"You thought you were so smart, not giving me her phone number. But I remembered Horse hadn't had a phone long. I called information and got the number from the phone company. So I'll just call on her."

"No! No! I—I'll bring you the money. Where do you want me to meet you?"

Dusk closed in on the rest park as Raid went with the driver to the big truck. "My name's Raymond. My friends call me Raid," he told him.

"Me llama José." José opened the door on the driver's side. "Get in and see if you can drive this truck, *si?*" He encouraged Raid as he got settled behind the wheel. "Is easy, *no es verdad?*"

"All right." Nodding, nervous, but feeling like he could handle it, Raid got in and took the wheel.

Great, it's an automatic transmission. All I've got to do is remember how long and big this thing is.

José got settled in the passenger seat. The keys were in the ignition. Raid started it and slowly pulled out of the parking place.

"Let the others go ahead," José told him.

"All right." Raid waited, then pulled out and followed the pickup truck. "You going all the way to the border was lucky for me." He smiled at José, feeling better.

"Is maybe lucky for me, too. Maybe not so many trooper cars stop us with a gringo driving." José's grin showed a gold tooth next to a gap where one was missing.

For some reason, his smile made Raid uneasy. He concentrated on keeping the pickup truck's lights in sight ahead of him.

Mickey gave directions to Happy about where to meet him. Happy asked him to repeat part of them. "Okay, I've got it. I'll be there."

As if it made any difference, punk. You'll get as far as you need to.

Mickey left the pay phone and crossed the lot of the all-night mall. He lost no time hot-wiring the car he had picked out before he called Happy. It was a dark green SUV and heavy enough to do the job. He pulled out and drove a few miles under the speed limit to the place he was going to intercept Happy.

Having been close to the place he had chosen when he called, Mickey parked and waited. The SUV was in position to get a fast start for what he had to do.

It wasn't long till he heard Happy's motorcycle coming. Mick gave the heavy car some gas and headed toward the overpass he had checked out earlier in the week.

Happy didn't notice the SUV with its lights off. He was concentrating on his own lane and on keeping Mickey away from Maggie when he heard the roar of the engine over his own. He didn't even have time to cry out before the big car hit him broadside and knocked him and his motorcycle over the bridge to the rocky waste below it.

Mickey got out to look over at Happy's body sprawled beside the motorcycle, then jerked his attention back to the street. The lights of an oncoming car lit the area. Mick hurried back to the SUV and left.

He parked the car in the slot he'd stolen it from and got out. He felt proud of himself as he pulled off the cheap gardening gloves and tossed them into the car floor before he closed the door and walked away.

Raid's gone, Happy's out of the picture. Two down, one to go . . . Miss Maggie . . .

Raid was proud of the way he took to driving the truck. He even enjoyed it enough to give some thought to trying to get a job driving a truck in Mexico when he got there.

They stopped often to relieve themselves, rest and get water for the water bottles they carried with them. Raid and José swapped up driving and didn't talk very much due to Raid not understanding much Spanish and José not being too good with English, plus the noise the truck made.

Once they had pulled over and José motioned for him to move over and drive. The cars Raid had noticed in the distance turned out to be border patrol cars. They passed without incident, and Raid kept his eyes straight ahead.

It dawned slowly on Raid, but it did dawn on him, that every place there might be much traffic or a border patrol car around, José had him drive. *I hope all they've got back there is cantaloupes. I don't need more trouble than I've already got.*

As they began seeing highway signs giving the mileage to El Paso, José pointed and smiled at Raid.

He smiled back. *Must be going to cross into Juarez there*, he thought. His insides began to knot up at the thought, hoping there would be no trouble. The traffic being much heavier didn't help.

The phone woke Joe up. By the time he got to it, there was no one there, but he played the message that had been left.

"Joe, this is Alan. I'm sorry to wake you up with bad news, but there's been a wreck I know you would want to hear about. A bad one. The victim is Happy Harris. He's in critical condition, but he's alive. I'm headed down to the hospital now. I called in case you and Maggie want to come see how he's doing. It looks bad, Joe."

"Oh, Happy's been hurt? And he said it looks bad. I wonder what happened." Maggie had come to his side and heard the message.

"We'll find out when we get there. If you want to go."

"Yes, I do. I'll microwave us a cup of instant to drink while we get dressed."

Alan had called Happy a victim. I hope that doesn't mean

261

someone tried to kill him. Joe didn't share his thoughts with Maggie.

At the hospital, they learned Happy Harris was in surgery and not much else. They found Alan pacing the hallway outside the waiting room. He went to them, glancing at the people hurrying by, and gestured toward the waiting room.

"Those people in there, the man and woman, are Happy's parents. I don't want to upset them any more than they are. Right now the only thing on their minds is hoping Happy will live."

"You said it was bad?"

"Broken legs, both of them. Broken left arm. Head injury, spleen damaged, internal bleeding. He did have his helmet on. I don't think the head injury is too bad. It's the internal injuries."

Joe held Maggie's hand. "Did they say anything about what his chances are?"

"They won't be sure till they can find out about the internal injuries and bleeding, but they're hopeful. Fifty-fifty chance hopeful."

"What happened? You said he had his helmet on. Was he on his motorcycle?"

"Yes. I talked to some of the nurses in emergency. They're at a loss to know why he was out at that hour or where he was going."

"When did it happen and where?"

"According to the location on the report, it wasn't far from their house, at an overpass. Around one or two in the morning."

"One or two in the morning? Must have been Mickey or Raid called him to meet them somewhere for him to be out at that time."

"That's what I think, too. But he never got there, wherever it was. As he went up the overpass a car hit him and knocked him and his motorcycle over the railing, and he fell about twenty feet down. One of his legs was pinned under the motorcycle."

"At that hour, I suppose there weren't any witnesses? How do you know it was one or two in the morning?"

"We did have some luck. There was a witness."

Maggie and Joe's hands tightened on each other.

"The witness was coming from that all-night drugstore at the mall and saw a big, dark car hit the motorcycle. He couldn't see all that well, but there was only one light on the vehicle coming over the overpass, and he thought it was a motorcycle. The car, he thinks, was a dark-colored SUV. A man got out and looked over the bridge, then got back in the car and left."

"Did he see the man well enough to identify him?"

"No, just general things. Average weight and build, about five ten, he thinks. The lucky thing is he called an ambulance and they got to Happy soon enough to get him here and give him a chance."

Maggie clung to Joe's arm, feeling guilty about the times Happy had called her.

"I haven't spoken to Mr. and Mrs. Harris yet. I'll talk to them after you do. Go on in, and I'll be in there in a few minutes."

Maggie led the way, going to Mrs. Harris. "I'm Maggie Murphy Driver, Mrs. Harris. Horace Murphy was my husband."

Mrs. Harris took her outstretched hand, looking as miserable as she felt.

"I'm so sorry to meet you at a time like this. I met Happy after Horace's accident. He's such a nice boy. I—we came when we heard about what happened. I'm married again now, and my husband came with me to see if there is anything we can do to help."

"Thank you," Mr. Harris answered for both of them. "I don't know of anything to do but pray he will be all right. He's in surgery now."

"I know." Maggie nodded. "We asked at the nurse's station out there."

"He was on his motorcycle," Joe said. "But he was wearing his helmet?"

"Yes," Mrs. Harris said tearfully. "I always reminded him, and he was good about it. I don't know why he was out on the streets so late."

"That's what I was going to ask," Joe said as Alan came in. "This is Captain Alan Hill. He's looking into what happened."

Alan shook hands with Mr. Harris. "I'd like to ask you some things. It can wait if you would rather come down to my office tomorrow."

"No, no. It's all right. What is it you want to know? We don't know much about it ourselves," Mr. Harris told him.

"The first thing that comes to mind is why he was out at such a late hour, as Joe was asking. Did you say you didn't know he was out on his motorcycle?"

Mrs. Harris nodded. "That's right. I didn't hear him start it. And I don't know where he was going."

"Did he get a phone call? Someone call him to come and meet them somewhere?"

After a slight hesitation, Mrs. Harris shook her head. "No, I don't think so. At least, I didn't hear the phone ring if someone called."

"Where is the phone? Is it where you would normally hear it in your bedroom?"

"It's in the den, and there's an extension in our bedroom, but the one in the bedroom doesn't ring. I guess it's possible it could ring and I wouldn't hear it."

"You hesitated when I asked you about the possibility of someone calling. Is there someone you think might have called at such a late hour?"

"Happy had been very sick with some kind of a flu-like virus, and I don't know whether it was because I was listening for him to call me or I was just wakeful, but someone did call at midnight or after a couple of times while he was sick."

"Who was it?"

"I don't know. They called three times. The first two times were a couple of days apart and whoever it was, they just hung up. I thought it was someone who called a wrong number. But then they called again and I thought it must be teenage pranksters just playing with the phone. I was worried about Happy and hadn't had much sleep and I fussed at them for having nothing better to do. They didn't call again, that I know of."

"Did anyone say anything?"

"That third time, someone said, 'Who is this?' and I thought what an inconsiderate idiot to call someone's number and wake them up, not even sure they had the right number. I wasn't very nice," she confessed to Alan.

Alan was sympathetic. "I can't say I blame you, after two other calls. Did you recognize his voice?"

"No. It was a young man. I didn't recognize his voice and he didn't call back."

Alan glanced down at the notes he had taken. "You said you didn't hear the motorcycle when he left?"

"No, I didn't. I thought that was odd, too. But then, my husband and I are usually sound sleepers."

"Thank you. May I have your phone number in case I want to ask you something else?"

"Of course." Mr. Harris gave him the number.

Alan handed him one of his cards. "This is my office number. If I'm not in, leave your name and number and I'll get back to you as soon as I can. Thank you."

Joe strolled out with him. Maggie stayed to talk to the Harrises. "I'm the one who gave Happy Horace's motorcycle. I'm so sorry this happened."

Mrs. Harris smiled at Maggie. "No, don't you blame yourself. He had the motorcycle all fixed, and it was sweet and generous of you to give it to him. There was nothing wrong with the motorcycle. I'm sure it was just as they told us. A car hit him. Probably didn't see him, is what caused this accident. They don't know who did this, but it certainly isn't your fault, dear."

Out in the hall, Joe glanced back at the Harrises and asked, "You thinking what I am? That Happy pushed that motorcycle out on the street to start it and not wake up his parents?"

"I'd bet on it, given the hour and him not telling them or leaving a note. He's a pretty good kid, it sounds like to me. He wouldn't have just taken off in the middle of the night without a good reason."

"And one he didn't want his folks to know about. Who does that bring to mind?"

"Yeah, narrows it down. Jack Gardner is working and runs the other way when any of Horace's friends or a uniform comes in sight, so I don't think he's the one who called Happy. We've heard nothing from Raymond Wilson, and Mickey Lewis walked off his job. But I'd bet a bundle, whether we can prove it or not, we have heard from Mickey. That he's the one who's doing all these petty hold-ups around town."

"And he's the kind of dirty bird who would threaten Happy and not care about waking Mr. and Mrs. Harris up in the middle of the night."

Alan's cell phone rang.

"Alan Hill." He listened, his eyes finding Joe's.

Something's up—connected, maybe? Joe listened to Alan's side of the conversation.

"Yes. I do. Take it to the impound lot whether he objects or not. It's probably evidence. Do what you can to calm him down, but take it. Now."

"What? Impound what?"

"A man reported damage to his car. It was parked in the parking area of the all-night mall near where Happy had his wreck. It's got Sunshine Yellow paint on it, like Happy's motorcycle. They're taking it in."

CHAPTER THIRTY-ONE

Raid waited in line at the Mexican–U.S. border checkpoint, glancing uneasily around. He pulled the truck up on the weight scales as the uniformed guard directed him to do. He drove very carefully, feeling a little superior, along with being nervous because José was depending on him. He was wary, moving slowly. He tried to do everything he was directed to do.

The officer walked over and stopped beside Raid's window. "Get out and bring in your papers."

"It's not my truck," Raid explained. "I'm swapping driving for a ride down here. It's his truck." He gestured at José.

José took that cue to paste a broad, friendly smile on his face and nod several times. "No have too much Englais, but bring papers."

The officer nodded and beckoned to him. José got out and followed him.

Raid stood a little distance from the truck, wondering what was going to happen next. He looked across the border with hungry eyes, his heart beating fast.

That's Mexico! I can see it! I'm going to make it!

Two other officers passed by him on their way to the truck, one of them holding the leash of a large dog. They opened the cab doors and threw back the tarp at the back of the truck. The dog took his time sniffing and examining as they went.

Raid was hoping there was nothing under that tarp but cantaloupes, and was relieved to see the dog hadn't found anything when one of the officers came from the other side of the truck and beckoned to him.

"Yes, sir, what is it?" Raid was the soul of cooperation.

"You have any kind of fender bender or back into anything?" Raid looked confused. "Anything that would have damaged some of your cargo?"

"Not after I got a ride with them and started driving."

"Look at this." The officer touched wetness oozing out of the cargo and sniffed his fingers. "Doesn't smell like it's spoiled or anything."

"I don't know," Raid scratched his head.

"I'm going to take a look. You go back where you were and wait."

"Yes, sir." *That's all we need. How should I know about any damage to the cantaloupes?* He frowned. *The guy with the dog is going around there, too.*

The border guards came back, one of them carrying a cantaloupe in his hand, the other restraining the dog. His partner took José's arm and led him into the building. Neither of them spoke, but neither looked happy or friendly.

Inside, Raid took the chair he was gestured to. The man with the dog waited with him. *Am I in some kind of trouble?* Raid's hands were clenched into cold fists in his pockets to keep them from shaking.

The other officer took the cantaloupe into some kind of an office and closed the door.

There was no sign of José. Raid's eyes searched the area in vain. The mere closeness of the officer and the dog were as scary as the silence around Raid. *The dog looks like it's sitting at attention, too.* Raid bit his lip to stifle a laugh that would surely have turned into hysterics.

After a few minutes, the officer came out and beckoned to him. When Raid went into the office, the officer closed the office door after him and stood waiting beside it. Raid's eyes had gone immediately to the cantaloupe on the desk. He gasped.

"Oh, this is a big surprise to you, is it?" The man behind the desk looked like suspicion with skin on it. "Didn't know a thing about this?"

"No. No, sir. I didn't." He stared at the cantaloupe in horror. It had been cut neatly in two, hollowed out to within a half inch of the rind and a plastic sack of marijuana, seeds and all, had been packed into it. He tore his gaze away from it and faced the man behind the desk.

"I hitched a ride on the truck and was swapping driving for a ride here. I asked José what he was carrying, and he said cantaloupes. We even ate one of them on one of our stops. I didn't know there was anything on the truck except this load of cantaloupes."

The man pointed at Raid and then the door. The officer took Raid's arm and escorted him to a small room down a hall. José was in there, too. There were bars on the one window. Raid's heart sank as his knees buckled and he sat down on one of the two narrow bunks.

José saw the look on his face. "It will be all right. I told them you didn't know about the marijuana. That I give you a ride to help me drive. They let you go, I think." José nodded his head several times, trying to cheer him up.

"Thank goodness! I'm glad you told them. What's going to happen to you?"

José shrugged. "I work for people who will take care of me. They have lawyers. Deals can be made." He grinned, not looking worried at all. "If they let you out, I give you another lift sometime, *si?*"

Raid couldn't help but smile back at him. José was a friendly traveling companion and he'd tried to help him. "Well, I'm not out yet. But thanks for telling them I was just hitchhiking. And," he added, "good luck. You get a job driving with someone else, you'll do all right."

"*Gracias.*" José shrugged. "Maybe I retire."

Joe knocked on Alan's door. "Got a minute?"

"Long as it's just one. Don't have a seat."

"You've probably set southern hospitality back a hundred years. I just wanted to tell you I'm going by to talk to Millie and Pauline. I'll tell them the government agencies have Joséf Kranz, that he's the one who killed Mr. Wartz, and our local case is closed."

"Okay. It's not as if we had anything else we could tell them. Didn't you say Millie told you Wartz was at Auschwitz, and that his wife died there?"

Joe nodded. "Yes, he was a little older than Millie, but not much."

"I think she was there too. I didn't ask too much about it." Joe nodded. "Yeah, I think they should know." His eyes went to the phone. "Who have you got on hold there?" Joe eyed the blinking light.

"Checking on the invisible Michael Lewis. I've given copies of the picture that was in his personnel file at the electronics store to everybody I can think of to keep an eye out for him."

"Good. Good luck"

"If he's still in the area, we'll get him."

At the moment, Mickey Lewis was counting his money. It didn't take long. He cursed.

If that damned car hadn't come along, I'd have gone down and got the money Happy was bringing me. Tomorrow, I'll look for a place that looks like there will be some money in the cash drawer. May have to do two. If I get enough, I may just leave town. There's nothing anyone can prove against me. I may just go. But first, I've got to have some money . . .

He looked over several small shops, service stations and convenience stores in the neighborhood; then an armored truck caught his attention. He watched it pull up to fill up an ATM machine.

He stood in front of a store window with his back turned, watching the reflection from several yards down the street. *Hey, looks like I got lucky! Why didn't I think of this before?* It looked like the pot of gold at the end of the rainbow to him.

That's been here all the time! These things are all over the place, and I've been fooling with nickel and dime cash drawers!

Mickey looked at his watch, noted the name of the bank on the sign and looked for a likely, or at least available, car. He jumped into one that had been left running and burned rubber getting away, not looking back.

Mickey's heartbeat slowed down a couple of blocks away. He took care to drive the speed limit and went to where he'd seen another branch of the bank. He parked within sight of the ATM beside it, checked out the locations of the other ATMs listed in a nearby phone booth and wrote down the locations. Then he waited.

He watched as the ATM was serviced, then went to a nearby store and bought a can of pepper spray. The armored truck passed by as Mickey came out of the store, grinning in anticipation. He took a shortcut and parked to wait for it at the next location, hoping he'd guessed right. This one was in a less traveled place.

When he saw the truck coming, he strolled over to the ATM.

The uniformed man sat in the truck and waited until Mickey turned away from the machine.

I'm glad he can't see this is an out of date Visa card. Mickey smiled at the approaching man, his hand tightening on the can in his pocket.

The operation was another one of Mickey's ideas that just didn't work. When he aimed the spray at his quarry, the man's partner and backup was on Mickey before he knew what was happening, and pinned his arm behind his back.

"What do you think you're doing?" he demanded, outraged.

"I think I'm preventing a holdup," the uniformed man answered sarcastically.

His partner picked up the can Mickey had dropped and informed him, "If you're due an apology you'll get one." His eyes were hard, without mercy. "You'll get exactly what you deserve, punk."

Raid's harsh breathing slowed down and he relaxed enough to breathe comfortably, listening to what the man behind the desk was telling him. Since José had admitted that he didn't know about the load of marijuana added to the cantaloupes, it seemed there would be no charges against him.

He took a big breath to say thanks but before he could get the words out, a guard stuck his head in the door. He turned his head to regard Raid, then looked back at the man behind the desk.

"Warrant." That was all he said.

The man behind the desk gestured at Raid. The officer beckoned to Raid and escorted him back to the little room he'd just come from.

José was gone and the little window was set too high to look through. *Welcome again to the Cross Bar Hotel,* he told himself.

He sat down on one of the hard, narrow bunks that seemed designed for the maximum in discomfort and tried to remember if he had a speeding ticket he hadn't paid.

As soon as Maggie got in and got settled at her desk, she called Grace.

"What a nice surprise. How are you, Maggie? I was just thinking about you. Hank told me about them finding out who killed Mr. Wartz. He said they didn't know much except that it was the man we knew as Josef Kranz."

"That's right. It's more complicated than we thought it was. That's not his real name, of course, and they didn't tell us what it was. The man we thought was Josef Kranz was some kind of war criminal, and government agencies were looking for him. He was evidently afraid Mr. Wartz could identify him, is what the motive for the crime was. But they've got him now. He will be prosecuted for the crimes he was already convicted of, and he's not going to hurt anyone else."

"How awful! And he was supposed to be a friend of Mr. Wartz."

"I only saw him once. It was when I went with Floyd to take some papers to him. But he—I don't know how to describe it—"

"You mean he looked mean?" Grace supplied.

"Yes, but I don't think mean was bad enough. He looked downright evil. I remember saying to Hank he looked like the actors in old war movies who play the Gestapo parts. But since he was supposed to be Jewish, Hank said that couldn't be."

Grace laughed. "It's always easier to fool men than women," she said. "I knew he was not dependable when he didn't show up at the meeting I invited him to. Would you like to have lunch? We can gossip and discuss the weaker-minded sex." Her smile was audible.

"That's what I called you for. I mean, not to discuss the weaker-minded sex," she said with a giggle. "I want to take you to lunch and thank you properly for your and Hank's wedding gift. I've sent a card to you both from Joe and me, but I wanted to say thanks in person, too. I'll go in and thank Hank too, before I come to meet you. Where would you like to eat?"

"You'll probably have to remind Hank. He's famous for only seeing what's right in front of him to work on. And we can eat at the cafeteria near you or the little seafood place, if you know where it is."

"I do, and I like seafood. I'll meet you there as close to twelve-thirty as I can get there. Fatima goes to lunch from eleven-thirty to twelve-thirty."

Maggie went back to Hank's office and knocked. He looked up.

"Before you say certainly not, I'm not here asking for anything. I want to say thanks for what I've already got."

"That's nice. What? Job, house, great working conditions, chance to work with such intelligent, interesting people? All of the above?"

Maggie laughed. "All of the above, and with feeling! What I meant right now is, thanks for my and Joe's wedding present. We were just overwhelmed! After all of the above, that investment folder was really something. We both thank you from the bottoms of our hearts. And speaking of the house, I loved it from the first time you showed it to me. I just didn't see how I could get it. Sorry to be such a hard sell." She paused. "Hank, you sure you want to give us so much? That twenty-one thousand dollars was an awful lot of money. I wouldn't blame you if you want to reconsider. After all, Grace and Aunt Myrtle did all that arranging for our wedding."

"Reconsider? I'm famous for not even considering the first time around. And Grace handles most of our accounts. Does very well, too. So if Grace isn't worried, I'm not worried." He started to go back to work. "Oh, and you're welcome."

As Maggie turned to go, he snickered. "Hell, Maggie, the wedding reception entertainment alone was worth the price of admission." He laughed. "Have you heard if Joe's uncle got back to Australia all right with his—uh, ferret?"

Maggie's grin was as wide as his. "His—ah, ferret, is doing fine, and they're safe at home. Joe called him from New Orleans. Oh, and I'm going to lunch with Grace today and thank her too. And yes, I'll wait till Fatima gets back so there will be a warm body to answer the phone. I'm not so shaken up and addled I can't remember the rules."

"Good girl."

CHAPTER THIRTY-TWO

Alan's call was patched through to Joe while he was still on duty. "When you get in, stop by my office before you leave."

"Good news or bad?"

"Good."

"I'll do it. See you then."

Joe lost no time in getting loose and headed for Alan's office. The door was open.

"Come in. You don't need to close it."

Joe went to sit in the chair nearest the desk. "I hope you're going to tell me Mickey Lewis hanged himself." His mouth was grim.

"No, but the idiot made it a lot easier for us to do it."

"You got him? Who found him and where?" Joe pictured him lurking around his and Maggie's house somewhere.

"Nobody apprehended him from the picture. They just recognized him when he was brought in."

"Brought in. Another holdup?"

"Yes, but he's got a lot cuter since the last one. He tried to hold up an armored car."

"I knew he was nuts!" Joe spat out the words. "What happened?"

"He'd evidently watched the cars when they filled up the ATMs, and he decided he'd rob somebody with a lot more money rather than those penny-ante stores he's been living on. He got himself a can of pepper spray and went into the robbing armored cars business."

Joe rolled his eyes. "A can of pepper spray against an armored car?"

"Yeah, the lad's got confidence. No doubt about that. Must store it where a brain's supposed to be. It evidently didn't occur to him that the driver wouldn't be alone. When he started his little dance, the backup man grabbed him, cuffed him and brought him to us. He's now a guest of the city. But you know how he is." Alan's face contorted with disgust. "He doesn't appreciate it a bit. He's yelling about his rights and griping about the facilities."

"Shame. Can I have five minutes alone with him?"

"Heck, no! You'll have to get in line. He's so dumb, he doesn't even know how bad off he is."

"He doesn't know about the yellow paint from Happy's motorcycle on the car he stole?"

Alan shook his head.

"He doesn't know Happy is still alive?"

"You got it."

"Did they get enough DNA from the sweat on that cap of his to match up?"

"Yes."

"This is going to be fun. We could sell tickets."

"Remember the cheap gardening gloves he left in the stolen car? We're going to tell him or his lawyer—he's yelling for one—"

"It figures." Joe hissed through his teeth.

"We'll tell them about the DNA from his hat and that we got enough fingerprints from the glass he used in the Molotov cocktails to identify him, and that we took the gloves apart to get fingerprints, so it's all over for him."

"You were able to get fingerprints from those gloves?" Joe raised his eyebrows.

"You're not listening. I said we'd tell him we took them apart to get fingerprints."

"The good guys can't tell outright lies like the bad guys." Joe snorted.

"No, but we can have implications out the wazoo, and there's enough else that it will do the job."

"But right now, the idiot thinks he's home free because the armored car holdup didn't come off and he's got a good chance to walk."

"Right."

"I'd like to see the look on his sorry face when he realizes all you've got on him. I don't even remember too well what he looks like."

"Here, be my guest." Alan handed him a folder.

The picture showed a young man staring at the camera as if he didn't want to be bothered. Medium described his height, weight, brown hair and flattered his intelligence. The bored eyes and aggravated expression summed up his self-important opinion of himself.

"Yeah, that brings it back. You'd have to be pretty dumb to think you're as smart as he does. But you've got him locked up. He can't get out by hollering for a lawyer, can he?"

"We've got him for the next twenty-four hours. Then we'll have to see if he qualifies for an attorney at the taxpayers' expense. It's all going to take a while. I know you won't stop looking over your shoulder until he's put away, but the way he's been running, I don't think he's going to get bail."

"That's good. With all we've got, he's going to be put away for a long time. I'll tell Maggie as soon as I get home."

Maggie was as pleased as Joe pictured her when he told her the news.

"Joe, you were right about everything," Maggie admitted humbly. "I just couldn't believe anybody could do the things he did. And without any real reason! He's got to be unbalanced. If he was half as good as the others said he was at working with computers, he could have done a lot better working than trying to steal."

"If he doesn't know that now, he will soon. Do I smell something in the crockpot?"

"One of your favorites. Chicken, and I put some vegetables in. It's ready is why it smells good. After we eat, I'd like to go to the hospital to see Happy. He's in a room now."

"All right, we'll go. Does he know what happened to him yet? Is he talking?"

"I don't know. I called the hospital to ask about him, and all they would say was he had been put in a room. I didn't ring the number, not knowing whether his mother and father are there or not."

Joe nodded his approval. "He must be better with his chances looking pretty good for them to have put him in a room. I'm sure his parents will be there tonight."

"If he's able to talk, are you going to tell him about Mickey Lewis trying to hold up the armored car and being in custody?"

"I don't know. Probably better not. I didn't think to ask Alan about that. He may have already talked to him or be there tonight. We'll wait and see."

Maggie and Joe paused at the hospital room door, hearing voices. Joe stuck his head in.

Around Happy's bed were his mother, father and Alan Hill. Alan raised his hand in greeting.

"Hi, Maggie," Happy grinned, then put two fingers on his upper lip. "Happiness hurts right now," he said through the fingers on his split lip.

"I'm still thanking the Lord he had his helmet on," his mother said.

Mr. Harris nodded. "There wasn't a concussion, and the little bump on his head will heal up in no time. The broken bones will take a bit longer."

"Happy, do you know who did this to you?"

Alan answered Joe. "I've already asked him that."

"But I didn't hear the answer," Joe insisted.

"Yes, I know. I didn't want to think it. But, Mickey called me. He wanted me to bring him some money. He told me where to meet him, so I guess he waited for me then hit me and knocked me off the bridge."

"You just agreed to meet him, just like that?" Joe asked.

Happy glanced at Alan as he answered. "He-he said he had Maggie's phone number and if I didn't come, he'd ask her for some money."

Alan looked pained. "I didn't think to ask him that. Is there anything else I should have asked?"

Happy shook his head. "All I know is he wanted money, and when I said I didn't have any he asked how much I had right then. Then, even though it wasn't very much, he said to bring it to him. I didn't want to but he said he had Maggie's phone number. I was afraid he might have found out where she had moved, too."

"And that scared you, didn't it, Happy?" Joe pursued. "Because you know he threw those Molotov cocktails into the house where she used to live, didn't he?"

Happy hung his head. "Yes. I knew. Raid told me."

Alan spoke up. "When did he tell you, and where is he?"

"He told me a while back. Maybe a week or two before that call from Mickey, I guess. I don't know where he is. He said he was going to leave town soon as he could get some money. I didn't have any to give him. I felt bad about it. He was afraid of Mickey, too. He said he was going to try to get to Mexico."

"Why was he afraid of Mickey?" Alan interrupted.

"Mickey was always a little strange, suspicious of everybody, but he'd got paranoid. He was always asking me what I told Maggie. I told him I didn't tell her anything except what time Horse—Horace—left that night. But he didn't believe me. And he was afraid Raid would tell about the warehouse robbery they tried to pull."

"Warehouse robbery." Alan thought back. "The electronics place where one of the watchmen was shot?"

"Yes, sir, that's the one. Mickey had found out when a truckload of electronic equipment was coming in and he wanted to steal it because he thought he could sell it fast for a lot of money. But it just didn't happen. They didn't get anything."

"Was that the thing they wanted Horace to do? Was that what he refused to go along with?" Maggie asked.

Happy nodded. "They should have known he wouldn't have anything to do with anything like that. But they—Mickey, I mean—he got worried that I had heard them and told Maggie about what they'd planned. Then Mickey got it into his head that Raid would talk about it, too. There's no telling what he would do. That's why I went to meet him when he said he'd call Maggie."

"That watchman died," Alan said. "Mickey was afraid he'd be up for murder as well as trying to hold up the warehouse, wasn't he?"

"Yes, sir. That's what he was afraid of. He—he didn't want any witnesses." A tear slipped out and rolled down one cheek. Maggie reached over and squeezed his hand.

"Happy, we've got Mickey Lewis in jail. He tried to hold up an armored car. Will you testify against him? That you saw them put something in Horace's drink, and tell what Raid told you about the warehouse job?"

"I don't want to, but I will if you need me." Happy looked

worried but determined. His parents smiled at him, giving their approval.

"Do you have any idea where Raymond Wilson is?" Alan pushed. "It would be better if we could get his testimony that he and Mickey did that warehouse job. Raymond could get off lighter by cooperating. Make a deal by testifying against Mickey, if Mickey forced him to go along. You said he was afraid of him."

"He is. Raid would never have thought of doing something like that. It was Mickey who planned it and made Raid go with him. He didn't get anywhere with Horace." Maggie smiled at him. "And, there's something else."

After a second of silence that seemed like an eternity, Happy continued. "Mickey is the one who killed the watchman. Raid saw him do it. He told me. That's why he's so afraid of him. To think he would kill someone like that, and Raid saw him do it."

"We'll do our best to find Raid," Joe promised. "We've got a warrant out for him and hopefully, he'll turn up somewhere soon."

"Happy, if you think of anything else you want to tell me or that I didn't think to ask—" Alan smiled. "Call me." He put one of his cards on the bedside table. "Thank you for your help."

Joe walked out with Alan, then went back in to find everyone smiling. "What did I miss?"

"Happy just told me he's going to be healed up and raring to go by next September, and he's going to college."

"That's good news. But I think from the way it looked when I saw it, you're going to have to shoot your bike." Joe grinned at him.

"That's been taken care of," Mr. Harris said. "We're selling what's left of it to the garage and going to use that for a down payment on a used car with a roof on it."

"Yeah, I may paint it sunshine yellow too." Happy forgot and laughed, putting two fingers on his lip again.

Chapter Thirty-Three

Maggie listened to the ringing phone, wondering if Aunt Myrtle was out. She was about to hang up when she answered.

"Aunt Myrtle? I was afraid you were out. Are you busy? Should I call back later?"

"No, no. I was out watering my roses and didn't hear the phone. Is Joe working tonight?"

"Yes. I thought I'd call and get you caught up on all the news."

"Why don't you come on over? I've got a roast in the crock-pot and squash from the garden. Last time I talked to you, you said they found out who killed that man—"

"Wartzy. Mr. Wartz. They did, and there's lots more."

"Come on right now. It's formal though, so wear shoes."

Maggie drove defensively. Now that the two cases were nearly all over, she watched other cars in case Mickey Lewis had somehow managed to get out of jail.

It took so long for Joe to convince me I was really in danger I missed out on a lot of good worrying time. She laughed at herself.

Aunt Myrtle gave her such a big hug, Maggie winked at Doug over her shoulder. "Must have been longer between visits than I thought. Or does time just fly faster for old married women?" She raised her eyebrows at them.

"What are you asking me for? I'm just married, not old!"

"Yeah, what she said." Doug came over to get his hug. "I'll

285

help you get things on the table. I want to hear all the news, too."

"Okay. Let's see. Josef Kranz killed Mr. Wartz."

"You told me that, but why?"

"The FBI and some other government agencies were in on that case and were watching Josef Kranz but weren't sure yet who he was. Not till Joe managed to get his fingerprints and they sent them in to identify. Other agencies here and in other countries were looking for him, and the FBI, too. When they got those prints, they came and took over the case."

Aunt Myrtle handed her a glass of tea to keep her going. Doug sat fascinated, picturing the agents swarming into police headquarters flashing their badges like Scully and Mulder on *X-Files*.

"They didn't even tell Joe and Alan what Josef Kranz's real name is, but he killed Wartzy to keep him from telling who he was. Wartzy was at Auschwitz. His wife died there. That's why he was killed. He must have recognized Josef Kranz. All they told Alan and Joe was that he is the fugitive they were looking for from the Nuremburg trials, and the local case is closed."

Maggie paused only a second for breath. "And about that mental case who threw the Molotov cocktails into the house where I used to live—"

"They've got him?" Doug asked.

"Yes. Well, I mean, they've got him in custody. But they will get him. He's as good as convicted and in jail. And Aunt Myrtle, he's just as crazy as Joe thought he was. When he stormed in and moved me to my new house in the middle of the night, I thought Joe was the nut case, but he was right all the time."

"I knew Joe was smart."

"Then when we went on that river trip with the garden clubs, he nearly killed Fatima and me. He's the one who pushed that crate off the roof. But they've got him. They've got the DNA off that cap of his that he dropped. The sweat," she explained when Doug opened his mouth. "He's the one who threw the Molotov cocktails, too. They've got two or three prints off the broken glass—"

"How did they get him?" Doug was interested in the blow-by-blow excitement.

"They had a picture of him they circulated and were watching for him, but where he messed up is that he tried to hold up an armored car with a can of mace."

"A can of mace?"

Maggie nodded. "He knew the armored truck would be coming to fill up the ATM machines he was watching. But the really craziest and worst thing he did was try to kill Happy Harris."

"No! That nice young boy who told you Horace was trying to get home? Tell us about it. Or do they know what happened?"

Maggie told them about Mickey's call to Happy, the threat to call her, and how Mickey had stolen a car and hit Happy's motorcycle as he went over an overpass.

"Oh." Aunt Myrtle cringed, rubbing goosebumps on her arms as she pictured poor Happy's motorcycle going over the railing. "He's a cold-blooded thing. He tried to kill Happy and he tried to kill you, too. Twice! That's the terrible thing. He's got to be deranged or something. He tried to kill both of you."

"Yes, and Raid—Raymond Wilson—is afraid of him, too. They think he's probably left town. Raid, I mean."

"But, what is he so afraid of that he's trying to kill you and his friends? I guess I just don't know how to think like a criminal." Aunt Myrtle wrinkled her brow.

"Well, you do very well thinking like a woman, and that's devious enough." Doug patted her hand.

"Thank you, I think."

Maggie explained about the warehouse holdup and finished

with, "But he's being held in custody right now and they have enough evidence against him to convict him, even if they don't find Raymond Wilson."

As they put away the dishes, Doug said, "I'll go water the lawn in front, since you've already done your roses."

"Good. Maggie and I will have another glass of tea in the swing."

Maggie put more ice in their glasses and followed her aunt.

"The roses are beautiful, Aunt Myrtle."

"It's water, fertilizer and love. I think they like to be appreciated like people do."

"The one where Horace's urn is must have twenty buds and blooms on it."

"I snip the dead ones off. Makes it bloom more. You thought any more about scattering his ashes, not that it makes any difference to me."

"Yes. Just haven't got around to it yet. I will, though. I'd better start home before it gets dark, Joe might call me."

"He won't panic now that that mental case is in jail, will he?"

Maggie shook her head. "It may take a while not to panic. But I think they will convict him of that warehouse robbery and put him away for a long time. There's no more need to worry."

Joe knew their worries were probably over now that they had caught up with Mickey Lewis. But before he went to work, he went by where they were holding him, just wanting to see what he looked like. He spoke briefly to the officer on duty without even slowing down. "I just want to walk by and make sure he's there."

The uniformed officer shrugged. "Okay. Don't want to go in or question him?"

"No."

Joe walked down the narrow hall between the cells then

turned and came back. He paused a minute outside Mickey's cell. Mickey looked up. Neither spoke, but there were questions in Mickey's eyes.

You don't look a bit better than your mug shot. Joe's eyes bored into his. *I'm the guy who's going to kill you if you insist on it.* Joe turned and went back out, feeling better when he left.

Joe entered the cafeteria at St. Olaf's with mixed feelings. Alan was right; he couldn't give Millie and Pauline much in the way of details. But he could let them know Wartzy's killer was on his way back to face the war crimes he'd been convicted of. He would face the punishment for both his known and only guessed-at crimes against humanity.

"Hello, Officer. Glad to see you again." The elderly cashier grinned. "I know freebies are against your work ethic or something else I can't spell, but I'm going to give you one of them offers you can't refuse."

"I'll decide about that when I hear what it is." Joe returned his grin. "All I want is a cup of coffee."

This brought on a delighted cackle. "That's exactly what it is! I'm getting ready to refill the coffee urn and make more, so coffee's on the house right now. I'd just be pouring it out, so it won't cost us anything." He reached for a cup. "Okay?"

"Okay. I'll take you up on it just this once. Thank you."

He turned to see Millie waving wildly at him across the room. He smiled and moved toward the table where she and Pauline were sitting.

"Thought you'd forgot the way over here," Millie greeted him.

Pauline smiled a welcome as he sat down. "We've been wondering if you'd found out anything else about Wartzy?"

"Yes, we've got the man who killed him and closed the case." Joe spoke softly and they both leaned forward to listen.

"We didn't see anything in the papers," Pauline said.

"Or on television either." Millie's red bangs bobbed, her eyes holding unspoken questions.

"You probably won't, or you'll just hear that the case is closed. I can't tell you much. The government agencies that took over the case didn't tell us much."

"Government agencies?" Pauline cast a bewildered look at Millie. Millie sat silent and waiting, almost as if she knew what was coming.

"The FBI and others had been watching the man who stabbed Mr. Wartz," Joe continued. "They suspected him of being the fugitive they were looking for. When we managed to get fingerprints and asked for help identifying them, they knew he was their man. They entered the case and took over. He's gone now to pay for other crimes he's guilty of. War crimes he is already convicted of. They gave us the identity of the prints on the knife used to kill Wartzy and just enough to let us close our local murder case."

"Government agencies? War crimes? A fugitive from Nuremberg?" Millie narrowed her eyes. Smoke from her cigarette curled up around her face, giving her the sad, knowing look of an ancient wise woman.

Joe nodded. "Josef Kranz. That's not his real name, of course. And they didn't give it to us." He looked at Pauline. "Bigot wasn't a bad enough word for him."

"You could almost tell, just by looking at him. The superior master race, humpf!" Millie ground out her cigarette. "Nothing they do to him will be bad enough."

"I know. But rest assured, they'll try," Joe assured her. "And he's gone now. He may die before they execute him."

"I hope not," Pauline spat, holding Millie's hand. "I just really, sincerely, do hope not."

Raid sat in the old converted school bus in a daze. Bouncing along the highway. The heat and humidity were bad, too bad to try and close the window against the blowing dust, sand and occasional insects.

Probably won't work anyway.

Sweat stung his eyes and ran down his back. He looked out at the scenery he had struggled through to get to Mexico, only to be sent back in that rattletrap to Shelby County, Tennessee.

He rested his forehead briefly against the bars on the windows. It actually feels a little cool. *I wonder if that's where I'm headed—behind bars, going back to go to jail? But what for? They surely wouldn't do this for a traffic ticket, and I haven't got any I can remember. Maybe I parked in a wrong place before my car quit on me.*

He was shaken up and down as the old bus ate up the road. *This thing is probably stuck together with duct tape; it's even older than my car was. Wonder what the Spanish words are for shock absorbers? Not that anybody on here would recognize one if it bit him on the butt.*

He laid his head back against the hard seat's high back. His troubled thoughts wouldn't let him rest. He wondered if this warrant had something to do with Mick, though he didn't see how Mick could have been picked up for the attempted warehouse robbery.

Surely he didn't try something else. Raid's eyes flew open as a cooler breeze blew in from the window and an unexpected shiver crawled up his spine. *I wouldn't put much past Mick. He's turned out to be a real mental case.* He closed his eyes again, trying not to think about Mickey or anything he might do.

One of the three other passengers was snoring loudly. The guard kept his eyes on all of them, his gun across his knees.

Joe stuck his head in Alan's door. Alan smiled and he took a seat beside his desk.

"Does that good humor mean things are going well with Mick the Slick?"

"That's a good name for him. I hear you went by to take a look at that budding genius?"

Joe nodded. "I did. Should have known it would get back to you. All I did was look. That should have got back to you, too."

"Yeah." Alan's half smile was amused. "There aren't any secrets in this place. What did you think of him?"

"Run of the mill smart aleck punk. Looks as bad as his mug shot. I didn't speak, and he didn't either. Only took a minute." Joe's brows drew together. "But I'll know him if our paths cross again."

"I don't blame you for not crossing him off your worry list till he's convicted and behind bars. But that is going to happen. He's as good as gone."

"Is the public defender taking his case?"

"Yes. I was in on their first meeting with them. He looked a little shook, out of his depth. The district attorney's office must screen for scary expressions." He grinned.

"Mickey trying to deal?"

"He's not that smart. Thinks he's safe. We told them about the prints on the glass from the Molotov cocktails. Mickey didn't think there would be enough left to get prints from and screamed bloody murder. The lawyer calmed him down. He's young, but a lot smarter than his client, and I laid it all out for him. We also told them about the cap he dropped when he pushed the crate off the roof and the witnesses who saw it fall off his head. We have the DNA from that."

"What about Happy? Did you lay that one on him?"

"Sure did. We've got the paint from Happy's motorcycle on the car that hit him. Mickey tried to look innocent and said he didn't own a car like that."

"He's even dumber than I thought he was. He must think

we'd never heard of stealing a car to do a job."

Alan shook his head at Mick's stupidity. "I just looked at him like he was a kindergarten kid with the wrong answer and told him we cut the gloves he left in it to get his prints. It was dumb as dirt to leave them in the car."

"What did he say to that?"

"He'd finally realized by then he was in deep doo-doo. He didn't say anything. No deal is on the table yet, and the lawyer wants to confer with his client now that they both know what they're up against."

Joe sighed. "He thought from the beginning he was smart enough to get away with murder. It took me a scary long time to convince Maggie she was in any danger. The Molotov cocktails did it."

Alan nodded. "It takes a while for it to dawn on the victim he or she is in any danger. Then they blame us because we can't do anything until the perp breaks the law." He grimaced. "Ain't it hell?"

Maggie sat in her Aunt Myrtle's swing with her aunt, sipping iced tea and admiring the roses.

"Doug is sweet to do all this watering and help you." She looked at him across the yard.

"Yes, he's a dear. Don't know how I ever got along without him." Myrtle frowned, "Not too well, if I remember right."

Maggie laughed. "Well, you certainly had me fooled. You were my tower of strength. I don't know what I'd have done without you."

"Oh, you'd have made it fine. You've got more strength than you think you have. But speaking of Doug, I invited him to join our Eden Extended Garden Club."

"Oh, and is he going to?"

"Not now, but he said he might visit some time. But just

between us, he's got a friend whose minor was in horticulture or something and retired from teaching when Doug did. If he happens to decide to join a garden club, hopefully ours, maybe Doug will too. We'll just let nature take its course. He's circling the idea right now. Sort of like a dog would circle a porcupine."

Maggie stifled a laugh, picturing that. As she turned away, her eyes fell on the rim of Horace's urn near the pink roses. Her smile turned serious.

"Aunt Myrtle, I've been thinking about doing what Horace wanted me to do. About scattering his ashes, I mean. I think I've found where I want to do it."

Aunt Myrtle sat quietly, listening.

"I thought about a commercial raceway not far from town, but it's too busy and noisy. And people there aren't going anywhere exciting. It's somehow . . . I don't know. I guess *confined* is the word."

"And you've found a place he would like better?"

Maggie nodded. "It's an overpass that has a sidewalk over a freeway. You can look down at the freeway running north and south below it. People going north to the Indy Five Hundred, or south to Daytona. I think Horace would approve, and I did promise."

"It sounds like what he had in mind."

"Yes, that's what he wanted, and the place sounds good to me. I believe I'll do it. I don't know when, but soon."

Aunt Myrtle squeezed her arm. "Take your time. Let me know when, and I'll go with you."

When he was ready to leave for home, Joe glanced toward Alan's door. Alan appeared and jerked his head toward his cubicle of an office. Joe followed him toward his office. "Guess who's turned up?"

"With any luck, was it Raid?"

Alan smiled.

"Where? How?"

"The warrant. He was driving a produce truck. They picked him up trying to cross into Juarez from El Paso."

"Produce truck. Was it carrying anything besides produce?"

"Yes. About half their load of cantaloupes was full of marijuana."

"They holding him?"

"No. Seems he was hitchhiking, swapping driving for a ride. The man on the truck confirmed that and cleared him. But they checked him out and found our warrant. He's here. I haven't talked to him yet."

"He may not know what Mickey Lewis tried to do to Happy, but he sure as heck knows about Horace's doctored-up drink, and we know now he was there and in on the warehouse plans, too."

Joe's lips formed a grim line. "Probably will try to tell us he doesn't know anything about the Molotov cocktails either, since he doesn't know Happy told us about that." Joe looked grim. "I guess five minutes alone with this one's out too?"

"Yeah. What do you think this is, your birthday? Besides we want enough of him left to take to court. How much he knows depends on when he left. But he told Happy about the Molotov cocktails before he left, and there's no way he couldn't know about the drink and the warehouse job. He's got to figure out he might as well cooperate if there's going to be any hope for him at all."

"When are you going to see him? Tomorrow?"

Alan nodded. "How is Happy Harris doing?"

"He'll be going home soon, and he'll be all right." Joe glanced at the door. "I'll be home if there are any late bulletins."

Raid sat down on the hard bunk in his cell. He was the only

one in it, and from some of the noises he heard from down the hall, he was grateful for that. Someone farther away sounded like a loon or a peacock screeching until an officer went to see what the problem was.

As the guard passed his cell on the way back, Raid thrust his hand through the bars.

"Excuse me?"

The policeman stopped but didn't get any closer. He waited for Raid to speak.

"I . . . is it possible for me to make a phone call? It's just a local call," he added hurriedly, his eyes pleading.

"I'll check on it and see."

After a few minutes the officer came back to him and escorted him up the hall. "One call. Local. Be brief."

Raid quickly dialed Happy's number. His heart sank when the phone kept ringing. The policeman was watching him, and Raid had almost given up when someone picked up the phone.

"Hello?" It was a woman's voice.

"Mrs. Harris? Are you Happy's mother?"

"Yes. We were just leaving for the hospital."

"Hospital? Is Happy in the hospital?" Raid's hands clutched the phone tighter. "What's the matter with him?"

"He got hurt on his motorcycle. Who is this?"

"You don't know me. My name is Raymond Wilson. Happy and I used to ride together sometimes."

"Oh. Happy hasn't had his motorcycle very long." Mrs. Harris sounded suspicious.

"Yes, ma'am, I know. I'm sorry to hear about his accident. Is Happy going to be all right?"

"Yes. He'll be in the hospital a while, but he will be all right."

"I'm glad. Please tell him Raymond Wilson called and I'm sorry about his accident. Do you know how it happened?"

"Someone in a heavy car knocked him off the overpass near

our house."

Raid gulped, "Who? Who—"

"We don't know. It was a hit and run. We're just glad Happy's going to be all right. And I've got to leave now. I'll tell him you called, Raymond."

Raid stood there as if frozen with the phone in his hand, listening to the dial tone.

The policeman took the phone and hung up for him. "Where'd you call? A haunted house?"

Raid tried to smile at the jailhouse humor but he couldn't. His smile muscles were still in shock like the rest of him. He silently followed the policeman back to his cell.

Alan picked up the phone at home.

"Captain Hill?"

"Yes."

"This is Officer O'Toole at the jail. I'm sorry to interrupt your dinner, sir."

"You didn't. It's all right. What is it?" Alan was picturing everything from an escape to Raid hanging himself in his cell.

"The suspect you had the warrant on, I let him make a local phone call."

"That's all right." He knew better than to draw a breath of relief at that point and braced for more.

"He made his call, all right. But, when it was over he just stood there like he was in shock or something. You should have seen the look on his face. I had to go take the phone out of his hand and hang up for him."

"Do you know who he called?"

"No, but I think it started with an H."

"H. Harris? Could it have been Harris?"

"Yes! I think that's what it was. Harris. I thought you might want to know."

"You thought right. Thanks."

Maggie turned away from the cabinet where she was putting away dishes when the phone rang.

"I'll get it," Joe called. "Hello?" Joe had a fleeting second to wonder if Mickey had managed to get out.

"Joe," Alan's voice sounded weary. "We aren't going to get to see Raid's reaction to what happened to Happy."

Guilt and anger clashed as Joe reacted to that news. "He didn't . . . don't tell me he's the one who—"

"No. No, nothing like what you're thinking. One of the men from the jail just called me and said Raymond Wilson asked to make a local phone call."

Joe's hand cramped. He was holding the phone like it was the back of Mickey Lewis's neck. He relaxed his grip, waiting.

"Officer O'Toole told me about the call. He said Raymond looked so scared, he asked him if he'd called a haunted house." The brief pause was dramatic. "He talked to someone named Harris."

"Nuts! There goes our element of surprise, all right. But it shook him, did it?"

"Maybe it's just as well, Joe. He knows about Happy's wreck now, knows it's the truth. Happy is in the hospital, and Raid heard it from one of his parents. We don't have to convince him about somebody nearly killing Happy, and he'll also know it's got to be Mickey who did it. I called the hospital before I called you. Mr. and Mrs. Harris had just got there and I asked if I could bring Raymond to see Happy. They asked Happy, and he talked to me."

"I guess he doesn't believe Raid would do the things Mickey planned?"

"No. He thinks Mickey pushed him into whatever trouble

they got into. I think it would be good to let these two talk. I'm going to take Raymond to the hospital with an officer to escort him. Do you want to be the officer?"

"Are you at the jail?"

"Yes."

"I'm coming."

Maggie came to meet Joe at the kitchen door and slipped her arms around him. "Trouble? Work?"

He took her hands and kissed them. "I hadn't got around to telling you yet, but Raymond Wilson was returned to Shelby County today."

"Returned?"

"There was a warrant out for him. He tried to cross into Mexico, and they saw the warrant on him and sent him back. That was Alan who called. He hasn't had a chance to talk to him yet, but Raymond's called from the jail and found out Happy's in the hospital. Alan and I are going to escort Raymond to talk to Happy. When he sees what Mickey's capable of, he may open up and testify against him."

"I'll get my purse."

"Not this time, Maggie. Mr. and Mrs. Harris may have to cool their heels in the hall, too, while we talk to them." He tried to console her. "You understand, don't you?"

Maggie nodded and obediently locked the door behind him when he left.

How am I going to be the neck in this relationship if I melt and run down in my shoes every time he says "please"?

CHAPTER THIRTY-FOUR

Just as the news came on, Joe arrived home with a half gallon of pecan praline ice cream and a big smile on his face.

"I can tell by your face the news is good. And by the ice cream. You know all my weaknesses. I guess you're going to use them to your own selfish advantage?"

"Naturally. One of the best ways of staying married until the twelfth of never."

"Hey, that's the day I'm swearing off ice cream! Tell me what happened before we eat ourselves into a stupor."

Joe sat down at the kitchen table and started talking as Maggie got bowls and spoons.

"Getting Raid to the hospital to see Happy was the best thing we've done yet. Raid wasn't much more than a bystander in the warehouse holdup and will testify against Mickey. He saw him shoot the watchman, though he's not sure if the gun went off accidentally or not. We'll let his lawyer worry about that."

"Lawyers should be against the law," was Maggie's sage comment.

"Yeah. Some of them are. Raid knows Mickey was threatening to get rid of all witnesses, and Happy chimed in about his getting your phone number—"

"How?" Maggie gasped. "You never did tell me that."

"Called information and got the new number listing. I forgot I didn't tell you."

Maggie shivered at his having got information about their

whereabouts in spite of their precautions.

"We've got a couple of fingerprints on the Molotov cocktail thing, DNA from the cap he dropped when he pushed that crate off trying to crush you and Fatima, Raid's testimony about the guard at the warehouse, and no one is going to have to worry about Mickey Lewis again for a long, long time."

"What about Raymond Wilson?"

"Alan thinks he will probably get probation, and asked him about his parents."

"Do they live here?"

"No. His mother was a widow and lives in Florida. She's just remarried. Raymond is happy for her and doesn't want to cause her any trouble or embarrassment. He's going to stay here when we get all this straightened out. Happy's dad said he could stay with them till he gets a job. He had been in his sophomore year at the university when he dropped out."

"He's going back to school then?"

Joe nodded. "He'll be all right. He even asked me some questions about getting into the academy. Said he had an uncle who retired from a force somewhere in Michigan."

"That's good. And so is this." Maggie pushed back her bowl. "I'll wait a few weeks before I go near the scales."

"Didn't you say you had something to tell me before dinner and all this excitement?"

"It'll keep."

"I won't. What is it?"

"Anyone ever tell you you've got more curiosity than a litter of kittens who just got their eyes open?"

"That's a lot." Joe grinned. "And besides, it comes in handy. Now, what is it you've got to tell me?"

"I've decided where I'm going to scatter Horace's ashes."

Joe took a few seconds to think that over. "I remember you saying that's what he wanted. Maybe over some raceway, wasn't it?" An expectant grin spread over Joe's face. "Are we going to Daytona?"

"You wish! His second choice was a freeway, and I've found an overpass over a busy one where people pass going to raceways north and south or wherever, and there's a good place I can stand to scatter them."

"Fine," Joe nodded agreement. "Is Aunt Myrtle going with us?"

Us?

There was no traffic on the chosen overpass and very little on the freeway beneath it when Maggie, Joe and Aunt Myrtle arrived. Horace appeared as they got out of the car on the broad shoulder and walked up the sidewalk of the overpass with them.

Joe had loosened the top of the urn, and Maggie held it tightly against her heart as she stopped and looked over the rail at the road beneath.

"I'll wait over here," Joe said quietly. He crossed to the other side of the overpass. He walked right through Horace, who was wandering around, peering at the expressway from all angles and both sides, an expectant expression on his face.

"Should we say a few words?" It wasn't really a question, and Aunt Myrtle closed her eyes. "Lord, this is Horace Murphy. He was a good man and a good husband and we all loved him. We will miss him. May he rest in peace and let perpetual light shine upon him in his heavenly rest with you. Amen."

"That was beautiful, Aunt Myrtle. Thank you."

Pausing only slightly, Maggie closed her eyes. "Lord, Horace was trying to come home when he rode his motorcycle through the pearly gates. He was turning away from temptation and coming home. We know that now, and I'm sorry I ever doubted he was trying his best to come home like he said he would. We love him and will miss him. Amen."

Maggie opened her eyes and lifted the urn. She stood holding the top open far enough for the ashes to pour slowly through. After several seconds, Horace reached out and hit her elbow, making her lose her grip on the urn.

Maggie stood horrified, watching openmouthed as the urn fell as if in slow motion, turning and scattering the ashes as it went, then shattered on the concrete shoulder below.

Joe turned. Sensing something wrong, he was there in an instant. Aunt Myrtle simply stood, not knowing what to do.

"I d-dropped it!" Maggie was horrified.

Joe put his arms around her, holding her close and cradling her head on his chest. "It's all right. It's all right. You've done what he wanted you to do, Maggie."

Aunt Myrtle nodded, glad it was over.

Horace nodded his approval with a sad little smile. His eye fell on a conical pile of ashes on the rail as a playful wind began to swirl them upward. Horace raised his arms in an upward dive position and rose with them, not looking back.

ABOUT THE AUTHOR

Jackie Griffey would probably have to toss a coin to decide whether it's more fun to write or to read cozy mysteries. Her favorite place is anywhere with a book in her hand. Her life away from the keyboard is filled with her grown children, two large cats and one tiny Chihuahua who thinks he's a (huge and dangerous) watch dog. She lives in Arkansas and she's currently working on another cozy mystery.